# CASTLE OF SHADOWS

# CASTLE OF SHADOWS

by Ellen Renner

illustrated by Wilson Swain

HOUGHTON MIFFLIN
Houghton Mifflin Harcourt
Boston  New York  2012

First U.S. Edition copyright © 2012 by Ellen Renner
Illustrations copyright © 2012 by Wilson Swain
First published in the United Kingdom in 2010 by Orchard Books

Houghton Mifflin is an imprint of
Houghton Mifflin Harcourt Publishing Company.

www.hmhbooks.com

The text of this book is set in Garamond Premiere Pro.

Library of Congress Cataloging-in-Publication Data

Renner, Ellen.

Castle of shadows / by Ellen Renner.

p. cm.

Summary: A feisty eleven-year-old princess embarks on a dangerous mission to find
her missing mother, uncovering dark secrets inside and outside the castle walls.

ISBN 978-0-547-74446-9

[1. Princesses—Fiction. 2. Kings, queens, rulers, etc.—Fiction.
3. Missing persons—Fiction. 4. Secrets—Fiction.] I. Title.

PZ7.R2902Cas 2012

[E]—dc23

2011039907

Manufactured in the United States of America
DOC 10 9 8 7 6 5 4 3 2 1
4500342842

For Kit and Zubin

# The Royal Castle of Quale

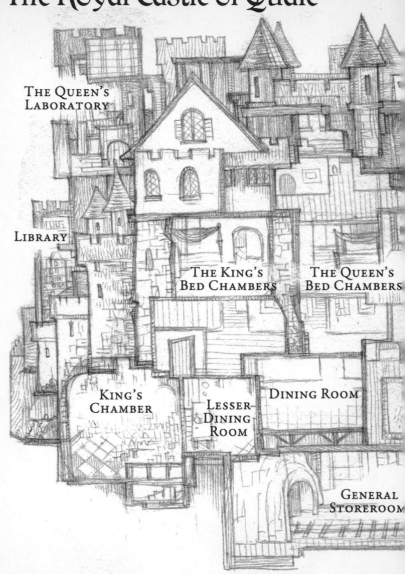

THE QUEEN'S
LABORATORY

LIBRARY

THE KING'S
BED CHAMBERS

THE QUEEN'S
BED CHAMBERS

KING'S
CHAMBER

LESSER-
DINING
ROOM

DINING ROOM

GENERAL
STOREROOM

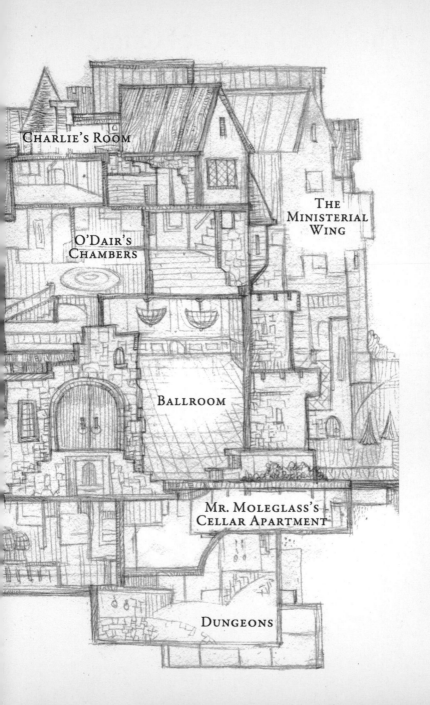

CHARLIE'S ROOM

THE MINISTERIAL WING

O'DAIR'S CHAMBERS

BALLROOM

MR. MOLEGLASS'S CELLAR APARTMENT

DUNGEONS

# Prologue

In the midnight darkness of Quale Castle, a woman emerged from the Queen's chamber. She carried a small carpet bag and wore the travelling clothes of an upper-class servant.

The woman mounted the stairs to the second floor, her shadow trailing in the candlelight. At the top of the stairs she hesitated, glancing round as though fearful of being overlooked. She hurried down the corridor, eased open a door and slipped inside.

A four-poster bed, its hangings pulled against the treachery of draughts, stood in the middle of the room.

The woman placed her candlestick on a table. The flame grew long and thin. She pulled back the bed-curtains and stood gazing down at a sleeping child, a small girl with a pale face and a tumble of dark red curls. The woman sighed once, softly. As if a spell had been broken, the child's eyes opened. "Mama?"

"Go back to sleep, Charlie. I didn't mean to wake you. Sleep now. I love you. Remember that."

The woman took her daughter's face between her hands and stared at it until the child felt the breath catch in her throat and the first cold squirm of fear uncurl in her belly. Her mother kissed her, then rose and left the room without a backward glance. The glow-worm trail of candlelight faded. The bed-curtains gaped, but darkness hung thick as velvet.

The child's fear returned—and grew . . .

# One

*Five years later . . .*

"Hold it there, you scrounging, nibbling limb of Satan!"
A bony fist grabbed the back of Charlie's dress. She was
lifted into the air and shaken like a rat in the jaws of a
terrier.

She stuffed the stolen food into her mouth and
chewed furiously, trying to swallow before either the
cheese or the shaking choked her dead. She had a
mouthful of dry flakes and no spittle to wash it down.
Crumbs spewed from her mouth and nose. The fist

gave a ferocious shake, and she coughed out the cheese. It plopped onto the flagstones in a dusty heap. Charlie followed it.

"Oh, look what you done!" moaned the fist's owner. "That were to be my dinner. Been looking forward to it all week. Kept it from the rats and from that nasty old Watch scrounging my kitchen at night worse than any rat. I been dreaming of rarebit sizzling and golden on a thick slice of toast. And now look at it! Not fit for the cat!"

Charlie stood and rubbed elbows and knees. "Sorry, Maria, I didn't know you were saving it for yourself."

The cook bent down, elevating her skinny behind and resting her large red hands on her knees. She considered the grey mess between her boots. Then she raised her long neck and considered Charlie. Charlie did not think it was a friendly consider. She got her running muscles ready. Maria had a good strong throwing arm.

"I don't know what is going to become of you." The cook unfolded and speared Charlie with a look of severe disappointment. "Or any of us, for that matter. But you didn't ought to steal. It may be all right for some, but princesses didn't ought to steal."

"I'm hungry!"

"Then you should have asked for summat," Maria snapped. "You know I'll always give you a morsel if you ask nice. Providing I got a bit the old witch won't miss, that she ain't counted and catalogued and marked down in her book."

"An apple?" Charlie wheedled. "Just one wrinkly old apple?"

"Might of done," Maria said, "if you'd not just spat me dinner out all over the floor. Now scat!" She reached a lanky arm for a wooden platter. Charlie gave a squeal of dismay. She made it through the door a second before the platter.

She paused for breath in the servants' hall. Maria wouldn't leave the warmth of the kitchen for the slender joy of thumping her. The hall was a gloomy brown room with a trestle table where the servants perched along a narrow bench to eat their meals, like so many shabby starlings. Charlie's eyes swept the room in vain: not a crumb to be seen, not a biscuit tin, a jam jar, a sticky spoon in sight.

Footsteps approached the door. She was trapped. None of the cupboards were big enough to hide in. If it was the O'Dair . . . Charlie squeezed into the corner made by the dresser and wall, as the door swung open and the upper parlour maid and third footman clattered in.

"... seven crates of playing cards I toted up there. Have you seen that room? And himself? Upside down and wisty? Fair give me the collywobbles!" The footman shivered until his rusty black coat-tails flapped.

"Course not," snapped the parlour maid. "Not my business."

"He ought to be put away."

Crammed in her corner, Charlie felt sick. The servants never talked about her father in front of her. She had long ago guessed what they must think of him, but hearing it was different. Worst of all was her fear that they might be right.

"You keep a civil tongue in your head, boy," said the maid. "He is the King, cards or no cards."

"What good is he?" The footman was new—a gangling, yellow-haired boy with acne. "Worse'n no king! We should have had a revolution same's the Esceanians. Cut off his head! He'd never miss it! Mad as an hatter and no blame use to anyone. Country's going down the plinker, and he's playing at jackstraws!"

Charlie darted forward. She wanted to hit the footman, to kick him as hard as she could on both his skinny shins. Anything to fight the wave of panic sweeping over her. Years ago, the last king of Esceania, King Charles the Twelfth, had been executed by guillotine. There was a large painting of his last moments (with the King looking very heroic, if rather plump) in the library. The image floated in front of her eyes, only it was her father she saw kneeling before the guillotine, hands tied, head raised in calm defiance. She blinked back tears and paused long enough to look for a weapon. Something heavy and hard!

Martha, the parlour maid, turned a scandalised face on the footman. "Don't you let O'Dair hear you talking that way, Alfie Postlethwaite," she gasped. "She'll have your scalp! She don't put up with no Republican nonsense."

They saw Charlie and snapped their mouths shut like a pair of carp.

"You shouldn't be here!" Martha had gone bright red. "You know O'Dair don't allow you in the servants' quarters."

"I heard you!" To her fury and shame, Charlie's voice

wobbled. She stood in the middle of the room and shook from head to toe, unable even to speak.

"Yeah?" The footman smirked at her. "What you gonna do about it? Tell Daddy on us?"

"Stow it, Alfie!" snapped the maid. "You got no reason to be nasty to the kid. You'd best make yourself scarce," she said to Charlie. "O'Dair'll be along any minute."

Charlie gave Alfie Postlethwaite her most evil glare before stalking from the room.

"Poxy-nosed scarecrow!" she muttered. "I'll show him!" She slid out the scullery door into the back yard that served the kitchen. She was not supposed to go into the Castle gardens without permission: Old Foss, the gardener, had complained one too many times to Mrs. O'Dair about stolen apples and inventive booby traps. But today she would risk being caught out of bounds, even if it meant a week on stale bread and cabbage water.

The yew hedges had not been pruned for years. They leant over the yard, tall green-black waves threatening to crash onto the cobbles. Charlie stopped for a moment and cocked her head like a robin, listening. Then she darted to a corner of the yard where the hedge was leggy and sparse. In a moment, she had wriggled through. She crouched at the base of the hedge, scouting for enemies.

The autumn sunshine was so sharp it made the air vibrate. For a moment, she wanted to twirl like a wild thing, crunch through the frosted grass in the tree-shadows, run and run until she collapsed in a heap. But she didn't dare. Besides, she wasn't here to play. She was here to pay out Alfie Postlethwaite.

Charlie took off, sprinting across the shrivelled grass and into the old orchard, weaving through the corpses of apple and pear trees. Her heart was thudding from running and the thrill of disobedience.

In the distance, beneath the trills of birdsong, Old Foss's grumble wormed through the undergrowth. She sped up, skirting the high brick walls of the kitchen garden, where the gardener did daily battle against weeds and old age. Breathless, she peeked through the gate. He and the boy were inside, hoeing the endless rows of winter cabbages. Charlie slipped past the gate, and her heart sang with victory. She trotted past the end of the wall, past blinded greenhouses and rotting sheds, past hillocks of mouldering compost. And there it was: the brown and black mountain of strawy manure, steaming in the sunshine. Her nose wrinkled at the rich smells trickling out of it. She pulled a rusty pencil tin from her skirt pocket and squatted to scoop the tin full of the ooziest lumps she could find, using a spoon she had stolen from the scullery. It was absorbing work, and she grinned, imagining Alfie's face in the morning.

"Oi! Get out of it!" A hand grabbed her shoulder and spun her round. Tin and spoon went flying. Charlie's foot slipped, and she plopped, with a squelch, onto the manure. The gardener's boy stood looking down at her, hands on hips, eyes dancing. "Little Princess Muckheap," he said and laughed.

"You rotten toad!" She scrambled up, fists clenched. Then she stopped. Tobias was a year older—a year taller and stronger—and she knew from experience that if she hit him, he would hit her back.

"Give me one good reason," he said, his eyes narrowed thoughtfully, "why I shouldn't call old Fossy."

"Because that would make you a snivelling, sneaking worm—as well as a toad!" spat Charlie.

Tobias grinned. His light blue eyes gleamed in the midst of his brownness—brown hair, brown face, brown freckles. She longed to punch his brown nose and see if he still smiled. In all their years of warfare, she had never once managed to make him lose his temper. It was one of the things she hated most about him.

"Toad or worm," he said, "either one can get you nicked. And then Fossy'll take you straight to Devil O'Dair. I *might* not fetch Fossy, but it'll cost you."

"What do you want?" As if she didn't know. The smugness spread over his face was past enduring.

"Let me think." He scratched his head. "What could you possibly have that I'd want? You ain't got no money, and I don't play with dolls—"

"Neither do I!"

"—so I guess it'll have to be another book. It's called *One Thousand and One Arabian Nights*. Bring it to the summerhouse eight o'clock tomorrow morning."

"Tomorrow morning!" Charlie's heart sank. He meant it. If she didn't deliver, he would serve her up to Fossy and smirk while he did it. Rot and blast Tobias Petch! "That's not enough time!" she grumbled. "What if I can't get in the library tonight? Watch might be hanging round. And the morning's the worst time to try and get out of the Castle. I'd have to get past O'Dair and Maria."

"That won't wash, Charlie." He shook his head. "Climb out a window if you got to. You done it plenty of times. And make sure you hang on till I get there. 'Tain't always easy getting away."

"What if I can't find the book?"

"Then Fossy'll learn about your visit to the muck-heap."

"You make me sick!" Charlie said.

"Good." Tobias grinned the self-satisfied grin of the victor. "I'd be going if I was you. Fossy's nearly done weeding."

There was nothing to do except leave. She rescued the pencil tin and spoon. Most of the manure was still in the tin. She closed the lid and shoved everything in her pocket.

"What do you want that stuff for anyway?" Tobias asked.

"To put in your porridge!" She stuck out her tongue and ran.

# Two

Charlie knew all about the dangers of air: its currents, eddies, disastrous gusts. Air, being invisible, was all too easy to forget. Charlie never forgot. With the ease of years of practice, she slipped through the door of her father's chamber, lowered herself onto the floor and tried to breathe as little as possible.

Twenty feet above her head, the King hung upside down from a scaffold pole. His long red hair was tied back and, as an anti-gravity measure, his jacket was buttoned to his trousers. He was about to place the final card on top of the thirty-seventh tower of his castle.

Charlie held her breath. Thirty-seven towers would be a new record.

A wall of windows formed the south side of the chamber. Five and a half years of dust overlaid the glass, interrupting the sunlight and mingling with it, until the King seemed to float in a golden haze of dust motes. Gingerly, holding the card between the tips of his two longest fingers, he stretched down and, with the merest flip, slid it into place. Although the impact could not have been greater than that of a feather, it was enough to make the entire tower quiver. The shaking slowed and stopped. The tower was complete.

Her father hung by his knees for a moment, admiring his handiwork. Then he reached out an arm and began his descent, swinging from his hands like an orangutan. He glided from one scaffold pole to another, twisting between towers, skimming over crenellations. Charlie almost forgot her worries as she watched. He was a magical sight: every movement slow and controlled, calculated to weave through the air with the least possible disturbance. He landed with the grace of an acrobat and stood with his arms crossed, gazing up at his creation.

She stared at his back. Was this the right time?

Should she wait a while longer? All day her ears had been ringing with Alfie's voice saying, *"Cut off his head!"*

It wasn't the footman she was afraid of—it was those he was parroting. Alfie was the sort of dim-noll who never had his own thoughts but borrowed other people's. Charlie often stole scraps of the newspapers the maids used to lay the fires. She knew times were hard and agitators were at work in the Kingdom: Republicans and worse—Radicals and Revolutionaries—who hated the very idea of a king. She feared Radicals and Revolutionaries more than she feared the dark.

She would have to risk it. "Father?" She spoke in barely a whisper and waited. "Father?" she said again, a touch louder.

"What? Is someone here?" The King's voice was faint from disuse.

"Behind you, Father," she whispered. "Is that you, Charlotte?" He turned to gaze at a spot a few inches over her head. "Are you well?"

"Quite well, Father."

"Good, good. Run along, child. I've just completed the thirty-seventh tower, you know."

"Yes, Father." Charlie took a deep breath. Talking with her father was like making friends with a kitten someone had beaten. You had to be patient, or he would take fright and scamper away. "A new record."

"Clever girl. Just so. A new record. And now I'm planning the thirty-eighth. So run along. Creep along, I mean . . . you know what I mean. Good girl. And mind not to breathe too much as you go." He made vague shooing motions with his fingers.

"Please, let me stay." Desperation made her voice shake. "You know I can be quiet! I won't move at all. But first . . . may I speak with you? It's very important!"

The King frowned. His face clouded, and she held her breath. "I don't know, child . . . oh, very well. I will talk to you in a little while. You must be patient. Proceedings are at a delicate point. If you stay you must promise not to disturb the air."

Charlie almost gave a gusty sigh of relief. She caught her breath just in time. "I promise."

"Good girl." He smiled at her right elbow, turned away, leapt onto the scaffold tower and began to climb.

*Creak . . . groan.* Something wheezed through the antechamber towards them. Dangling above the portcullis, the King tilted his head, listening. He sighed. "It's her, Charlotte. A pity. Perhaps she won't stay long." Charlie could have shouted with frustration. But she allowed herself only a stifled groan. She pressed against the wall as Mrs. O'Dair swept into the room, a colossus in black silk. The housekeeper's corsets creaked. Her long skirts billowed, rousing the air, chasing the dust into miniature tornadoes. Charlie smothered a sneeze. The card castle shivered and shifted.

"Please! Madam!" The King's voice floated down. "Your skirts, madam! Control your skirts!"

"Nonsense!" rapped Mrs. O'Dair. But she stood still, and the billow of black subsided.

Charlie was close enough to O'Dair to smell her: a mixture of mothballs, oil of cloves and cold mutton. She edged away, praying she hadn't been spotted.

"The child will leave." The housekeeper's massive head, its black hair subdued into a knot at the back of her neck, never moved. She did not even glance at Charlie.

"Father!" Charlie cast an imploring look at the King.

Her father turned to gaze up at his towers. He cleared his throat. "Charlotte would like to stay, I believe. I think she can be trusted to keep still, Mrs. O'Dair. You needn't worry."

"The child will leave," O'Dair repeated. "I have brought your medicine. I insist you come and take it now. And then you must rest."

Her father sighed and began the climb down. Charlie blinked back tears. Hatred burned like a lump of coal in her throat. She swallowed it and edged past the housekeeper towards the door. A hand the size of a dinner plate shot out and grabbed her shoulder. "What is that awful smell?" Mrs. O'Dair's large nose curled in disgust.

Too late, Charlie remembered the pencil tin. Still full of manure. Still in her pocket. She had lived with it so long she no longer smelt it. Thoroughly warmed, the contents of the tin exuded odour with renewed vigour. The smell was richer, deeper, exquisitely pungent. Charlie stank.

"It's um . . . it's only . . ."

"You filthy little—" The hand on Charlie's shoulder tightened like a vice.

"What's all this?" The King leapt to the ground. He peered at the air beside Mrs. O'Dair's left ear. "Is there a problem?" he asked.

"No, Your Majesty, not at all," soothed Mrs. O'Dair. "Merely that I believe Princess Charlotte to be in need of a bath."

The King's gaze hovered over Charlie's head. He sniffed the air. "Oh dear," he said and cleared his throat. "You are somewhat . . . fragrant, child. Perhaps a bath—"

"I shall see to it myself," Mrs. O'Dair said. "Once you have taken your medicine." Her grip slacked. Charlie flinched away and dodged out the door, the housekeeper's hiss of anger hard on her heels. But even as she fled, she knew her escape was temporary. Mrs. O'Dair might forget to feed Charlie or give her new clothes. She never forgot to punish her.

Scrubbed raw as a new potato, her stomach a knot of emptiness, Charlie lay in bed and hated Mrs. O'Dair. Then she hated Alfie for wanting to cut off her father's head. Finally, she settled down to hate Tobias Petch. She had plenty of practice.

Charlie had woken one morning, soon after her sixth birthday, to find that her mother had disappeared. Weeks later, when she was able to notice things, Charlie found that Foss had a new gardener's boy. Although she knew it was stupid, she couldn't help connecting the two: her mother's departure and Tobias's arrival.

It didn't help that from the very first he had refused to play with her when she managed to escape into the gardens. Or that he was a year older and thought he was cleverer. Or that when she told him her secrets, he never told her anything at all. All of that made it easy to hate Tobias Petch, but the thing that made it easiest of all was his mother.

In the months following the Queen's disappearance, Charlie's life had changed completely. Her father hid himself away in his private apartments and began his first, tiny card castle. Courtiers and guests vanished from the Castle, along with most of the servants. Soon afterwards, the housekeeper dismissed Nurse and banished Charlie to the east attics, where she was expected to stay out of sight and hearing. Charlie grew larger, but her meals did not grow with her. If she demanded more, she was locked in her room with nothing to eat except stale bread and cabbage water. At the end of that first, horrible year, despite everything, Charlie had grown so much that she struggled to get into her clothes, and O'Dair had grudgingly sent the Castle seamstress to her attic room. The woman uncurled her tape measure and stretched it around Charlie's chest and waist, and along her shoulders and arms. "Oh dear," said the seamstress, as she jotted down the measurements.

"Is something wrong?" Charlie liked this woman. She was gentle and nervous, with dark hair the colour of conkers and sad brown eyes. She had curtsied to Charlie and called her "Your Highness"—something Mrs. O'Dair and her new servants never did.

"Don't mind me, ma'am," the seamstress said. "It's just that you're so very thin. You need to eat up more, if you don't mind my saying so. Why, my Toby would make two of you!"

Charlie stared at her, amazed. It had never occurred to her that the gardener's boy might have a family or, indeed, exist at all outside the Castle grounds. "Are you Tobias's mother?"

"Yes, ma'am, I'm Rose Petch," she said, and blushed. She bustled about, tidying her things back into her basket, but Charlie had seen love and pride flare in the brown eyes, burning away every trace of sadness and timidity. Rose Petch, she knew, would never abandon her child the way Charlie's mother had abandoned her. She whirled away from the pain of that thought and attacked her clothes, wrestling into her worn petticoats and tight dress. She shoved her arm into a sleeve and heard the sound of ripping fabric.

"Gracious!" Rose cried. "That dress is half rotten, child. Take it off again, and I'll mend that quick as blinking. Come, let me help you."

Charlie stood, trembling, torn nearly in two by jealousy and longing, as Rose helped her undress. She turned her face away so that Tobias's mother would not see the tears in her eyes.

Now she stared up at the darkness, remembering. Her eyes were dry. The pangs in her stomach had settled into a steady ache, and she pushed all thoughts of her mother out of her head. She'd had practice of that, too. She threw off her covers, shivering as the chill struck her. She pulled on her boots, took the pencil tin and one of her precious candles, and crept out of her room. Even without Tobias's blackmail, her fear of the dark would not have kept her in her room tonight. At least there was a moon. Watery light seeped in at the windows—just enough to keep her heart from pounding and her breath from gulping.

Charlie pattered down three staircases without pausing. Each was larger and better carpeted than the last. She knew where she was from the thickness of the carpets: thin drugget for the attics, smooth flat weave for the fifth floor, thin pile for the fourth. When her boots sank into the plush of the third floor, Charlie knew it was time for caution.

No one slept on the third floor now. Moonlight cast dim shadows between the windows, chequering the corridor in silver and black. She fled from shadow to shadow, running silently on the thick carpet, feeling the emptiness behind the closed doors, listening for Watch. She reached the stair to the west wing without incident and began to climb. Her luck was holding.

The servants' bedrooms were in an attic like her own, with bare wooden doors and a narrow strip of drugget carpet tacked down the centre of the floorboards. Faint snores and sighings muttered through the doors. Beside each stood a pair of boots. The Castle no longer kept a boot-boy. As the youngest and newest footman, Alfie's first job of the day was to clean all the boots.

She fished the pencil tin from her pocket. There were only three footmen: three pairs of men's boots. Two pairs had worn heels and scuffed toes. That left the last pair, its leather stiff and shiny. She emptied the contents of the pencil tin into the shiny boots. A snore gurgled beneath the door. Charlie grinned.

All her nerves had disappeared by the time she got

to the library. It had been an easy journey: no sign of Watch. And the library was one of her favourite places, a room of long windows, leather sofas and high-backed chairs made for snuggling into. Books marched around the walls and into the room itself, dividing it into nooks and corners smelling of inked paper and ageing leather. She struck a match and lit her candle. Her luck continued: it only took an inch of the precious wax to find Tobias's book. She tugged its heavy weight off the shelf and carried it to a table to have a closer look. She put down the candlestick and leant over the book, touching the faded gold letters of its title with her finger. The ghost of a memory teased her. She knew this book. She had once before traced her fingers along these very letters. But when? She was trying to remember when the door rattled.

Charlie blew out the candle, grabbed Tobias's book and dived behind the nearest chair. The door thudded open. Lantern light invaded the room, followed by a thin man dressed in a greasy leather poacher's jacket and baggy trousers. He had a thatch of grey hair and hollow cheeks. His nose and chin curved to meet each other. Her luck had run out: it was Watch.

# Three

Charlie squeezed her eyes shut and tried to grow into the back of the chair. She heard Watch sniffing, and in her mind she saw all too clearly his nose twitching and snuffling.

Watch hunted largely by scent. He had a nose like a bloodhound, Maria said, and could smell out a fruit cake be it wrapped in ever so many layers of grease-proof. Charlie thought of the contents of the pencil tin and was almost sick with relief that she had emp-tied it. Watch would have sniffed her out and taken her straight to O'Dair. As it was . . . she crouched, barely breathing, listening to Watch shuffle further into the library. What was keeping him? Did the tin still reek? Could he smell it?

She heard the sound of springs groaning. A muttering, a shuffling and squeaking. Long minutes dragged by. Charlie didn't dare move. She spent the time thinking of twelve very unpleasant things she would do to Tobias the first chance she got.

The silence was splintered by a gasping, rasping snort. Then another. Inch by inch, she pulled herself up and peeked over the back of the chair. There, on a long leather sofa, stretched the lanky figure of the night watchman. Snores burbled out of his nose. His kerosene lantern sat on the floor beside him and hissed in unison. Watch had settled in for the night.

Drat the lazy gannet! Why did he have to choose the library for his midnight nap? Charlie waited for her heart to slow down, then stood, clutching Tobias's book to her chest. This was all his fault! She stepped from behind the chair and tripped over her candlestick. As Charlie tumbled backwards, she watched *One Thousand and One Arabian Nights* fly from her arms, arc through the air and crash to the floor with an almighty thud.

She scrambled to her feet, scooped up the book and raced for the darkest corner of the library. Watch spluttered and rolled off the sofa with an oath. He staggered up, grabbed his lantern and swirled it round, raking the room with light. He was sure to find her now. Even Watch would soon figure out that there were two people in the library—she had left the candlestick behind.

Charlie shoved *Arabian Nights* on top of the nearest row of books, stubbing her fingers on the shelves which rose like rungs in a ladder. She tucked her skirts into her drawers, her hands reached high, her toes scrabbled and pushed. She climbed quickly. When her head bumped, she bent over and climbed higher still, until her back pressed against the ceiling, and she was crouching twelve feet above the floor, clinging to the bookshelf like a squirrel on the side of a tree.

She couldn't see Watch—but she could hear him. He must have found the candle, because he was searching now. The yellow gleam of the lantern strode up and down the rows, approaching ever nearer. It turned the corner, and Watch stood below her.

He held the lantern high, and the light shone about his head and puddled onto the floor. It did not reach the curtain of darkness at the top of the room. Watch turned away. The lantern continued its circuit of the library, then dithered for a moment in the middle of the room. "I knows you're in here!" His voice creaked into the silence. "Might as well come out now, you little snip, from wherever you be hiding!" The voice grew wheedling. "If you comes now, I'll not fetch Mrs. O'Dair. I'll let you nip off to bed and no one the wiser."

Charlie scowled at the yellow glow. Watch was a terrible liar. O'Dair would give him double rations of beer for a week if he caught Charlie out of her room at night—and they both knew it. "Right then, you little devil! I'm locking you in here and off to fetch the missus. She'll sort you!" The lantern swayed from the room, and Charlie, left in darkness, heard the door slam and the key rattle.

She was at the bottom of the shelves in two seconds. She had decided what she was going to do, and she needed to do it quickly, before fear changed her mind. She found Tobias's book and tucked it beneath her arm—it had cost too much to leave behind now. Her pewter candlestick glinted in the moonlight. She scooped it up, broke the candle off and shoved both in her pocket. She climbed onto one of the window seats, opened a casement window, squeezed through and jumped. Gravel crunched beneath her feet, and she stretched up and pushed the casement shut. With any luck, no one would notice it wasn't latched. Charlie turned and ran.

Her heart was banging in her chest. Now that it was happening, she couldn't believe she was doing this. The Castle hounds roamed the grounds at night. If they caught her they wouldn't stop to ask if she was a princess of Quale. They would tear her to pieces, and O'Dair would be delighted to attend her funeral!

She skirted the Castle at full pelt, making for the scullery door. Its lock had been broken ever since she could remember. It wasn't far—it had seemed no distance from inside the library. But she had forgotten about the hedges to squeeze through, the weeds that entangled, the roots that tripped. She was taking too long.

Charlie had spotted the yew hedge surrounding the kitchen yard when a deep-throated bay boomed out of the darkness to her left. Then another. Then there was nothing but the sound of her own rasping breaths and the crash of heavy bodies hurtling through vegetation.

She dived forward and wriggled between two thick trunks of shaggy yew, banging her head and scraping her knees, tucking her feet as jaws snapped, snaking after her. Large bodies thrashed and scrabbled as the hounds tried to push into the gap. Then a mournful howl rose into the night air.

She stumbled across moonlit cobbles, pushed the door open and threw herself inside. She slid to the floor, and Tobias's book fell with a thump beside her. As she leant against the wall, panting for breath, Charlie thought of twelve new and even more unpleasant things to do to the gardener's boy.

She slipped through the door of the summerhouse and crunched into a hillock of leaves. The morning sun slanted through the broken windows. Charlie swept a window seat clear of frozen leaves and shattered glass and curled up to read Tobias's book. There was no telling how long he would be.

As she read it, Scheherazade's tale of *Ali Baba and the Forty Thieves* swam up through her memory to greet her, the words spoken by a voice that made her heart thump and her throat seize tight. A draught rustled across the floor, and she looked up to see Tobias step inside the summerhouse. He pushed his hair out of his eyes and left a streak of mud on his forehead.

"You're not touching this book with hands like that!" Charlie's eyes were burning with unshed tears. She grabbed her anger in relief.

"Morning to you, too." He scooped a handful of leaves from a bench and rubbed them to powder between his palms. "Never washed me hands in leaves before. But it seems to work. Any trouble getting it?"

"Enough."

"Good book, is it?"

"Yes. I want it back when you've finished. Don't you forget!"

He grinned at her. "Don't get in one of your snits, Charlie. I always give 'em back. There. Clean enough?" He held out his hands.

"Barely."

"Give us the book then."

"In a minute." She clutched it to her, not wanting to give it up, making herself concentrate on the other reason she had risked the dark and Watch. She frowned at Tobias. "You live in the City, don't you?"

"So?" His smile faded. "What's it got to do with you?"

"You must hear things."

"What sort of things?"

Now that it came to it, it was hard. She had never before asked Tobias for anything. But the image of her father kneeling before the guillotine refused to go away. Putting manure in Alfie Postlethwaite's boots wasn't going to stop him and others from thinking that her father was a bad king. Charlie studied the floor. "Rumours. Gossip. What people are saying in the City." She looked up at him. "About my father."

"Oh." His eyes grew wary. "I don't listen to gossip. You shouldn't either."

"But it isn't just gossip, is it? I know about the recession. I know that crops have failed for the second year in a row and there are food shortages. The Republicans and Radicals want a revolution, like they had in Esceania. I need to know how much support they have. How much people are blaming my father . . . Tell me what they're saying. Please!"

He looked at her, a slight frown between his eyes, and she felt a flair of hope. Tobias shook his head. "I got no time for this. Fossy'll be looking for me any minute. Give me the book."

It was no use. She should have known. Tobias Petch

kept himself to himself, and he wasn't about to change just to help her. Disappointment turned to anger. "Right!" She jumped up from the window seat and threw the book at him. It whirled through the air in a flurry of pages. He caught it in one hand.

"Missed."

She glared at him. "It wouldn't hurt you to tell me! You can get out of the Castle. I can't."

He sighed. "Forget it, Charlie. There's nothing you can do about any of it."

"Would you forget it? If it was your father?"

"I ain't got no father."

She hadn't known. For a moment she felt a tug of sympathy. "I'm sorry. What happened to him?"

"None of your business. Now, I got to get back to work." He turned to go, and all her sympathy vanished.

"You're selfish, Tobias Petch! You're a grubby, ignorant guttersnipe! I hate you!"

He turned back. To her fury, he was grinning. "And you, Princess, are an ugly little goblin. I reckon the fairies stole the real princess at birth, and you're nothing but a changeling. Maybe that's why you never learnt to smile."

She had nothing left to throw, so Charlie charged

at him, fists flying. She got in one good punch before he shoved her into the pile of leaves. He stood looking down at her, rubbing his shoulder where she had hit him. He wasn't grinning now. "You and your flaming red hair! I'll give you this much help, Charlie. It's time you learnt to control that temper of yours. You ain't some snarky little kid no more." He turned on his heel and left.

She scrabbled upright, trying to think of something cutting to shout after him. But he was already gone. Charlie sighed, rolled onto her knees and saw something white poking from the leaves. A piece of paper. One of the pages of the book must have fallen out when she threw it. But as soon as she touched it she knew it wasn't a page from the book. The paper was too thin.

Almost, she tossed it back to the leaves. It would be some old love letter or a laundry list or a receipt for making lemon curd. Idly, she turned it over and over. Her anger had vanished along with Tobias. He had refused to help her. Well, she had been a fool to expect anything else. She had always had to help herself. That was not going to change. Her fingers unfolded the paper.

It was a letter after all. Or the beginning of a letter, for it ended halfway down the page, in mid-sentence. But it wasn't a love letter. And although it was unsigned, she knew the handwriting—each sloping, spidery curl. At one time, Charlie had collected every scrap of it she could scavenge—although this sample seemed to have been written in haste and the familiar loops were uneven. She heard the voice again, as if her mother were sitting beside her, reading *Arabian Nights* once more, as she had done all those years ago. Only this time, her mother's voice read out the words of her letter:

My dearest Bettina,

I sit in the sanctuary of Charlie's nursery, watching as she sleeps. I have been reading her bedtime story. Tonight was to have been Henry's turn, but I forestalled him. These last few days I have spent every possible moment with her . . . and now that she sleeps, I may write to you in safety, unobserved.

You have never seen my two dear ones. Charlie is the image of her father, except for her hair. Though it is as red as Henry's, she has inherited my unruly curls. She would have them off, to save the pain of tangles, but I cannot bear to cut it. It is her only beauty, although her strength of character (you would doubtless call it stubbornness!) is already evident. She is my greatest joy, but as I watch her now my heart is breaking. My pain is all the greater because I fear I am about to do her untold damage.

Please excuse the unsteadiness of my handwriting! I have scarce slept for days. Something, my dear friend, something beyond imagining, has happened. You know I have, these past two years, devoted every spare moment to work essential to the peace of my country. Alas, I have drawn no closer to that which I sought, but instead have discovered something . . . something of which I dare not write! I am filled with the greatest unease. You are the only person I can turn to. I must ask . . .

And there the letter broke off. Charlie stared at the scratchy handwriting, shivering as the meaning of the words sank in.

When her mother disappeared, strange men had invaded the Castle, asking questions, peering and poking and prying. She later learnt that they were private enquiry agents hired by her father when the police and army failed to find the Queen. But the enquiry men failed too. No clue about where the Queen had gone or why she had left had ever been found. Until now.

She sank back into the leaves. Melting frost soaked into her stockings and the skirt of her dress, but she hardly noticed. A stray breeze crept through a broken window, stirring the leaves. Thoughts chased themselves, round and round.

Her mother must have run away because of something to do with her science. Once, Charlie had dared the trip to the north attics, hoping to explore her mother's old laboratory. But the door had been locked. Was the answer to her mother's disappearance somewhere inside that locked room?

Who was Bettina? Had her mother run away to her? If Charlie could find Bettina... Her heart skipped a beat. Her eyes scanned the paper, devouring the words over and over: *"... my two dear ones ... my greatest joy ..."*

Charlie never cried. Crying didn't help. It hadn't brought her mother home. Something round and wet plopped onto her mother's letter. Charlie blinked and wiped her face with her sleeve. She folded the letter and hid it in her pocket.

As she hurried back to the Castle, listening for any

hint of Foss, climbing in through the window, dodging the maids in the corridors, her hand kept creeping back into the pocket, her fingers searching out the folded edge of her mother's letter.

# Four

The ground-floor corridors, with their dark panelling and moulded plaster ceilings, stank of beeswax and mildew. Charlie's ancestors frowned from every wall, trapped forever inside gilded frames. The midday sun penetrated the gloom far enough to pick out glinting eyes, petulant mouths, frothy lace, sabres in jewelled scabbards. A rat scratched behind the panelling. Perhaps it knew, as she did, that Mrs. O'Dair was safely at her lunch. Charlie shuddered (whether at the thought of the rat or Mrs. O'Dair, she didn't know) and hurried on.

She pulled open the serving-room door and stepped into a long cupboard of a room. A row of tables lined one side. Set in the wall above them was the door that hid the dumbwaiter. Charlie clambered onto a table, tugged the dumbwaiter door open and crawled inside. She took a deep breath and pulled the door closed, shutting herself in the dark. Her fingers fumbled to find the pair of thick cables, fastened around the right-hand one and pulled. For a moment, nothing happened. Then the dumbwaiter lurched and, with a protesting squeak of gears and pulleys, slid down its wooden shaft towards the cellars.

Charlie hauled on the rope with a fury born of panic. After counting down three floors she fought the dumb-waiter to a halt, flung open the door, exploded out in a flurry of elbows and feet, and sat in an inch-thick layer of dust.

*"Aaaa-choo! A-tishoo!"* She grabbed her outraged nose and squeezed it shut as she scrambled to her feet. Dust swirled through the air. It lay in drifts across the stone floor. Overhead, tiny square windows pierced the very top of the walls, where the Castle sprouted from the earth. Dust swam up to the windows and slid back down on feeble beams of light.

Empty cupboards lined the walls either side of her. She glimpsed her reflection in one of the glass doors and saw that Tobias was right: she looked like a scrawny goblin, its hair bristling in a halo of tufts. She scowled and shook her head, spraying dust like water. She should have thought to wash; maybe even tried to brush her hair.

She dug the remains of a handkerchief from her pocket, spat on it and rubbed at her face, patted her hair and scraped at the black crescent moons under her fingernails. The reflection looked as grubby as ever. She gave up and waded through dust drifts down the corridor.

Light oozed beneath the door. She knocked and waited. And waited. Mr. Moleglass valued patience. Finally, the pattering of footsteps seeped under the door along with the light. The door creaked open to reveal a small, egg-shaped man wearing a morning suit and starched collar. His feet were clad in slippers of finest red leather, and he wore gloves the exact pigeon grey of his waistcoat.

"I see." Mr. Moleglass peered at her as though from a great height, although he was barely taller than she was. "On the scrounge again, Your Highness?" His voice was soft and sharp at the same time, like a slice of lemon cake. The ends of his moustache curled. The better his mood, the curlier the ends. Today, they barely curved out of the horizontal.

"You had best come in." He held the door wide for her. "Although I warn you, I've little enough food for myself these days."

"You always say that, and it's never true. You're quite as fat as ever."

"And you, ma'am, are quite as rude as ever." Mr. Moleglass shut the door behind her and padded across the room to the table which stood near the fireplace. "Please be seated." He pulled out one of the chairs and waited with the infinite patience of the professional. The visit was turning into a disaster.

"Oh, please stop butlering!" Charlie pleaded. "I need to talk to you about something really important, and it isn't my fault you're in a bad mood."

When Charlie was five years old, her parents had taken her on a trip to the seaside. While paddling on a shingly beach, she had met a seal with a sleek dark head and anxious brown eyes. The eyes had been wise and kind and sad. They had asked her a question she could not answer and disappeared into the blue-green water.

Mr. Moleglass reminded her of the seal. It was one of the reasons she loved him.

His eyes gazed at her in just that way now. "You're right," he said. "Let us start again. What do you wish to discuss?"

"My mother! I need to know about my mother, Mr. Moleglass."

He raised both eyebrows. "What can I possibly tell you about your mother that you do not already know? She was the Queen; I was her butler."

"I need to know about her work."

"Ah!" he said, and smiled. "She did her job very well. We were a brilliant team, your mother and I. She had flair and elegance, and I . . . well, I have a genius for organisation. Precision, timing and attention to detail." He sighed. "Detail is so important and yet so often overlooked."

"Stop teasing! You know I don't mean all that: I mean her real work, her—"

"Are you saying that running a castle isn't real work?"

*"Please, Mr. Moleglass!"* She hadn't meant to shout.

His eyes widened. "I apologise, Charlie. I did not realise . . . Sit here, please."

He fetched another chair and perched in front of

her. "You ask about your mother's scientific research. I fear I can be of little help. She seldom mentioned it in my presence. Now, something has happened to you. What is it? Why is your mother's research suddenly so important?"

Her stomach twisted into an even tighter knot. Mr. Moleglass knew everything about the Castle. It had never occurred to her that he might not know about her mother's work. She reached into her pocket and pulled out the letter. "I found this."

Moleglass took the letter, slid his spectacle case from his inside breast pocket, clicked it open, balanced a gold pince-nez on his nose, and glanced down. His eyes darted up to hers, then fastened once more on the paper. When he finally looked up at her, his face was grim. "Where did you find this? *Have you shown it to anyone else?*"

The look in his eyes scared her. "I-I found it in a book." Why was he so upset? "A book I took from the library. I remember my mother reading it to me just before she disappeared. And of course I haven't shown it to anyone else."

"Good! Do not! *Promise me.* Let me keep this letter

for you . . . or, better yet, let me destroy it—" He made a movement towards the hob and its glowing fire.

"No!" She jumped up, snatching the letter. "I need it!"

"Very well, Charlie." He held his hands up in defeat. "Sit down, sit down! I'll not try to take it from you, child! But you must promise me never to let anyone see that letter!"

"I promise, but—"

"Keep it if you must, as a memento, but I advise you to forget you ever read it!"

She stared at him in amazement. "Don't you understand what this means? My mother didn't abandon me! She left because of something to do with her research. She discovered something dangerous. I have to find out what it was, and I need you to help me."

He shut his eyes in dismay, but she pressed on. "It's no good, Mr. Moleglass. I can't just forget about this! Do you know who Bettina is?"

"No. I never heard your mother mention anyone of that name. She must be a friend from her life before she was Queen." He stood and strode to the sink, table and cupboard that served him for a kitchen. "It is lunchtime. We will think more effectively without hunger to distract us."

Charlie groaned. Worry always made Mr. Moleglass ravenous. "How can you think of food now? I'm not hungry!"

He ignored her. He placed the kettle on the hob and began to bustle about, exploring the contents of his cupboard, unwrapping interesting packages, covering the table with a crisp white cloth. A curl of steam rose from the kettle.

Charlie gave up. She had lied, anyway: she was starving! And despite everything, the room was working its magic on her. It was her one true place of refuge. Outside was a world of dust, but inside this room every surface was burnished until it shone in the red glow of the coal fire. Against her will, she felt a thread of comfort begin to uncurl deep inside and rise, like the steam from the kettle. And she found she could not help wondering about the contents of those interesting packages.

Mr. Moleglass turned to her with a smile. "Luncheon is served."

The sight of the table made her eyes grow large. "It's a feast! Oh, Mr. Moleglass—it's wonderful!" There was sliced bread and butter, a wedge of yellow cheese, a thick slice of pink ham, and sponge cake layered with strawberry jam and sprinkled with sugar. Charlie hadn't tasted butter or jam for months. She stood in silent awe. "Where did you get it all?" she whispered.

"That is not your business. And if you expect to eat any of it you had better wash your hands. They are disgusting."

Mr. Moleglass filled her plate, put rather larger portions on his own, and for some time the only sound was that of contented munching. Charlie licked her finger and mopped up the last of the crumbs. She could have eaten more: she could always eat more; but she was aware of the blissful feeling of having had enough. The butler leant back in his chair.

"Now. This letter. Your mother disappeared over five years ago. Whatever reason she had for leaving—"

"Her science. The letter says—"

"Whatever the reason, she has not returned. Which means that either whatever threat she foresaw still exists, or that she is . . . unable to return."

The meaning of his words hit her. *"She isn't dead!"*

Moleglass bowed his head. She couldn't tell whether he was agreeing with her or merely refusing to argue.

Finally he looked up. "Perhaps. But the truth is that your mother was Queen of Quale, and whatever this threat is, she could not beat it." He paused, and she saw doubt darken his eyes. "A grown woman and a queen. You are a child. How can you hope to succeed where your mother failed?"

For a moment it felt like she was back in the dumbwaiter with blackness pressing in from every side. But she knew that, even if Mr. Moleglass was right, she couldn't stop now. If she could find her mother, everything that was upside down in her life would right itself. Her father would get well and be a good king, and there would be no more talk of revolutions and cutting off heads. Mrs. O'Dair would be sent away, and Mr. Moleglass would move back upstairs. And her mother ... her mother would be home again.

She wanted to tell him all this, but the only thing she could say was: "You're my friend. You're supposed to help me!"

His mouth fell open in protest, and his face flushed pink. "You are right," he said at last. "I apologise. I will help in whatever way I can."

"Good!" Charlie bounced upright in her chair. She

reached out for her cup, took a sip of tea. "I need a lock-smith."

*"What?"*

"Or the keys to my mother's laboratory. I need to get inside."

"But the keys—"

"Are with all the others dangling from Mrs. O'Dair's waist. I know. That's why I need a locksmith."

"Just like that?" He gave his left moustache a fierce tweak. "I'm to magic a locksmith into the Castle without that rather astounding circumstance coming to the housekeeper's attention? Or did you intend to tell her of your plans? Perhaps ask her to come along and supervise?"

Charlie held onto her temper. She knew he was frightened. He had always refused to tell her why he had moved to the cellars after her mother's disappearance, but she knew it was something to do with Mrs. O'Dair. He could hardly bear to speak of the housekeeper. "You promised to help," she said, fixing him with a stare. "Or did you mean only when it's easy?"

His eyebrows shot upwards in outrage. But almost immediately the eyes beneath them began to sparkle.

"Do not be so hasty, my child. I shall not find you a mere locksmith. I shall procure for you a genius of locks!"

Charlie groaned. "Please, Mr. Moleglass. Stop joking!"

"But I am most serious. And we shall not have to pay our locksmith, I think. Which is just as well, as neither of us is in funds at the moment." He paused, to give his announcement full effect. "Come to tea tomorrow, Charlie, and I will provide you with something more interesting even than cake and jam."

And, no matter how she pleaded, he would tell her nothing more.

# Five

Charlie crept along the abandoned corridors of the east wing until she found the room she wanted. The door to her mother's study thudded behind her. She shivered: cold had seeped into the very bones of this room. Some six-year-old part of her still expected to see her mother look up from the desk in the window and turn to Charlie with the smile she saved especially for her. It had been years since she had come here, or allowed herself to remember that smile.

Several hours later she had looked in every drawer of the desk, every cubbyhole of every cabinet, and rifled the pages of all the books on the shelves. She took a stolen apple from her pocket and climbed onto the window seat. She had found nothing. No hint of what her mother had been researching nearly six years ago. And none of the diaries, address books or old letters contained the name "Bettina." There was still the laboratory, she comforted herself. Surely she would find something there. *If* Mr. Moleglass kept his promise about the locksmith.

The apple was old and tasted of cloth, but she worked steadfastly at it and had nibbled it nearly to the core when she heard footsteps clattering down the hall towards her. "Blast and botheration!" Charlie squeezed behind the nearest curtain. It pressed against her, shrouding her in cold and mildew, clinging to her face like damp cobwebs. The curtains had been eaten into a filigree of holes by sun and moth. She found that if she bent over slightly she could see the room through a halo of frayed fabric.

Martha, the parlour maid, bustled into sight. Trotting at her heels was a maid Charlie had never seen before, a girl of about sixteen or seventeen, with brown hair neatly tucked beneath her cap. Martha marched to the desk and swiped at it with a grimy cloth. "You have to dust and sweep the carpet and clean the window, mind. Dusting's once a week; sweeping once a fortnight, cleaning glass once a month."

"There's a mort of glass in this place," the girl grumbled, shrugging her shoulders as if they were already sore from polishing. She picked up a feather duster and dabbed at the bookshelf.

"Well, it's gotta be done." Martha rubbed at the desk. "Waste of time. She'll not come back."

"The Queen?"

"Dead!" Martha stopped rubbing and looked at the new maid with narrowed eyes. "Some say murdered."

Inside the curtain, Charlie gasped. It felt like someone had punched her in the stomach. Martha hitched up her skirt and sat on the desk. The new maid left off dusting. "Really?" she asked, her eyes wide. She clutched the feather duster to her bosom. "Who would want to kill the Queen? She was so beautiful."

"Jealousy does funny things to a man's mind," said Martha.

"You don't mean . . ."

Charlie couldn't breathe. She watched Martha shrug

her shoulders and smile. "Everyone knows the Kingdom's cursed," she said. "All the bad things started happening after the Queen disappeared. That's also when a certain person lost his marbles. You figure it out."

Charlie yelled. She roared. She tore the curtain open and rushed at Martha, fists flying. The parlour maid caught her wrists. Charlie kicked out, and Martha grabbed her by the shoulders and shook her. "Stop that! You little tyke! If you don't want to hear nasty things then don't hide in the curtains and eavesdrop."

Charlie stopped screaming and stood still. She thought she might be sick. She glared at Martha, shivering.

"Who on earth is that?" gasped the new maid.

"That?" Martha asked. "Believe it or not, that is Her Royal Highness, the Princess Charlotte." They stared down at Charlie.

*"My father did not murder my mother!"* Charlie's voice was barely a whisper and she was shaking worse than ever. She looked at Martha until the parlour maid's eyes flickered and dropped. The new maid did not look away. Charlie saw pity in her face and, at the sight of it, she turned and ran from the room.

————

She castled too soon. As soon as she switched the positions of her king and rook, she knew she had made a mistake. Mr. Moleglass's eyes glowed with delight. His bishop swooped out of nowhere and captured her remaining knight. "When's he coming?" she asked for the tenth time.

"Patience, Charlie," chided Mr. Moleglass. "He will come as soon as he can. It is your turn," he said, tapping the chessboard to draw her attention. "You are in danger of losing in less than ten moves. Really, Charlie, it becomes embarrassing!"

As she struggled to concentrate, Charlie became aware of a squeaking which grew rapidly louder. The squeaking was joined by a trundling. They arrived outside Mr. Moleglass's door. *THUD, THUD!* The door shook on its hinges.

"One moment, please," called Mr. Moleglass. He rose from his chair, dusted his jacket, neatened the creases in his trousers, straightened his gloves and strolled to the door. Charlie struggled for breath.

Mr. Moleglass swung open the door to reveal a wooden wheelbarrow loaded with coal. Behind it stood Tobias. "Excellent!" crowed Mr. Moleglass. "Come in! You are most welcome."

Charlie's heart fell into her boots. She threw Tobias her dirtiest look. He ignored her and grinned at Mr. Moleglass. "Will I fill the scuttle, then?"

"If you would, my boy. But wait just a moment." Mr. Moleglass scurried away and returned with an armful of old newspapers, which he proceeded to lay in a path across the floor to the fireplace. When he had finished, Tobias wheeled the barrow across the papers and began to shovel coal into the large brass scuttle. Mr. Moleglass stood and rubbed his hands with pleasure. Charlie kicked her feet under her chair and wished Tobias in twenty different uncomfortable locations.

"Thank you most sincerely, Tobias," Mr. Moleglass said when the barrow was empty. "Now please put the barrow outside and return here. I want a brief word."

Tobias shrugged and wheeled the barrow out. He edged back through the door and stood, scuffing his feet. Mr. Moleglass tidied away the papers, filled the kettle and put it on the hob. Charlie and Tobias watched him with identical expressions of discomfort.

"Wash your hands, Tobias, and join us for a cup of tea," said Mr. Moleglass.

"Ah, well . . . I'd best be off, Mr. M. Got work, you see—"

"Mr. Moleglass! Have you forgotten? We're expecting—"

Mr. Moleglass could not have heard them. He turned from the larder cupboard, holding a jug of milk. He set six shortbread biscuits on a plate and put plate and jug on his dining table. Charlie shot a glare at Tobias that could have boiled eggs.

"The sink, Tobias," Mr. Moleglass said. Tobias stumped to the sink and splashed briefly. "Be seated, please." The boy threw a puzzled look at him but scuffed over to the table. "Now, Charlie. Your hands could doubtless use some attention. Please wash them and join us."

He ignored her look of outrage. She stamped to the sink, washed her hands and sat as far away from Tobias as possible. Mr. Moleglass sat between them and poured the tea. Charlie had never enjoyed any cup of tea less. She glared into her teacup.

"Ah," sighed Mr. Moleglass into the silence. "There really is nothing quite like that first sip to rinse away the strains of the day."

She could not stand it any longer. "Mr. Moleglass!" she hissed. "The boy's had his cup of tea. Now send him away! You know that we're expecting someone."

Mr. Moleglass looked at her. It was the look he gave

her when she made a particularly stupid chess move. "Your locksmith, Your Highness, has arrived."

Charlie stared at him. She turned and looked at Tobias. He stared back, an appalled expression growing on his face. "Mr. M!" The hurt in Tobias's voice was plain. He stared at the butler as though Moleglass had betrayed him.

"I'm sorry, Tobias. But this is important. You know I would not—"

"Locksmith!" interrupted Charlie. "He's not a locksmith! He's nothing but a gardener's boy. And he's not even very good at that! Foss is always shouting at him for skiving off."

"Enough, Charlie!" snapped Moleglass. "Or don't you want to get into your mother's laboratory after all?"

"Of course I do, but—"

"Then I suggest you stop antagonising the only person who can help you."

Charlie's mouth fell open. She stared at the butler, then at Tobias, who had jumped to his feet. "You promised," he said to Mr. Moleglass. "I trusted you!" His face had closed down. "I'm off." He turned towards the door.

"Tobias, please!" Moleglass darted forward, put a

restraining hand on the boy's arm. Tobias whirled to face him and, for a moment, Charlie thought he would shake off the butler's hand. What was going on?

They were the same height, she noticed—the plump, immaculately dressed butler and the tall boy in his mud-stained clothes and shabby boots.

"I'm sorry, Tobias," Mr. Moleglass said. A note of pleading entered his voice. "I would not involve you in this if I did not believe that Charlie is to be trusted, and if this matter was not of the greatest importance. Please listen to what we have to say before making your decision."

Tobias frowned at the butler for a moment, then shrugged. "I'll listen. I reckon I owe you that."

"Thank you. Charlie has a problem," Mr. Moleglass said in a quiet voice. "And you are the only person who can help her. I think you are not so unkind as to refuse to help someone who is in need, if you are able? Well?"

Tobias sighed. "All right then. What's up?"

"Charlie," said Mr. Moleglass, "show Tobias the letter."

"But you said—"

"If Tobias is going to share a secret with you, then it is only fair that you do the same. I would not ask if

I thought we could not trust him not to tell anyone about this. Surely you cannot suspect Tobias of having anything to do with your mother's disappearance?"

She hesitated. Tobias was staring at them both in amazement. "Oh, all right." She fished the letter from her pocket and handed it to him. He unfolded the paper, and she watched as he read it, once quickly, then again, more slowly, before pursing his lips and giving a low, tuneless whistle. "Sweet Betty!" He raised wondering eyes. "How long have you been sitting on this, then?"

"I found it yesterday," she said. "It fell out of the book I stole for you."

"Stole?" said Mr. Moleglass. "What are you talking about, Charlie?"

"Strike me sideways!" Tobias studied the letter again, his face solemn. Then the familiar grin returned. "See? I done you a favour, Charlie. Reckon you owe me."

"I don't understand. Why would you steal a book for Tobias?" The butler's voice was plaintive.

"I don't owe you anything, Tobias Petch. But I might. If you really can unlock the door to my mother's laboratory. It is true?"

He looked at her, considering, then nodded. "I'll do it. I reckon this is important. To more folks than just you. I'll get you in, but don't get your hopes up."

"What do you mean?"

"Nothing." He shrugged. "You need to find out why your mum left, and that's as good a place to start as any. What about tomorrow? I can slip away from Fossy for an hour midday. He always nods off in the greenhouse after lunch. But if you ever tell anyone about me, I'll . . . well, just you keep your mouth shut if anyone ever asks how you got in there. You understand?"

His blue eyes were cold, and for the first time in all the years she had known him, Charlie was frightened of Tobias Petch.

They left together. Neither spoke. Charlie started for the dumbwaiter but froze when she noticed Tobias wheeling the barrow towards the servants' lift. "You're never going to use the lift?" she blurted. "O'Dair will hear it. She'll find you out!"

"O'Dair knows." Tobias gave her a withering look. "How d'you think I got the barrow down here to begin with, you gurnless idiot?"

Charlie was so astonished she ignored the insult. "O'Dair knows? She lets you bring coal to Mr. Moleglass?"

"She don't *let* me. It's her orders. I been bringing him coal and food and such for years. I'm off. It's all right for some, larking about. I got work to do."

"But why?" Charlie darted in front of the barrow, blocking it. "Why does the O'Dair give it to him?"

Tobias let go of the wheelbarrow and stood staring at her, his arms crossed. "That's none of your business," he said. "I reckon if Mr. M wants you to know, he'll tell you himself. Now, outta my way, or I'll bump you."

Charlie jumped aside. "I was only asking," she said, as he wheeled to the lift and began opening the mechanism. "Mr. Moleglass is my friend, too!"

A grunt was all the reply she got. Tobias pushed the barrow into the lift.

"Wait! Tobias!"

He paused in the act of closing the inner grille and looked at her impatiently. "Well?"

"It's just . . ." She gazed longingly at the spacious lift with its glass roof, air vents and pair of glazed lanterns.

"What?"

It wasn't worth the risk—just because she was afraid

of the dark. "Nothing," she said. And, because she was disappointed, she snapped: "Don't be late tomorrow."

"And don't you go bossing me around."

The lift door clanged shut, and the mechanism clanked into action. Charlie stood listening to the gears yanking the lift to the upper floors. Then she turned and began the dark journey back to the attics.

# Six

Charlie was hiding inside the abandoned butler's pantry on the ground floor of the north wing, her heart thudding in an irritating fashion. She pressed her ear against the panelled door and listened to the groan of approaching whalebone, the slither of starched bombazine. Like the windings of an enormous serpent, the sound of Mrs. O'Dair slid past the butler's pantry and hissed away down the corridor.

"Can we get on now?"

"Hush! She might have heard you!" It wasn't really

a lie. A few seconds earlier, it would have been true. She wasn't enjoying sneaking Tobias into the attics. Unless he was on an errand for O'Dair, the gardener's boy wasn't allowed in the Castle. But Tobias was Maria's special pet. It wasn't fair the way the cook spoilt him, slipping him treats and stopping work to make him cups of tea whenever he poked his head into the kitchen. But Charlie had to admit it had been useful today. Maria had merely shrugged when Tobias slid through the scullery door, then gone back to peeling parsnips.

Charlie knew O'Dair's schedule by heart. It was just past one. The housekeeper had spent the last hour devouring an enormous lunch. Now she would be settling her black bombazine backside into the well-cushioned armchair beside the fire, easing off her boots and propping her large, stocking-clad feet onto an ottoman. She would rest in her office for at least an hour, snoring until her corsets creaked.

Charlie counted to fifty, then crept out of the butler's pantry. Motioning Tobias to follow, she tiptoed to the servants' stairs and began to climb. The narrow wooden steps twisted round and round. A shaft of light dropped from a window far above, and the dry patter of their footsteps fell with it, down the dim brown well of stairs all the way to the basements.

The door on the sixth landing squeaked as she eased it open, a rusty screech. She jumped. Tobias snickered. She dug an elbow in his ribs. "Shut up, you!"

The door opened onto a dark, narrow corridor. The only light came from the stairwell behind them. Charlie had not been up here for years. The dusty floorboards creaked under their feet, and the noise of their footsteps seemed to echo endlessly. "Shhhh!" she hissed.

"There's nobody to hear us, Charlie." Tobias pushed past her and strode down the corridor towards a pair of large double doors. He tried the door knob. It was locked.

"Well?" she said.

He grinned at her. "You don't reckon I can get in there, do you? Well just you watch!" He fished in his pocket and pulled out a buttonhook.

Charlie stared at him. He was mad. "What use is that? Unless . . ." Her mouth fell open. "You're not . . . you can't . . ."

His grin grew wider. He squatted, stuck the buttonhook in the keyhole, wiggled it for a few seconds, and

Charlie heard a click. "How did you learn to do that?" she asked, awed in spite of herself.

Tobias shrugged. "Me stepdad was a thief. But just you remember to keep quiet about it." He pushed the door open, and Charlie walked into a room outside her imaginings.

The light that fell from enormous skylights dazzled her, and she stood still for a moment, blinking. She saw tables: rows of tables laden with brass microscopes, boxes of prepared slides, white ceramic dishes, burners, copper and iron vats, small and large charcoal ovens, wooden geometric models, stands holding coloured wooden balls arranged in intricate patterns, and racks of glass tubes, both empty and full. A blanket of powdery grime lay over the whole room. No one had been in here for years.

Tobias slowly revolved on one heel, digging a divot in the dust. "Blimey!" he breathed at last. "What a place! What *is* all this stuff?"

"It's my mother's equipment, of course."

"I know that, you gurnless girl. What's it do? What sort of things was she working on?"

"That's what I need to find out." She wandered among the tables, moving on each time her eye caught something new. A cupboard filled one wall. Through its glass door she saw ceramic jars with strange words written on them: selenite, beryllium, protosulphate of iron, antimony, tellurium. On the opposite wall stood an even larger cupboard full of crystals of every shape, colour and size, each carefully labelled.

"Sweet Betty!" Tobias was craning over her shoulder, reading the labels. "Didn't even know words like them existed," he said. "Right clever, your mum."

"You can go."

"What?"

"Go away! Go back to work. I don't need you now. You got the door open, and I'm grateful. I owe you another book. Don't worry! I'll pay you."

He was irritating her, wandering around her mother's laboratory, his sharp eyes peering, his clomping boots tracking through dust that had lain undisturbed for years. She wanted to be alone here. "Just go away!" she snapped, as he ignored her and sauntered across the room to peer inside another cabinet.

"I ain't going nowhere, Charlie. So just get on with what you want to do and put up with it."

"Why not? This is my mother's laboratory. It's nothing to do with you!"

He turned to her, wearing his most annoying smile. "And it's kept locked, ain't it? How you gonna lock it when you're done? Didn't think of that, did you? You want Watch to find this door unlocked next time he bothers to get his spindly shanks this far north, and go running to O'Dair?"

"Show me how to do that trick with the button-hook. Then you can go."

Tobias stared at her, then roared with laughter. "Just like that, eh? You want to learn lock-picking in five minutes? Thinking of starting a career as a cracksman, are you, Charlie?"

"Blast you, Tobias Petch!" She stamped through the dust to the desk which stood beneath a dormer window. A minute later she had forgotten him. One of the desk drawers was crammed with letters from other scientists, and Charlie scanned the names eagerly. No Bettina. She pulled out some of the letters to take away and read more carefully.

A pneumatic messenger had been installed to one side of the desk. Its brass body was tarnished greenish black, but the wire catch basket below was still full of the brass capsules used to carry messages. She unscrewed them, one by one, but they were all empty.

No long-forgotten message lay curled inside. She even lifted the flap of the pneumatic tube itself to make sure a forgotten capsule hadn't stuck in its throat. Then she gave up and turned to the pair of filing cabinets standing nearby.

Over eight years of research was carefully documented in her mother's spiky writing; each experiment recorded in precise detail and filed in chronological order. But the last paper in the cabinet was dated November 1843. Her mother had disappeared in May 1846. The vital two and a half years of research were missing.

A noise made her look around. She was startled to see Tobias. She had forgotten him. He was scuffing round and round a machine that stood at the other end of the room. It was nearly six feet tall and wide and sprouted glass tubes, brass wheels and gears. He caught her eye and grinned. "Look at this, Charlie! I do believe it's one of them machines for making electricity!"

She shuffled over and stood, looking at the machine. Tobias swiped at a brass plaque with his sleeve. "Read that," he said.

Charlie leant over. Through the greenish tarnish she could just make out the words: *Epsalom Tidbury's 6,000-Volt Generator. Patent Pending.*

"That's no help! What sort of use do you think that is, Tobias Petch?"

"Didn't find nothing, then?" His tone was conversational. She was grateful to him. She couldn't have stood sympathy.

"No!" She kicked Epsalom Tidbury's Generator and wished she hadn't.

"Here!" Tobias pulled her away. "Don't be daft—you'll break your foot. You didn't really expect things to be that easy, did you? Your mum was clever. She wouldn't have left her research here to be snaffled by whoever was after it, would she?"

It was appallingly obvious, and she hadn't wanted it to be true. The miracle of finding the letter was supposed to transform her life, give back her mother, make up for all the years of loneliness, all the years of Mrs. O'Dair and her father's card castles.

"You've still got the name, Charlie." Tobias's voice broke through the blackness of her thoughts. "This Bettina might know something, and there's got to be a way of tracking her down. I've got to go now, it's nearly been an hour. Fossy'll be waking up, and he don't appreciate me taking leave of absence."

Bitterness lay beneath the words, like mud on a river

bottom. He was smiling, but she wasn't fooled. She knew Tobias tended to skive off work whenever he could, but had never occurred to her that he might really hate working for the old gardener.

"He doesn't beat you, does he?" It was a horrible thought. Not even the housekeeper had ever dared strike her. But she knew that many children were not so lucky.

Tobias looked at her with narrowed eyes. For a moment she thought she had made him angry. Then he shrugged his shoulders. "Fossy? Course not. But he moans on at me for hours on end. A beating would be a sight quicker."

She grabbed the pile of letters from the desk and watched as he locked the laboratory door behind them.

"Would you teach me to pick locks?" Charlie asked, as politely as she could. "So I can get back in here?"

He glanced up at her, sighed. "Just get a buttonhook and practise, Charlie. Ward locks ain't hard. But you got to find the knack. Some never manage. Now let's shift." And he was gone, nipping down the servants' stair and out of sight, leaving her to follow, clutching the bundle of letters and the last of her hope.

# Seven

Charlie's supper was a bowl of cold parsnip soup and a hunk of stale bread. All her meals were left outside her bedroom door on a tray, and if she didn't collect them promptly, the rats got there first. She gulped the soup, shuddering at the taste, before racing downstairs to the library, anxious to get there and back before the gas lights were turned off for the night.

None of the letters from the laboratory had mentioned a woman called Bettina. She had pored over them for hours, looking for that name and for any clue to her mother's last project. All she had learnt was that her mother's work involved something called "synthesis." She was going to the library for a bit of research while it was safe. Mrs. O'Dair and most of the servants would be arrayed round the trestle table in the servants' hall, digging into something more appetising than parsnip soup.

She rounded the last corner and slid to a stop, surprised to see the door to the library open and light flooding out into the dimly lit corridor. She pressed into the wall and sidled as close to the door as she dared. Watch's voice drifted out. The words were mushy, as though struggling to find room in a mouth doing double duty.

"—mighty kind of you, Toby-boy. You know how fond I be of Maria's meat pies. Ain't no one conjure up pastry like that woman." There was a pause filled with chewing sounds.

". . . just have a look . . ." Tobias's voice was fainter.

"Look all you want, Toby. I'm too busy to notice if a book or two goes missing. Now, about Maria. You promised to write out that letter for me. You ain't forgot?"

". . . haven't forgotten, Watch. But I don't . . ."

"Leave the thinking to me, boy. Women likes love letters and such rubbish. Sweet talking will get you almost anything, and Maria's worth sweet talking more'n most. Not many women can cook like that one. And there ain't a female yet didn't want to get hitched. She's a rare one, but she ain't no spring chicken. Boy?"

Tobias's reply was muffled.

"Well, hurry up about them dang books. Then I'll tell you what I want in this here letter. You do this for me, son, and you got free range all over the Castle. My word on it."

Charlie eased back the way she had come. Her research would have to wait. A thief! That's all Tobias Petch was. Just like his stepfather. A thief and a swindler and not to be trusted. How dare he bribe Watch in order to steal her books! She only wished Maria knew the company her precious Toby kept, and what he got up to with the food she gave him.

Early next morning, Charlie visited her father again. She knelt on the floor of his chamber and watched as he demolished his castle. The King climbed his scaffolding until he was just above the highest tower. Dangling from his knees, he plucked the topmost layer of cards, harvesting them neatly, sending them fluttering to the ground. Her job was to creep about the floor, gathering the cards and sorting them into decks. They worked without speaking, the silence broken only by the whirr of falling cards.

Charlie loved watching the cards float down, spiralling like strange, rectangular leaves. But today . . . She knew she must choose her time, make him listen. And pray that they would not be disturbed again by the O'Dair. She watched and waited, her fingers gathering in the steady drizzle of playing cards.

The crenellations of the first tower took over three hours to demolish. Charlie's hands were stiff from sorting cards into packs, her knees sore from kneeling. The King drifted to the ground with the last of the cards. He counted the packs and stacked them in neat piles against the wall. "One hundred and two. Excellent! I needn't remind you not to bend them, Charlotte. A bent card is a wasted card."

"Yes, Father."

The King turned to gaze up at the remaining thirty-seven towers. This was it: in a moment he would be up the scaffold, and it would be another three hours. She reached out, caught the hem of his trouser leg, gave it a gentle tug. "Father!" she whispered. "I need to talk to you."

"What?" He turned and stared at Charlie's left ear distractedly. "Whatever for?"

"Have you heard of someone called Bettina?"

"Bettina?" He shook his head. "I don't think so, my dear. It isn't a Qualian name, you know. Sounds Durch to me."

Charlie sighed. Another dead end. Her father turned away, and she caught his trouser leg again. "Wait, Father. There's something else. Something important."

He sighed. "Please, Charlie. Be brief. I am busy."

"Something's wrong."

"Wrong?" Her father looked both puzzled and irritated. "Of course nothing's wrong. What could possibly be wrong?" His eyes widened in fear, and his hands wrung themselves in a flutter of anxiety. "It's not the playing cards, is it? They haven't stopped making my playing cards, have they? They wear out so quickly, and I haven't had a new shipment for months."

"It isn't the playing cards, Father!" She tried again. "Things are bad in the Kingdom ... and you need to know ... there are horrible rumours about you.

77

The papers are full of stories about Republicans and Radicals—"

But he was once more standing with his arms folded across his chest, gazing up at his castle made of cards.

*"Father!"* This time she did not bother to whisper. A dozen card towers shivered.

The King frowned at his daughter. For the first time in five years, he nearly looked at her. "Charlotte! You know the rules. If you cannot obey them you must leave."

"But the Kingdom's in danger! *You're* in danger!" Charlie blinked back tears of frustration. *"Listen to me!"*

"Nonsense! Alistair would have told me if anything were amiss. He has everything well in hand, as always. You are imagining things, child."

Her mouth dropped open. Of course! But there wasn't time to think about it now. He was turning away. "Father! Please listen—"

It was no use. The King was gone, swinging hand over hand high into the scaffolding. He didn't look back at her. He had forgotten she was there.

———

Charlie knew what she had to do. She didn't bother with the servants' stairs. She raced down the main staircase to the ground floor and pelted along the corridor. But she had forgotten that on Wednesday mornings the housekeeper supervised the cleaning of the state rooms.

"Where do you think you're going, young lady?" Mrs. O'Dair hove into sight, a battleship of black bombazine and starched linen running at full sail, her corsets creaking and groaning like ship's tackle under strain.

Charlie was going too fast to stop. She slid straight into the prow of the Battleship O'Dair. There was a smothering moment as the black bombazine yielded slightly beneath the invader, then the O'Dair rebounded, and Charlie found herself flying backwards. She hit the floor with a *whump!* that knocked the air out of her.

The housekeeper loomed above her. Charlie lay gasping on the floor, unable to speak, looking past the mountain range of Mrs. O'Dair's bosom, past her starched lace collar and the double chin it struggled to contain, past the beaked nose, straight into the clever dark eyes glaring down at her.

With a sudden creaking of corsets, O'Dair leant over and, with one large square hand, plucked Charlie off the floor and dangled her for a moment, before dropping her like a mother cat discarding a kitten. "Well?"

"Sorry, Mrs. O'Dair," Charlie muttered.

"You were running! Princesses do not run. To help you remember that fact when you are next tempted to run in the corridors, you shall have no supper tonight." She swept on in a rustle of starch and linen, then stopped suddenly and creaked round to spear Charlie once more with her stare. "What are you doing here, by the way? You have no business in this part of the Castle."

"I . . . I was going to the library." Charlie was painfully aware of her heart thumping and a drip of sweat beading down beside her left ear.

"Indeed," the housekeeper said at last. "You know perfectly well that you are not allowed to choose your own books from the library. No more books for a week. Then, if you ask me, I shall select something suitable for you. And now," concluded Mrs. O'Dair, "I shall lock you in your room, where you will stay for the remainder of the day."

The key clicked in the lock. Charlie crouched beside the door and listened to the housekeeper's corsets squeak and wheeze down the corridor. *"No supper!"* they taunted. *"No supper tonight!"* She ignored them. No one was going to stop her. Certainly not the O'Dair. She had known what she must do since the moment her father reminded her about Alistair Windlass.

Not that she had forgotten him. The man was impossible to ignore. *The People's Enquirer, The Illustrated News, The Dispatch* and *The Morning Chronicle* disagreed about most things, but on one subject they were united: Quale's brilliant young Prime Minister was the only thing standing between the country and disaster.

What Charlie *had* forgotten was that Alistair Windlass had been one of her parents' closest friends. He had often dined with them privately, and was always to be found at their grand evening parties. On these occasions she had been allowed a brief visit to the minstrels' gallery above the ballroom.

She would pull herself up onto her toes and peer over the banisters at the gentlemen in their dark suits and the ladies in their silken frocks of butterfly colours.

Her father was the best dancer of them all. She watched him, a slender figure in black, his dark red hair burning in the gaslight like the flame on a match, twirling among the pinks and purples, blues and golds, waiting for him to remember to look up at her and wink. She shivered with delight at the vision of her tall, golden-haired mother. "The most beautiful lady in all of Quale," Nurse said. Nurse delighted in pointing out the grandest of the guests. "And that's the Prime Minister, Mr. Alistair Windlass, dancing with your mother. Isn't he a handsome man? And not yet thirty. Youngest Prime Minister in history!"

How could she have forgotten that he had been such good friends with her parents? He might even know who the mysterious Bettina was. It was her last hope. It was also her great good fortune that a few years ago Alistair Windlass had moved his headquarters from Parliament House into her father's old office in the ministerial wing.

She tucked the skirts of her dress and her red flannel petticoat into her drawers, opened her bedroom window and clambered out onto the parapet. A north wind sliced through her clothes. The Castle roofs stretched before her: a maze of parapets, lead gutters, slopes and alleys. The wind snarled, snatching at her hair and the dag-ends of her tucked skirts. She hesitated for a moment, then began to climb.

She knew every inch of these roofs: they were her summer playground. But she seldom visited them once the autumn winds grew boisterous. She didn't like the feel of the wind today, but there was only one place where she need be cautious. Concentrating on where to put her hands and feet made it easier to ignore the cold and, to her relief, by the time she reached the ridge the wind had stopped gusting and blew steadily.

The ridge was a flat strip of lead sitting atop a section of the chapel roof. She would have to walk its length to reach the ministerial wing. It was six inches wide and nearly ten feet long, and the roof it belonged to slid away on either side. There was no parapet to catch a falling body—nothing but the cold flagstones of the inner courtyard forty feet below.

The sky was a cloudless, bitter blue. Beyond the sprawl of tiled roofs, the sullen brown worm of the River Quale twisted towards the docks. Charlie balanced against the push of the wind. Knowing that if she didn't go now she never would, she stepped onto the ridge. She had crossed it countless times.

She was three feet from the other end when the wind suddenly caught its breath, dying away to nothing. She wobbled and steadied herself. Her heart was pounding. That had been close. The wind roared back, slamming into her. Charlie felt herself falling and launched forward, diving for the opposite roof. She crashed onto elbows and knees, her feet dangling over empty space. She pressed her face and body into the cold lead of the roof as she gasped and shuddered.

Five minutes later, Charlie slid open the attic window of a small, unused room over the ministerial wing and climbed inside. She was frozen with cold, but it was the shock of having nearly fallen that kept her shivering as she began the last leg of her journey to the Prime Minister. Soon she was shivering for another reason. Alistair Windlass was the last chance she had to find her mother. He *must* help her. Life couldn't be so miserably unfair that it would nearly kill her on the chapel ridge only to present her with yet another dead end! On the other hand, life hadn't exactly played fair with her so far . . .

The offices on the upper floors of the ministerial wing were abandoned. She reached the first floor without seeing a soul and started down the wide marble steps. Everything was grand here: from the glass dome in the ceiling to the floor that looked like a giant chessboard made of grey and white marble. Enormous panelled doors lined the marble hall. Directly opposite the stairs stood the largest door of all. Gilded carvings of fruit and birds sprouted all around it, and a statue of a lady wearing hardly any clothes stood above. She had reached the Prime Minister's office.

There was just one problem: a big problem wearing a red and gold uniform and enormous black moustaches. Stationed outside the office of the Prime Minister, obviously on duty and complete with rifle and sabre, was a corporal of the Castle Guard.

Charlie and the corporal saw each other at the same moment. Their mouths fell open in unison. The corporal blinked first. His bushy black eyebrows floated up his forehead and disappeared beneath his helmet.

"How did you get here, missy? You've no business here! Run along at once before you get into trouble."

Charlie was desperate. She couldn't turn back now.

If the O'Dair found out she'd been here there wouldn't be a second chance. "Please," she gasped. "You don't understand. I must see the Prime Minister!"

A cavern appeared beneath the moustaches. The corporal roared with laughter. "The Prime Minister don't see little kids like you. He's got important matters to deal with. Now hop it! Go on home to your mum before you get in real trouble, there's a good girl."

Charlie was used to being ignored, but she wasn't used to being anonymous. She didn't like it. She stretched herself up and focused her most freezing look on the corporal. "I am not a good girl," she said. "And my mother, the Queen, vanished five years ago. I am the Princess Charlotte Augusta Joanna Hortense, and I want to see the Prime Minister. Now kindly open the door and announce me!"

The corporal's eyebrows grew together into a caterpillar of a frown. His ears glowed pink, and he began to splutter. "Princess?" he roared. "What do you take me for? D'you think Princess Charlotte would go round in a dirty dress and torn stockings? You've had your little joke, kid, now be off. Go on, or I'll box your ears!"

He took a step forward. Charlie was rooted to the spot, unable to move, watching in horror as he raised a giant hand. Neither of them had noticed the door swinging open, or the man watching them from the threshold. Now he cleared his throat. The corporal snapped to attention.

"Your Royal Highness," murmured the Prime Minister, bowing deeply. "How may I help you?"

# Eight

It felt strange to be back in her father's old office. It was every bit as grand as she remembered, with high ceilings, sparkling chandeliers and gloomy paintings of important-looking people. A large portrait of her father in his coronation robes, looking stiff and nervous and hardly older than Tobias, hung on the wall behind the Prime Minister's desk. Charlie's eyes kept flitting up to it as she shifted nervously on her chair.

"A biscuit, Your Highness?" Alistair Windlass reached into a drawer and pulled out a large tin. She hadn't seen biscuits like them for years. Her fingers hovered over thick chocolate; her eyes lingered on pink icing. She darted a look at the Prime Minister and scooped up one of each. As she took a bite, she glanced up and saw him watching her. A crumb lodged halfway down her throat, and she began to cough. He waited until she spluttered to a stop, then said: "It is, of course, a pleasure to renew your acquaintance, Princess Charlotte. But I hope nothing is wrong. Please, to what do I owe the honour of this visit?"

Something about the sound of the word "honour" made Charlie swallow the last of her biscuit and sit quite still, staring at him. Even in shirtsleeves and waistcoat, Alistair Windlass was nearly as elegant as Mr. Moleglass. He was tall and slender. He had long, curving eyebrows above blue eyes—eyes watchful as a hawk's. His hair, thick and straight, was the colour of faded straw, and his mouth quirked up on one side when he smiled. He was undeniably handsome, but she preferred her father's funny, long-nosed face.

His smile grew a shadow of impatience. "Come now, Your Highness," he said. "I'm a busy man, and I would hate to think that you have disturbed my work this morning for no reason. Tell me why you are here. Quickly, now, or I shall have to ask you to leave."

Surely she could trust him. Her fingers crept into her pocket, found the letter. She glanced up to see Windlass watching her. She pushed the letter deeper, pulled out her handkerchief and began to wipe smears of icing and biscuit from her hands. She kept her head down, lying without knowing why she was doing so. "I overheard a rumour," she began. "One of the servants—"

"Ah," he said, and in that "ah" Charlie heard exactly what he thought of little girls who listened to servants' gossip. She felt her face blush as red as her petticoat.

"One of the servants," she repeated grimly, "said that the Kingdom is cursed."

"That's an old tale. I advise you to disregard it. I'm surprised you believe in such nonsense." He glanced down, selected a portfolio from one of the tidy piles on his desk. "Now, if you will excuse me—"

"You don't understand!" She needed time to think. If she didn't show him her mother's letter, at least she must talk to him about her father. "I know people have said the Kingdom's been cursed since my mother . . ." She paused, surprised by a tightness in her throat.

"Most unfortunate." He did not look at her. He snapped open the portfolio and picked up a pen.

Suddenly she was furious. How dare he sit there, refusing to listen, making her feel stupid and small? And now he expected her to slink away. She found she had jumped off her chair and was shouting: "*Unfortunate?* The Queen disappears for five years, and you call it *unfortunate?* In case you haven't noticed, it's the Kingdom that's been unfortunate! The country's in recession! Crops have failed again! People are out of work and hungry!"

His head jerked up. He stared at her, but Charlie couldn't stop the words pushing out: "Of course I don't believe the Kingdom is cursed! I'm not an idiot! What matters is that people are looking for someone to blame for the bad times. And from what the servants are saying, I think they've decided to blame my father! Haven't you heard of the Republicans? The Radicals? Some of them want to cut off my father's head, like they did thirty years ago to the Esceanian king! There's a revolution brewing, Mr. Prime Minister, and I want to know what you are doing about it!"

He put down his pen. "Just what have you overheard?" His eyes were a blue so pale as to be almost silver. His mouth was smiling, but the smile didn't reach his eyes. They were as cold and empty as a winter sky at twilight. "Tell me," he said softly, and Charlie knew she had no choice.

"Some people think that my father . . . murdered my mother," she whispered. Other than a slight widening of the eyes, his face showed nothing. She shut her own eyes for a moment, feeling sick. When she opened them, he was leaning forward, watching her.

"This has all been upsetting for you," he said. "Please don't worry about your father. It was brave of you to come to me, but I already knew of this rumour and dozens like it."

He leant back in his chair, but his eyes never left her face. "You see, ordinary people need rumours. They like to blame their problems on some agency, whether human or supernatural. They like to think that there is a reason for the things that happen to them, both good and bad, rather than to accept that most things happen through a combination of chance, circumstance and their own lack of foresight. You understand this already because you are an intelligent girl. Oh yes," he smiled at her—and his smile was a gift. It made her blink and look at the floor. "You take after your mother.

A woman of remarkable intellect. Her thesis on refractive crystals—"

Relief hit her like a punch in the stomach. She *had* been right to come after all. He had been her mother's friend. The warmth in his voice was unmistakeable. And he knew about the science. Her fingers crept into her pocket, touched the letter. She had been a fool not to show it to him straight away. She could have ruined everything, but he had forgiven her outburst. It wasn't too late.

"I want to find my mother," she said.

"Of course." She felt his attention sharpen. The sympathy in his face was tinged with concern. "We all do. Your father . . . But you must know we *have* searched. For years." His voice barely changed, but she suddenly knew that he wanted her mother's return as much as she did. She came to her decision.

"A few days ago," she said, "I found this." She pulled the letter from her pocket and handed it to him.

Windlass spread it out on his desk and read it. A look of blank amazement flowed across his face. Then, for a moment only, there was a look of such pain that she felt embarrassed, as though she were eavesdropping on a private grief. He looked up, and she thought she must have imagined it: his face was perfectly calm. He handed the letter back to her. "Thank you for your trust in me, Your Highness," he said. "I believe this to be the first clue to your mother's disappearance ever found. It explains a great deal. I only wish she had felt able to confide . . ." He paused. "Obviously, I know what your mother was researching. Indeed, she was working at my request."

"On what?"

"I'm sorry." He smiled. "I can't tell you that. It concerns national security. But I assure you, everything possible was done—is still being done—to locate her. This letter advances us, but only a little. Try not to hope too much."

"But she left because she discovered something. Something horrible!"

"So it would seem."

"What was it? What was she frightened of? Why didn't she go to you? Surely you and my father could have protected her!"

"If only she had trusted us to do so. We must hope that she is still alive, and that she has not fallen into the wrong hands." He paused. "I'm sorry, Your Highness.

I've shocked you. I should not have said that. There is much I cannot tell you, and I think it best if we don't discuss this further. But please believe that I will not rest until I have engineered your mother's safe return."

"Do you know who Bettina is?"

"I'm very sorry," he said. "I do not know the name. Obviously, I will endeavour to find out. You have given us a chance. If something comes of it, you will be the first to know. And now, I want to know a bit more about you, Charlie. May I call you Charlie? I heard your mother do so many times."

She nodded, dazed. Perhaps everything would be all right. Perhaps she had given him the clue he needed.

"You will excuse my impertinence, but why are you dressed like a ragamuffin? What is your governess thinking of?"

Her mouth dropped open. "Governess?"

His eyebrows raised. "Have you a lady's maid?"

She shook her head.

"Where are your quarters, Charlie?"

"I live in the east attics. I like it there!" she added quickly, seeing his mouth tighten. "I love my attic room! Please don't make me move."

"Do you receive any sort of schooling?"

She shook her head, blushing.

"But you can read, obviously."

"My mother taught me, before she . . ."

"I see." He paused, his face grown so cold and remote she was almost frightened. "I owe you an apology, Charlie," he said. "I have been so concerned with finding the mother that I forgot about the daughter. Don't worry. I will rectify my mistake. And now, I'm rather busy today and can't allow myself the pleasure of seeing you to your quarters. I trust you can find your own way back?"

"But my father? The Republicans?"

"I am well aware of each and every radical organisation at work in this country. They are observed and kept under control. Your father has entrusted the care of the Kingdom to me. I take that charge very seriously."

He rose from his chair, and she jumped up, feeling suddenly like a scared rabbit, although she couldn't imagine why, as he took her hand and bowed over it, smiling at her with real warmth in his eyes. He held the door open, and Charlie almost ran from the room. She had done the right thing, giving him the letter. He would find her mother for her. She knew it. But, kind

as he had been, something about Alistair Windlass un-
nerved her.

She pounded up the grand staircase, racing past the
corporal and his moustaches, the marble and crystal,
the pomp and polish and smell of power, without noticing any of it. The only thing she wanted was to get
back to her attic. Things were going to happen now.
Not just about her mother. Things about her. She had
seen it in Windlass's face. And Mrs. O'Dair was not going to like it. Charlie didn't know whether to be pleased
or terrified.

# Nine

"Stand still, girl! How do you expect Mrs. Petch to set the hem straight if you keep fidgeting?"

Charlie looked at the floor and tried not to move. It felt as if she had been standing on this chair in the housekeeper's office, with Tobias's mother pinning up the hem of her new dress, for hours. She avoided O'Dair's eye. For days now, the slightest thing sent the housekeeper into spasms of fury.

Charlie had not seen the Prime Minister again, but she thought about him constantly, and about his promise to try to find her mother. He was Prime Minister of

Quale. Surely he would succeed. When he did, her life would change again, and Mrs. O'Dair would no longer matter.

Her nose began to itch, but if she raised a hand to scratch it, the housekeeper would shout and poor Rose Petch would tremble with fear. She wrinkled her nose and tried to ignore the itch. The seamstress gave a weary sigh and leant back on her heels. "I've finished, madam. Shall I help the Princess off with the dress and take it away to hem?" She cast an anxious glance at Mrs. O'Dair, who was seated at her desk writing out the household accounts.

"One moment," ordered the housekeeper, rising from her chair. The seamstress gave a gasp of dismay and scurried to one side as Mrs. O'Dair stalked round Charlie with the deadly intensity of a buzzard circling for prey. "This silk is far too expensive to allow errors. The Prime Minister would have it, although I told him it was too dear. What a waste!" she hissed, shooting a vicious glance at Charlie. "Very well. You may take the wretched thing away. I want it finished by morning."

"Yes, madam."

Charlie was soon free of the heavy silk. Rose picked up her old clothes.

"You are not paid to help the girl dress." Mrs. O'Dair had not looked up from her desk, but her voice was heavy with menace. Rose's hands shook as she bundled her sewing together. She gave Charlie a timid smile and fled the room.

All the time she was dressing, Charlie felt O'Dair watching her. As she was pulling on her boots, she dared a glance at the housekeeper. O'Dair's black eyes were fastened on her, glistening with an emotion that made Charlie shiver and look down, her fingers suddenly clumsy as they struggled with the broken laces. She'd always known Mrs. O'Dair disliked her, but what she had glimpsed in the housekeeper's eyes was pure poisonous hatred. O'Dair lunged to her feet, corsets popping, sailed to the door and flung it open.

"Follow me, girl. You're to learn Latin grammar and Mathematics." O'Dair snorted derisively but did not speak again as she wheezed and creaked her way to the attics, moving so quickly that Charlie had to run to keep up.

Flinging open the door of a room, the housekeeper thrust Charlie inside. The thin, elderly man sitting behind the desk clambered to his feet. "I beg your pardon?"

"Your charge," Mrs. O'Dair snapped. "Make what you will of her, but you are to have her four hours a day, and that is four hours I shall not have to bother with the creature!"

The old man drew himself up. "The Prime Minister has given me his instructions for Her Royal Highness."

The housekeeper turned and left, slamming the door behind her.

"What a singularly unpleasant woman!" The old man collapsed into his chair, mopping his forehead with a large handkerchief. "Oh!" He stared at Charlie in dismay and bounced to his feet. "Do forgive me!" He waved his handkerchief in agitation. "May I sit in your presence, ma'am?"

Charlie's mouth fell open. "Why shouldn't you?"

"Protocol, ma'am. Protocol. Oh dear," he said as she continued to stare blankly at him. "The Prime Minister told me that you were sadly undereducated. I thought he meant academically, but I see you are unschooled in a range of subjects. Would you care to sit at that desk, ma'am, while we endeavour to find out the extent of your ignorance?"

Charlie looked where he was pointing and saw a brightly varnished school desk complete with inkwell and quill. Full of trepidation, she slid into the seat. Her teacher sat at his desk.

"First, allow me to introduce myself: Professor Archibald Meadowsweet. You may call me 'Professor.'" He jumped to his feet and bowed stiffly from the waist. Charlie found herself staring at the bald pink circle on top of his head and had to smother a hysterical giggle. Not certain what the polite response was, she stood, too.

"No, no!" said the Professor, shaking his head so violently that his white hair stuck out like a halo of candyfloss. "Do not stand, ma'am. Incline your head graciously, like this." He demonstrated. The top of his head now looked like a pink-eyed daisy. Charlie burst out laughing.

"Really, ma'am," he said, shaking his head sadly, "I see little that is humorous in our situation."

Two hours later, Charlie could only agree. She was eleven years old, and it seemed that she knew almost nothing.

"Mathematics, little; Latin, Greek, Modern Languages, none; Geography and Statecraft, none; Biology, Chemistry, none; Physics, none; History, little . . ." On and on droned the professor, peering at his notes, while

Charlie sank lower and lower in her chair. "Spelling and Vocabulary, good; Reading, excellent; Grammar, adequate; knowledge of Literature, haphazard; Etiquette, none; Deportment, little." The Professor sighed, took his handkerchief and mopped at his large forehead. "Oh dear," he said. "Where to start?"

Charlie trudged down the third flight of stairs. It was lunchtime, and she was exhausted. Half an hour each of History, Mathematics and Latin, followed by a lecture on Etiquette. Her brain felt wrung out.

The Prime Minister had ordered that she eat all her meals in the lesser dining room. Three times a day she had to sit all alone at the vast polished table with her plate floating in the middle of the shiny dark wood like a raft lost at sea. There was no question of reading at the table. She had to concentrate on the food. It made the mutton taste stringier, the vegetables soggier, the pudding thicker. Mrs. O'Dair had been forced to increase her rations, but she made sure the food served to Charlie was as unpleasant as possible.

Worst of all were the footmen. At every meal one of them stood beside the door, impersonating a chair or a lamp. In the awful silence created by someone pretending to be a piece of furniture, Charlie had to slurp her soup and chew her gristle. Every time she began to relax, the footman would silently appear behind her and whisk away her plate from one side while sliding a new plate in from the other. No doubt Professor Meadowsweet would say it was Etiquette. Charlie hated Etiquette.

Etiquette or not, she was hungry. She clattered down the last of the stairs and ran along the corridor leading to the lesser dining room. In front of the door stood a footman, staring straight ahead, pretending to be a potted plant. It was Alfie Postlethwaite. This was not a good day.

Instead of holding the door open for her, Alfie looked into the distance over her head and said, "Your Royal Highness is to report to the Prime Minister."

"B-but I haven't had my lunch yet."

"Your Royal Highness is to report to the Prime Minister at once." Alfie smirked. Smugness radiated off him like heat from a coal fire. She could have kicked him.

"Did you know, Alfred," she said sweetly, "that you've got a really disgusting spot on the end of your nose?"

The sight of his face flushing red as beetroot jelly cheered her as she began the long journey to the ministerial wing.

This time, the corporal smiled through his moustaches at her. "Your Highness is to wait in the office for the Prime Minister," he said. "He'll not be long." She smiled back at him, and he opened the door for her with a flourish. She held her head up and strode into the office, feeling slightly grand.

The door shut behind her. In the Prime Minister's absence, the room seemed much larger. Beneath the gaze of her father's portrait, she wandered around the room, noticing how it had changed. His battered old desk was gone. She remembered him picking her up and sitting her in the middle of all his papers, so that she could play with his blotter, rocking it back and forth and pretending it was a ship battling through a storm at sea. That desk had been replaced by a grand affair of polished mahogany and inlaid leather.

In the far corner, partly screened by a tall cupboard, she spotted another door and remembered her father's extraordinarily grand privy. She ran across and flung open the door. It was all still there—the most beautiful water closet she had ever seen. It had a giant wooden thunderbox and a large marble sink with a tap for hot as well as cold water. She couldn't resist. She turned on the hot tap. The water splashing into the basin was cool at first, but it soon warmed, and Charlie held her hands under the flow. What a marvellous extravagance! Warm water from a tap rather than icy cold in a jug that had been toted up dozens of stairs. No wonder Alistair Windlass looked so clean. If she had such a thing, she might enjoy washing too. Although she doubted it.

"... five minutes. I have an appointment."

Charlie froze at the sound of Windlass's voice. She felt her face burn red. He would think ... She turned off the water, hesitated, uncertain what to do. The sound of his visitor's voice decided her, and she pulled the door almost closed and stood beside it, listening.

"I'm sorry to bother you, I'm sure," said Mrs. O'Dair. Her words chewed the air like grindstones, ponderous and implacable. Charlie was shocked by the resentment snarling in the housekeeper's voice. How dared she speak like that to the Prime Minister? "But I requested a meeting last week. I have had no response. Not one word!"

"Pressure of work, dear lady." Windlass's voice was

as smooth and glossy as mayonnaise. "Come, seat your-self. I can spare a few minutes. Indeed, although this is not the ideal time, I have been intending to clarify my instructions concerning Her Royal Highness."

"It is precisely those instructions I wish to discuss," said O'Dair. "Five years ago you entrusted all domestic issues concerning the Castle and its inhabitants to me. Until now, you have expressed no dissatisfaction with my work. Indeed, I was under the impression that you had no interest in such details. I have devoted my life, these past years, to the efficient running of the Castle and to making sure you were not bothered with trivial matters. Now, suddenly, you issue specific instructions regarding one of my charges."

"One of your charges?" Windlass's voice was quizzi-cal. "Her Highness is not a domestic servant, O'Dair. Indeed, no domestic would have stayed to endure the treatment you appear to have meted out to the Royal Heir!"

There was the sound of heavy breathing. Charlie had a vision of O'Dair's face turning the colour of boiled ham.

"You have no experience of children, if you excuse my saying so, Prime Minister. Such things are best left to me. I'm sure you mean well, but your interference is not helpful. It confuses the staff and lessens my authority. In issuing these instructions, sir, you are intruding on my domain!"

There was a moment of silence. When Windlass finally spoke, his voice was so quiet Charlie could barely hear the words. "Your domain?" Something in his voice sent a shiver down her spine. It seemed to have a similar effect on the housekeeper.

"I-I didn't mean—"

"You are employed, Mrs. O'Dair, to follow orders. If you cannot do so, I will find someone who can."

"I apologise, sir! I—"

"I don't have time for this. Consider yourself lucky that I am too busy at present to find your replacement. But be aware that you are under scrutiny. I will not allow any more neglect of the Princess. You exceeded your instructions. Do not do so again. Do you understand? Good. Now . . . you may leave."

Charlie held her breath. There was the distant creak of corsets, the thud of a door. Then she heard brisk footsteps and Windlass's voice: "Her Royal Highness is late. Send word—"

"Excuse me, sir," said the corporal, astonishment in

every syllable, "but I let Her Highness into your office over fifteen minutes ago!"

Charlie squeezed her eyes shut. She wanted to sink into the floor and disappear. She listened to the sound of the door closing again.

"Please come out, Charlie. If you've quite finished."

She opened the privy door with a shaking hand and stood staring up at the Prime Minister. He looked back at her, taller than ever and impossibly elegant in his close-fitting frock coat and high-collared shirt. His waistcoat and cravat were the exact silver-blue of his eyes. The look in those eyes was both amused and sympathetic, and Charlie felt herself blush carrot-red to the roots of her hair. "I'm so sorry," she gasped. "I didn't mean to—"

He shook his head. "I know you had no intention of eavesdropping. It's unfortunate that you overheard that particular conversation. Try to erase it from your mind." He smiled and held out his hand. "And now, to business—"

"Please, Mr. Windlass!"

He paused, raised an inquiring eyebrow.

"My mother! Have you found out anything?"

"It's early days, Charlie." His smile was kind. "I've no

news for you yet, but I promise: I will find her. I am not in the habit of giving up." He guided her to a chair and bent to open a drawer in his desk.

"Forgive me for starving you, Your Highness, but I want to know how you got on with your lessons." Alistair Windlass held out the tin of biscuits. "Please, take some. You've worked hard this morning, I imagine, and I always find that thinking makes me hungry."

Charlie scooped up three biscuits. The ends of her fingernails were black with grime. Windlass's own fingernails, she noticed, were spotless. The Prime Minister sat on the end of his desk and crossed his arms. He raised his eyebrows. "And?"

She paused in mid-bite. He smiled encouragingly. She decided to tell the truth. "I like Mathematics. But I'm sure History ought to be more than lists of dates. And I *hate* Etiquette—it's stupid! It's ridiculous to have rules about when to sit or stand or how to hold your knife and fork!"

He gazed at her, so solemn she knew he was smiling inside. "I sympathise," he said. "But I wonder if you understand why I have arranged these lessons? And why I expect you to work hard at them?"

She looked up at him. His face gave away nothing.

"It's about more than just schooling, isn't it?" He raised an eyebrow. He was testing her, and it seemed suddenly very important that she pass this test. "Is it because of what we talked about?" she asked. "M-my father?" She looked down at the remains of the last biscuit crumbling between her clenched fingers, no longer hungry.

"Yes, Charlie." She looked up and saw that her answer had pleased him. It was a heady feeling. For the first time in years, she remembered what it was like to want another person's approval. Alistair Windlass did not, she imagined, grant his lightly. "Your father is unable to act as head of state. When he first became ill, that mattered less. But in the last few years the economic and political situation in Quale has changed. It becomes increasingly urgent that the people remember there is a Qualian monarch. That is why I moved into your father's office a few years ago. To connect the governing power with the Castle, and hence the monarchy. I have been acting as unofficial Regent. But you are old enough now to begin to represent your father."

He leant forward, and his eyes glowed with energy. "You can be of great service to your country. But you must work hard and learn, so that you can begin to fulfil some of his duties. Under my guidance, of course.

"Which brings us back to the topic of Etiquette. You are right," he said. "It is not important in itself. But it is useful. It will make your work and mine easier. It is one of the tools you will use to manage and control those around you."

She frowned at him. "I don't want to control people."

"Very noble," said the Prime Minister. "But one day you will be Queen of Quale. Part of your job will be to control people. Without government, civilisation descends into chaos. For now, your job is to learn. I'm glad you enjoy Mathematics. It would please your mother. Mathematics was the language she used to explore the world and its mysteries. I hope you will study hard, so that when she returns she will find a daughter of whom she can be proud."

The hunger she felt had nothing to do with food. "Did you know my mother well?"

"I knew and admired her. I was honoured to count her as one of my closest friends."

Charlie took a deep breath. "What was she like?"

He gazed at the floor as though looking into the past. "One of the most brilliant minds I have ever met. A great scientist. She overcame considerable family and social pressures to go to university, you know. I have always thought that it was one of the most imaginative things your father ever did, marrying your mother. The courtiers hated it." He looked up with a wry smile, then his face grew solemn. His eyes caught hers and held them. "She loved you and your father very much. Never doubt that."

Charlie blinked. She stared at her hands. The last of the biscuit crumbs dribbled onto the floor. She looked up to see Windlass watching her. His crooked smile was back. It grew teasing. "Your mother had a great regard for Etiquette. She also maintained the highest standards of personal cleanliness. She was particularly careful of her fingernails, as I remember."

This blush was hot and furious. Windlass stood and held out his hand. "I must let you go and eat your lunch," he said. "I would like you to visit me three times a week. I will arrange for you to have your lunch here, with me. You need lessons in Statecraft and, however capable the Professor, I think it best if you receive those from me. Mondays, Wednesdays and Fridays, after your lessons, if you please."

He towered over her, tall and elegant. She placed her

right hand with its grubby fingernails in his, and the Prime Minister bowed low over it. He raised his head, and his eyes shone like moonstones.

Charlie couldn't face the idea of the lesser dining room, Alfie, and a dish of congealed mutton. She wanted to be alone to think. She'd be in trouble later, of course. The footman could be counted on to make sure O'Dair knew she hadn't shown up. But later was later and, after all, there was little the housekeeper could do to her now that the Prime Minister was her friend. The idea was new and extremely delightful. Charlie smiled and began to run along the corridor towards a favourite ground-floor window. She was taking a half-holiday in the gardens.

# Ten

With the edge of her sleeve, Charlie wiped a peephole in the foggy greenhouse glass and peered inside. Half hidden by a jungle of withered tomato vines, Fossy was seated at a potting bench, his dinner pail in front of him, a battered tin kettle steaming on top of the kerosene heater. After his lunch the gardener would snooze under a horse blanket for at least an hour. That just left Tobias. Charlie took a detour through the kitchen garden, grubbing up a couple of carrots in case she got hungry, and ran on until she came to the overgrown pleasure gardens.

This was where her favourite climbing tree grew. The hornbeam sprawled as wide as it was tall, its lower branches resting massive elbows on the ground. She clambered onto one of these and walked up to the main trunk. She was soon high in the tree, sitting astride a branch. The air was cold; the sun bright. She was safe from Tobias up here. He never climbed trees, not even to chase after her when she managed to ding him with her peashooter.

She was rubbing one of the carrots clean on her sleeve when she spotted him. The carrot crunched between her teeth as she watched him sauntering through the gardens as though he owned them, whistling an annoying tune. He kicked through drifts of fallen leaves, obviously heading towards the summerhouse, probably to read one of the books he had stolen from her library.

Once he was out of sight, Charlie turned her mind back to the interview with the Prime Minister. He seemed all fine clothes and elegant manners, but she wasn't fooled. He had reduced Mrs. O'Dair to a quivering wreck without even raising his voice. She sighed with happiness at the memory. Alistair Windlass would make a bad enemy. He was an equally impressive friend. He would find her mother. The question was: when?

She was starting on the second carrot when another movement caught her eye. Tobias again? No. This person was wearing the black dress and white apron of a Castle maid. Charlie stopped chewing. The maids were not allowed in the gardens. The woman drew nearer, and Charlie saw that it was the new girl—the one from her mother's study.

Walking briskly, the maid disappeared in the direction of the summerhouse. Charlie shoved the remains of the carrot in her pocket and shinnied down the tree. Something was going on, and she was going to find out what it was.

Leaf-drift rustled as Charlie waded through it on hands and knees. It had rained last night, and the noise was slightly soggy, as were the knees of her stockings. She crouched at the base of the summerhouse and listened. Had she been heard? But the voices floating out the broken windows didn't pause:

"—need an answer from you, Toby. Are you with us, or not?"

"I ain't *with* nobody. You ought to know that by now, Nell. Not the Petches and not your blessed Resistance."

"I ain't working for the Petches! I told you, I broke with Zebediah! None of 'em'll have anything to do with me now. That's why I got to earn my own keep."

"Better'n thieving."

"This ain't about thieving."

"Seems to me that's exactly what it's about."

"I need your help to get past some locks, Toby. You're good with locks; the whole Family knows that. Uncle Barty used to say—"

"Barty's dead. Leave him out."

"Will you help?"

There was a long silence. Charlie's heartbeat hammered in her head. Who was this Nell? What was all this about Petches? Was Nell Tobias's relation or a Resistance spy? And what did she want with him?

"Well?" the girl's voice drifted out the window. "You can keep yourself to yourself and watch Windlass steal the country out from under us, or you can fight. What's it gonna be, Toby?"

"I already said I'd work with you, Nell. I'd work with the Devil himself against that man. But I won't turn thief on your say-so. Not unless I know exactly what you're looking for."

Another silence. Charlie didn't dare move in case

they heard her. What had Nell meant about the Prime Minister stealing the country?

"All right." Nell's voice was directly over her head. Charlie's legs ached with crouching. She began to wobble, and her fingers dug into the ground. She had to hold on! Just a few more minutes.

"I reckon I'll have to trust you, Toby. We need your help to break into the Prime Minister's office. We want information about a new-fangled weapon he's trying to make. A month ago, one of our spies got inside his laboratory up north. Our man got out alive, but only just. They caught up with him outside Quale and put a bullet in him. He lived long enough to say that it had something to do with the Queen."

Charlie gasped. Her right foot gave way, and she tumbled headlong into the leaves.

"Someone's out there!" shouted the girl.

Charlie scrabbled to her feet and ran. But her foot had turned into a block of wood. It twisted under her, and she fell. She yelped in pain as her foot exploded with pins and needles. Someone grabbed her arm and yanked her to her feet. She stared up into the furious eyes of Tobias Petch.

"I might have known! Can't you stop making

trouble for five minutes?" His hand tightened on her arm.

"Let go!" she shouted. She stood, glaring at Tobias. Nell appeared at his side, shock and dismay chasing across her face as she recognised Charlie.

"How much did you hear, girl?"

"Don't you dare call me 'girl' you . . . you *Republican!* I'm Her Royal Highness Princess Charlotte Augusta—"

"Stow it," Tobias said. "We know who you are. And you don't have to look so scared. No one's gonna hurt you. You startled us, is all."

"It ain't that simple," said Nell.

"No!" shouted Charlie. "You're Republican spies, both of you! When I tell the Prime Minister, he'll arrest you! He'll have you put in prison! He'll—"

Tobias grabbed her shoulders and shook her. "Shut up! You ain't gonna say one word to that man!" He spoke slowly and softly, and his eyes held hers like a rat in a trap. "I thought you were listening. Didn't you hear what Nell said? Don't you understand what it means? Windlass is the reason your mum run off! She ran away from *him!*"

Charlie went very still. The blood was pounding in her head. "You're lying."

"I'm not." His voice was even quieter.

"He was my mother's friend!" She heard herself gabbling. "You're wrong! He already knew all about her science—what she was working on . . . he told me . . . he asked her to do it in the first place! Why would she run away from the Prime Mini—"

"Told you?" Tobias's hands tightened on her arms. His eyes narrowed. "What do you mean?"

She gawped at him.

"Spit it out!" He gave her a shake.

"What's going on?" Nell shouted. "Toby?"

"Did you show it to him, Charlie?" Tobias's voice was grim, his face grimmer. *"Did you show him the letter?"*

"What letter?" said Nell.

Charlie just stared at Tobias. It couldn't be true! None of it. He must be lying. But he was too shocked, too angry. He was telling her the truth. Which meant . . .

"Damn it!" hissed Tobias. He'd seen her answer in her face. "You little idiot! Do you know what you've done?"

She was terrified that she did, and she kicked him, hard, on the shin. Tobias yelled and let go, and Charlie ran, faster than she'd ever run in her life. He was after her already, cursing. But she had a head start. She had reached the hornbeam and was halfway up when he arrived, panting and still swearing, at the bottom of the tree.

"Charlie! Don't be a fool! Get down here!"

She climbed higher. He wouldn't follow her, and she needed to be alone. She had to think. She had to deal with the fear trying to swallow her from inside out. She had to think what to do. To fix it. To fix what she'd done. *What had she done? How could she have been so stupid?* Her eyes were burning. It was hard to see where to put her hands and feet. She stopped climbing and leant into the tree, letting it hold her.

"Charlie?" Tobias's voice floated up. It was joined by Nell's.

"What's going on? What's this about a letter? What's she done?"

"Not now!" snapped Tobias. "Leave it. Get on back inside before O'Dair smells you out. That's all we need. I'll talk to you later."

"But—"

"Get out of it, Nell, or I won't be picking no locks!"

Nell stamped away through the leaves. Charlie clung to the tree. She blinked to clear her vision, climbed higher until she found a forked branch where she could crouch, half-sitting. She was shaking so hard the branches around her shivered.

"Charlie?" Tobias's voice was soft. He had finished being angry with her, then. She hadn't. She had never hated herself before. It wasn't a good feeling.

"Charlie?" Tobias sighed. "I wish you'd come down so we could talk this through. We gotta fix what's happened. No use blaming yourself. You didn't know." He paused, cursed softly. "I gotta go now. Fossy's shouting for me. Go to Mr. Moleglass. Soon as you can after supper. Don't let no one see you. And don't go near Windlass. Not the state you're in. The man's no fool."

The leaves crunched again, and she was alone.

The worst moment came, as she knew it would, when Mr. Moleglass opened his door. The fear in his eyes confirmed all Tobias had told her. It was true.

Tobias was already there, pacing from one end of the room to the other, hands shoved deep in his pockets. He didn't look up as she entered.

"Sit down." Moleglass guided her to his armchair in front of the hob. "Tell us," he said, "exactly what you have done."

Tobias turned. They both looked at her.

"I . . . I showed him the letter." This was the first payment for her stupidity. That look on Mr. Moleglass's face would stay with her forever. She tried to defend herself: "I remembered that the Prime Minister had been friends with my parents. I thought he might know who Bettina was. That . . . he would help me find her."

"I told you not to show the letter to anyone." Mr. Moleglass's eyes were dark with disappointment.

"You made me show it to Tobias!"

"Because I knew we could trust him."

"Well, you're wrong! He's working for the Resistance! The new maid, Nell, is a spy, and he's working with her. They're Republicans! They want to cut off my father's head!"

"The only head the Resistance is after belongs to Windlass," Tobias growled.

Charlie groaned. She clenched her fists and thumped the arms of the chair. "I don't understand! Alistair Windlass is the Prime Minister! He was my parents' friend. Or was that a lie, too?"

"It's true." Mr. Moleglass shook his head. "Although the man has always been something of an enigma. Little is actually known about him, other than that he was shipped down from the north by the Whigs to contest a marginal seat at the age of twenty-three and, against all expectation, won. He has great charisma and charm, of course. How could it be otherwise? A man of no background, lacking powerful friends to offer him advancement, and yet he becomes Prime Minister of Quale at the age of twenty-eight. Only a man of exceptional abilities could achieve that. His tragedy, and ours, is that he has chosen to misuse those abilities."

Tobias grunted and began to pace to and fro in front of the hob. Moleglass's eyes followed him for a moment, then turned back to Charlie. "But whatever his ambitions for power, the truly puzzling thing to me has been the fact that I am certain the Prime Minister's friendship with your parents was genuine! He was not only their friend, but their most trusted advisor. Indeed, he often visited your mother in her laboratory, especially in the months preceding her disappearance."

"He told me she was doing work for him!"

"So what?" said Tobias. "She ran away, Charlie. Your letter proves that. Who else would she run from? She was the Queen of Quale! Who other than Windlass had power enough to scare her off? Except your dad, and he wouldn't scare a flea. I don't know the ins and outs, but Windlass has taken over this country lock, stock and barrel since your daddy . . . Ask Nell. She'll tell you."

"And just who is Nell?"

"Nell Sorrell. My stepcousin. Her mum and my stepdad were sister and brother."

"You said your stepfather was a thief."

"So he was, till the day he died. So are all the Petches. Thieving's their trade and there's none better at it."

"But you're not a thief!"

"No." He grinned his slow grin. "My mum don't fancy the thieving trade for me. And to tell the truth, nor do I. But I ain't a real Petch. Only adopted. Nell ain't a thief either, in case you're wondering. She's a good girl, Nell. Bit bossy, but straight as they come. And you're wrong about something else: I never broke my word to you. I never told Nell about that letter. You're gonna do that."

"*What?*"

"The Resistance is your only hope," said Mr. Moleglass. "The Prime Minister will have set his spies on Bettina's trail. It will not be difficult for him to find her. And if she knows where the Queen is . . . But there is a chance Nell's friends might be able to reach her first."

Acceptance was sinking in, and with it, misery.

"Why didn't you tell me about the Prime Minister?" she wailed.

Moleglass blinked. "I am sorry. Since your mother's disappearance and your father's illness, I have remained in the Castle for one reason. To look after you. That is why I have put up with living in this damp—"

"Why down here? You would never tell me! And why do you let Mrs. O'Dair run everything?"

Moleglass sighed. Tugged his moustache. "The matter was taken out of my hands. I had no complaints about the housekeeper's work during her first years here. But afterwards . . . once your father became ill she dismissed most of the servants. All the ones who had served your father and the Old King before him. I remonstrated. Hiring and dismissing servants was my responsibility. But she laughed in my face. *That woman!*" Moleglass took a deep breath and continued.

"The Prime Minister wanted no one in the Castle whose loyalty lay with the King, rather than himself. She is in his pay; she is his creature. She gave me a choice: I could stay and serve her, or I could leave. I chose to do neither. I will not work for that woman, but I cannot abandon you, Charlie. So here I am. She allows me to stay because she still hopes that I will return to the servants' quarters and to my work! She knows my value. But I have refused. I live here, in the Castle, but not in her domain."

"Why didn't you tell me all this years ago?"

"To what purpose? So you would have hatred festering inside you? So you would grow fearful of your situation and frustrated at your powerlessness? Heaven knows you've had little enough childhood as it is! And what good would it have done to tell you of my suspicions about the Prime Minister? Your worlds did not coincide. You had forgotten his existence and he yours. It was safer for you to remain ignorant. If only you had never found that letter!" He sighed. "But once you had found it . . . Yes. You are right. I should have told you then. But . . . you are so intemperate, Charlie. I feared what you might do."

"Well, she's gone and done something worse," Tobias said. "And you can both stop blaming yourselves. The only person to blame for this mess is Windlass. Our job is to figure out what to do next, and that's easy. Give Nell the letter. See if the Resistance can find your mum before he does."

"Tobias is right," said Mr. Moleglass.

"No," Charlie said. The butler's mouth dropped

open. Tobias frowned. "I'm not giving Nell the letter," she said. "I'm not giving anyone the letter."

"Then Windlass wins!" shouted Tobias.

"No." She shook her head. "*I'm* going to talk to the Resistance. I want Nell to arrange a meeting as soon as possible."

Mr. Moleglass's eyes widened in horror, but Tobias's look of surprise melted into a broad grin. "Well done, Charlie," he said softly.

"Absolutely not!" Mr. Moleglass snapped. "You cannot leave the Castle. It is too dangerous!"

He meant for the best, but he was wrong. She walked over to the chess table and picked up a white pawn. It was carved of bone and felt cool and heavy in her hand. She had known and loved these pieces for as long as she could remember.

"This is what I've been, all these years," she said, holding it out. "But remember what you always tell me, Mr. Moleglass: never despise a pawn. If it succeeds in crossing the board safely, it becomes a queen—the most powerful piece in the game." She replaced the chess piece on its square and turned to the butler. "I won't be a pawn any more. I'm going to find my mother."

He stared at her, then turned to Tobias.

"She's right," said the gardener's boy. "Sorry, Mr. M, but it's checkmate."

Moleglass walked to his armchair and collapsed into it. He put his face in his hands. After a moment, he looked up, his eyes full of foreboding. "Very well," he sighed. "At least, include me in your plans. It's true that I have no turn for adventure, but perhaps I can be useful in other ways."

"I'll go find Nell in a minute," said Tobias. "Maria'll fetch her for me. We'll set up a meeting with the Resistance. All that's easy enough. The hard part's gonna be getting Charlie out of the Castle. It'll have to be at night, and blamed if I can think of a safe way to do it. I don't fancy trying to get her past the Guard *and* the hounds. It's too chancy."

Moleglass frowned in thought. "I think I know of a way. No one has done it before, but I cannot think why it would not work. *If* you are brave enough, Charlie. It will, for you, require much courage indeed!"

# Eleven

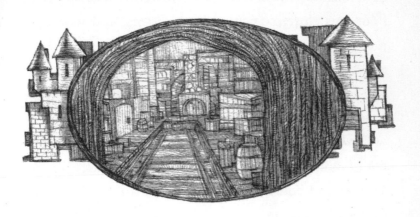

"I can't! It's no good."

"Then you stay here, Charlie, and Tobias takes the letter to the Resistance." Mr. Moleglass shrugged. "As you have been at pains to make clear, it is your decision."

She glared at him. "No!" she said at last. "I-I'll do it." She felt sick. Mr. Moleglass's plan was brilliant. It was also her worst nightmare.

It was the middle of the night, and they were standing in the freight room, examining a small wooden carriage sitting on a narrow railway track. The track disappeared into a hole in the wall. The freight room occupied the whole of the Castle's south cellar. It was an enormous room lined with towering shelves. The floor was cluttered with barrels, crates, and wheeled carts. But the most important object in the room was the steam engine which powered the pneumatic railway used to ship supplies from the City. The railway tunnel cut through the Castle hill and bored under part of the City itself. It had been installed in the 1830s by her grandfather, in the great age of pneumatics, when air-powered railway mania had swept the whole of the Eastern Hemisphere.

Supplies still arrived at the Castle daily, but now it was after midnight, and the freight room looked ghostly and abandoned in the light of a single kerosene lantern. Charlie stared at the tunnel's mouth, a hole carved into sheer stone. It didn't help to know the track was only a quarter of a mile long and ended in a modern, purpose-built building in the heart of the mercantile district. A quarter of a mile of dark tunnel was a very long way.

The hole was only two and a half feet tall and wide, and the carriage that travelled through it was built to carry freight, not humans. She would make the journey lying down inside that little wooden car. Mr. Moleglass would operate the steam engine that stood to one side of the tunnel, its furnace glowing red as Tobias shovelled more coal into it.

The carriage fitted into the tunnel like a bullet in a gun barrel, and had a row of bristles either end to form an airtight seal. The engine pumped all the air out of the tunnel, which created a vacuum. And the carriage, with her inside, would be sucked along iron rails from one end of the tunnel to the other. In the dark. Charlie shuddered. What if it got stuck? It had been known to happen. It was only slight comfort that Tobias would be going with her.

"That ought to do it, Mr. M," Tobias said, throwing the shovel back onto the coal heap and shutting the furnace door. "You sure you know how to work this thing?"

"I am not an imbecile, boy! The mechanism is perfectly simple. Now, make sure they send you both back safely."

"Nell's promised," said Tobias. "She's staying at my house tonight. Told O'Dair her mum was on her deathbed and got leave to sleep out. We'll see Charlie back safe and sound, don't worry."

They turned and looked at her. "Have you got the

letter?" Mr. Moleglass asked kindly. He knew she was terrified. She nodded.

"All set then?" Tobias jumped in the carriage and lay down.

Charlie took a deep breath and climbed in beside him.

"Ow! Mind your elbow!" he grunted. But he took hold of her freezing hand in his warm one and held it tight.

"Ready, Charlie?" Mr. Moleglass stood at the controls, his hand on the lever.

"Just do it!" She closed her eyes. She didn't want to see the darkness swallow her. The engine chuffed louder. Then there was a moment of sheer panic, as the vacuum took hold, and the carriage was sucked into the tunnel. The air in the carriage shifted, pressed on her. There was only this air now—the air trapped in the carriage with her and Tobias. It was all they had to breathe until they reached the other end. Panic welled up, flooding every inch of her. The cart trundled along the tracks, faster and faster.

"Hold on, Charlie!" Tobias shouted over the whirr of the wheels. "Only five minutes. Remember, the dark can't kill you!"

She wasn't sure. Her heart was racing faster than the click of the wheels. She was trapped in a wormhole beneath tons of rock! Five minutes? It had been forever! She wanted to scream. She clutched his hand even harder. She would do this or die!

And then they were out with a *whoosh!* and a rush of cold air on her face. Charlie opened her eyes as they hit the bumpers and jarred to a standstill. Her head thudded against the end of the carriage.

"Dang it!" said Tobias. "Should have faced the other way." He sat up, rubbing his head. "You all right?"

She struggled upright, dazed. Gulped air. Gradually her heart slowed. She had done it!

"Wasn't so bad, was it?"

Charlie ignored the remark and clambered out of the carriage. The very thought of getting back in it for the return journey made her ill. "Let's get out of here!"

They fumbled through the semi-darkness of the warehouse and found the door by touch. Tobias knelt, and Charlie heard the metallic clicking of the buttonhook. Then the door opened and released them into the moonlit streets of Quale City.

She stared about her in awe, the tunnel forgotten. She had not been out of the Castle since she was five, when there had been a long, stuffy carriage ride and the sea at the end of it. Quale City, even at night, silent and asleep, was a magical, unknown world.

So many buildings! And all crammed together, higgledy-piggledy, with no spaces in between. She stood in the middle of the cobbled street, turning slowly round and round, gazing open-mouthed at the shops and warehouses, tall and short, old and new, brick and stone, stucco and wood. She stared at the streetlamps glowing blue-white with gas light, at the gutter dividing the street, something smelly trickling along its length. She started across the street to take a closer look at the shop fronts. Tobias grabbed her arm.

"We ain't here to sightsee. Where's Nell? She's supposed to meet... *Look out!*" Half a dozen figures darted from the shadows. They were hooded and masked. Before Charlie could turn and run, or even scream, a sack dropped over her head. Tobias's hand was torn from her arm. Her own hands were grabbed and tied behind her, and she heard grunts and the muffled sound of a struggle.

"Be quiet and do as you're told," a man's voice hissed in her ear, "and you won't be hurt." His hands gripped her shoulders. Charlie twisted and squirmed, trying to kick out. "Stop that!" he muttered. A grunt and "Little devil!" as her foot made contact. He grabbed her round her middle, and she was dangling from her waist, writhing like a sack of eels.

She stopped wriggling long enough to gasp for air. The coarse fabric of the sack sucked into her open mouth. She twisted her head away and managed one scream, as shrill as Mr. Moleglass's kettle.

"Shut up! Make another noise and I'll shove me kerchief down your throat and see how you like that!"

She didn't have breath left to scream again. Charlie hung limply, fighting back fear so she could think. Who were these people? She had read horrible stories in the newspapers about children who disappeared, never to be seen again. Had she been stolen to work in the mills? Or deep underground in the northern mines, where she'd never see daylight again? That thought was bad enough, but a worse one wormed into her head: rumours of people snatched to make pies and dog meat . . .

Just as she felt she might vomit, the man carrying her lurched to a stop. He grunted as he lifted her and dumped her face-down onto a hard surface. A body thudded next to her. Tobias? She clung to that hope as the floor she was lying on swayed and began to move. She heard the clomp of horses' hooves, the grind of iron-rimmed wheels on cobbles. She was in a cart! Bile rose in her throat, and she swallowed it down. Being sick inside this sack was an unbearable thought.

The jouncing lasted fifteen or twenty minutes, then stopped. She was hauled out and guided through a doorway and up some stairs. A hand pushed her forward into a wash of light that filtered through the cloth over her head. When the sack was pulled off she was blinded for a moment by the brightness of several kerosene lanterns. Her hands were untied, and Charlie stood rubbing her wrists and blinking at her kidnappers. She was shaking so hard it was difficult to stand.

She turned her head and saw Tobias behind her, looking furious. The wave of relief dried in an instant when she saw who was untying his hands: Nell Sorrell!

"How *dare* you!" she shouted. "We trusted you! We were coming to meet you! How dare you treat us like this! I'll . . . I'll . . ." She stopped. She would *what*? She was powerless to do anything. The knowledge made her angrier still.

"I'm sorry, Char—Your Highness," said Nell, as she finished untying Tobias and stepped back. She was pale and nervous, hardly recognisable in a blue coat and skirt, her curly brown hair tied back with a ribbon instead of hidden beneath a maid's cap. "There's good reason for bringing you here like this. Let us explain."

Tobias said nothing. His face was white with anger. He glanced at her and shrugged. They were in no position to do anything but listen. Charlie took a deep breath and tried to calm down.

She turned to study the people in the room. Besides Nell, seven Resistance members were gathered around her and Tobias, some of them men holding masks and hoods. There were two other women and five men. One of the women was old, with a gentle face. She wore a black dress and an old-fashioned lace cap atop her white hair. The other was younger, dressed all in grey with a long face and spectacles perched on a sharp nose. Two of the men wore cloth caps and workmen's jackets; the third, a powerfully built man of about twenty-five, wore a brown suit.

The remaining two men were older. One was tall and balding and dressed like a banker, in severe grey and black. The other was altogether untidier, but it was he who held Charlie's gaze. This was the leader. She was sure of it. She glared at him. "Who are you?"

He smiled. He was not a tall man. He was not a handsome man. His nose and mouth were too big for his narrow face; his mouse-brown hair was long and untidy. But his eyes sparkled with intelligence and humour. He was thin and dressed in shabby clothes that hung from his body, but he moved towards her with a grace and confidence that reminded her of her father gliding through his scaffolding.

The stranger stood in front of her, his head cocked to one side, his entire body expressing an almost comical curiosity. But the smile in his eyes had steel behind it. "My name is Peter. I am in charge here. But you are wrong, my child. The question is, who are *you*?"

Charlie stretched as tall as she could. "I am Her Royal Highness, Charlotte Augusta Joanna Hortense, Princess of Quale, and *you,* sir, if you dare threaten me, tread dangerously close to treason!"

A snort exploded beside her, and she whirled to see Tobias trying to smother a spurt of laughter. "Trust you, Charlie!" He shook his head and shook the laughter away with it. His eyes grew angry again. "Nell!" he barked. "Speak up for us! You brung us here, and I for one don't much appreciate the reception we've got! If this is the way the Resistance treats its friends—"

140

"Is this your cousin, Nell?" asked Peter.

"Yes. It's Toby. Toby Petch. And she may not look like it, but she *is* the Princess."

"Yes, well. Looks can deceive." He smiled at Charlie again. "I apologise, Your Highness, for the rough handling. But we cannot afford to be careless. Alistair Windlass is not a man to miss a trick, and for all I knew, you might have been the bait to catch a fish which has long been eluding him. Indeed, Master Petch," his sharp eyes darted to Tobias, "how do I know you are not in his service, come here to spy on us?"

"I serve no one. And never shall." Tobias's face was as hard as stone.

"No? Perhaps not the Prime Minister, but what about your uncle? Zebediah Petch has turned profiteering into an art form in the last few years. In troubled times a master thief can gain new spheres of influence. He might think to dabble in politics . . . broker power. And he has a reputation for demanding loyalty from his family."

"I don't belong to the Petches. I ain't never met Zebediah. My stepdad was his brother, but I got nothing to do with the Family. Ask Nell if you don't believe me!"

"He's telling the truth, Peter."

The man shrugged. "I must apologise if I appear overly cautious. Trust belongs to gentler times. However, I do believe you, young man. You, I think, are an accomplished liar, but your cousin is not. Now, you have a letter to show us, I believe, Your Highness?"

"First," said Charlie, "Tell me what the Resistance wants. Are you only after Windlass, or do you intend to destroy the monarchy too?"

"Ah, politics." His eyes laughed at her. "Dreary, dreary politics. We are not politicians here, Your Highness. We are neither Republicans nor Anarchists nor Radicals. At least, none of us except Joseph." He smiled at the young man in the brown suit, who did not smile back. "We have no ambitions to topple the monarchy. We merely intend to rid Quale of a dangerous man who is preparing to betray us to our dearly unloved neighbours, the Esceanians."

"But who *are* you?"

Peter motioned towards the others, each in turn. "Bankers and builders. School masters and governesses and clerks. Shopkeepers, tradesmen, labourers, market gardeners, seamstresses, dancing masters and maiden aunts. Fathers and mothers. Grandmothers, even." The elderly woman in black smiled. "We eight here tonight are the Council of the Resistance, which represents all the people who have suffered under Windlass's government these last five years. And who will suffer still more if this country goes to war with Esceania! A war which, if Windlass succeeds in his treachery, Quale cannot win." His face had lost all humour: the joker had turned deadly serious at last.

"Please, ma'am," he gestured to a table and chairs standing in a corner of the room. "Let us talk properly. You have been locked away in the Castle for years. You will be ignorant of many things which concern your father's subjects. Will you allow me to enlighten you about a few of them?"

It would do no harm to listen. She nodded.

"Excellent!" He smiled his gratitude. "Nell? Perhaps you and your cousin would care to join us?" He held a chair for Charlie, and then Nell, with nearly as much grace as Mr. Moleglass, then seated himself. Tobias grunted as he settled next to Charlie. His face was expressionless as he watched the Resistance leader, but Charlie could tell he was still furious about being kidnapped. Joseph squeezed into a space next to Nell. The other Resistance members gathered near.

"First," said Peter. "You need to know that Alistair Windlass is loved by the people."

"I've seen the newspapers," Charlie said.

"He is an illusionist! He distracts them with impossible promises: he will stop the recession and make the crops grow, he will single-handedly see off the Esceanians! And all the time he is robbing the Exchequer in order to fund secret scientific laboratories and bribe Esceanian officials.

"All but the very rich have suffered. Food is scarce. People cannot afford to buy clothes, educate their children, or even pay for a doctor." He paused, closed his eyes. When he opened them, he became even more animated. But Charlie saw that the lines etched around his eyes and on his forehead had deepened. Something had happened to this man. Something bad.

"There is no longer any pretence of democratic rule," Peter continued. "When your father became ill, Windlass dissolved Parliament and set up that abomination that sits in its place. He is the paymaster for our military, and their loyalty resides in their wallets! The newspapers print what he dictates or the presses do not run. And the people cheer him! Once they stop believing his promises, they will have nothing left.

"Those who can see through the illusions and have courage enough, agitate and plot. Some blame the monarchy for our ills and dream of revolution and Utopianism."

Beside Nell, Joseph stirred, frowning across the table at Peter.

"I am a pragmatist," the Resistance leader continued. "Human nature is not perfectible. You only have to look across the Esceanian sea to observe the inevitable result of revolution. And Windlass would sell us to the Emperor!" His voice grew acid with scorn. "He is their man, bought and paid for. That is why I formed the Resistance. Quale will not become part of the Esceanian Empire if I can help it!

"My question, ma'am, is this. Will you help me to defeat the Prime Minister? We are not a threat to your father, or your own right to inherit the throne. I give you my word of honour." His bright eyes held hers with their intensity. She felt an instinctive liking for this man, but she had liked Windlass too, and the last time she had trusted someone . . . She glanced at Tobias, caught his eye. He gave an almost invisible shrug.

"All right," she said. "I believe you." She took the letter from her pocket, unfolded it and handed it to

Peter. His eyes travelled slowly over the contents, and his body tensed, like a cat which has just spotted an unwary bird. A smile curled across his face. "I thank you, Your Highness. We have a chance."

"Less than you think," said Tobias. "Windlass has seen that letter."

Peter's eyes flicked up, fastened on hers. "Is this true?"

She nodded.

"When?"

"Eight days ago," she said.

"*And you're only just now coming to us?* Even without a head start . . ." He clenched the letter in his fist, jumped up from the table and began to pace.

"I didn't know you existed before yesterday!" Charlie cried. She stood, took a hesitant step after him, swallowing as guilt thickened in her throat. "He may have found nothing."

Peter whirled to face her. "Alistair Windlass? My dear Princess, do not underestimate him. He will be on Bettina's trail already. He is a ruthless spymaster and does not tolerate inefficiency. But . . . there is still a slight chance. On the other hand . . ." His funny, mobile face took on a calculating look. Charlie felt the hairs on the back of her neck prickle. "You are, yourself, a node of power. Do you understand my meaning?"

It was all too familiar. A pawn. A tool. And she had liked this man! "You mean I could be useful to you. Because of who I am!" She didn't quite manage to keep the anger and hurt out of her voice. His eyes caught hers and softened. He shrugged and smiled, as though they shared a joke that was both sad and funny.

"Indeed, Your Highness. Insurrection. A princess of Quale would make a valuable figurehead in a rebellion against the Prime Minister." He shrugged again. "Alas, we are not well enough armed for that, nor are we professional soldiers. It would be suicide. The army obeys the Prime Minister." He frowned. "Still, I am reluctant to let you slip back under his control. It might be safer to keep you. And it would certainly unsettle Mr. Windlass. There is also the possibility of treating with the Durch and the Bohemians. Perhaps the North Islanders. With you in our hands, we might be able to rally Quale's former allies, although I admit the chance is remote . . . unless we can secure this weapon that Windlass seeks . . . but on the whole . . . No, I am not inclined to let you return to the Castle."

"That's for Charlie to decide," Tobias said. He had

moved to stand beside her. "We came here in good faith, and we're leaving when we choose, not you!"

Peter's eyes swivelled to Tobias. "I suggest, Master Petch, that you hold your tongue!" His voice was cold; his eyes colder.

Charlie sensed danger. A thief, no matter how talented, was of less use to the Resistance than a princess.

"Leave him alone, Peter!" cried Nell. "He's right. It's kidnapping! I won't have nothing to do with it!"

Tobias lurched forward. Charlie grabbed his arm and pulled him back. "I thought you wanted to beat Windlass!" she shouted at Peter. "Well, you won't do it unless you stop being so *very* stupid!"

His attention switched to her. Her temper didn't improve when she saw that he looked amused. "You have another suggestion, Your Highness?"

"Yes! You need spies in the Castle. That's why you sent Nell there. That's why you asked Tobias to pick locks for you, though I doubt he'll want to now! But you can do better. If you want someone to spy on the Prime Minister, use me!"

He blinked. "I am intrigued. Carry on."

"The Prime Minister has decided that I will make a useful puppet. He's teaching me Statecraft three times a week. He wants to show me off to the people to try and keep them loyal to the monarchy and keep them from turning to such as you." She paused for breath. Her heart was thumping hard. "I'll do a deal with you. You want to know about this weapon Windlass is trying to make. I'll find out whatever I can. You help me find Bettina and my mother. Do your part, and I'll do mine. Is it a deal?"

Peter gazed at her, his eyes thoughtful. "The weapon is the key. Windlass wants it more than anything and, therefore, I will do anything to stop him getting it." He bowed, a sweeping courtier's obeisance. It was beautifully done, and she guessed his profession at last: he was an actor. He straightened, grinning. "Agreed, Your Highness. Welcome to the Resistance!"

# Twelve

"I ain't gonna turn thief for that jumped-up jacka-napes!" Tobias snarled as he climbed into the carriage for the return trip through the tunnel.

"I'm sorry!" Nell was standing at the steam engine controls. It had taken half an hour to build up enough pressure in the boiler. They were all ratty with nerves, terrified that someone would spot the smoke rising from the chimney of a building which should be unoccupied. "Try to understand. We've lost so many people lately to Windlass's spies. Peter has to be careful. Or we'll all end up dead . . . or shipped off to the penal colonies."

"Yes, please shut up about it!" snapped Charlie. It was nearly dawn. She was exhausted, and she still had to go back through the tunnel. "The only thing that matters is beating the Prime Minister." She grabbed Tobias's hand and held it tight as the carriage slipped forward into darkness.

By the time they had emerged at the other end he had relented. "I did say I'd work with the Devil himself against Windlass."

"I know. Why?"

He ignored her question, squatting to open the fire-box door on the Castle's steam engine. "Good. That'll be cold by morning. O'Dair won't know we used it; unless she weighs the coal every day. Wouldn't put it past her."

"I asked you a question," said Charlie.

"So?" He turned round, wiping his hands on his trousers. "Don't mean I got to answer it."

"Why do you hate Windlass? Why get involved at all? And don't tell me it's to do Nell a favour. You don't do favours."

He looked at her, his head cocked to one side. She waited for him to tell her to mind her own business. "You don't know anything about me, Charlie. You don't know if I do favours or not. I'm helping the Resistance because Windlass is rotten and what he's doing is rotten. If you see someone doing something wrong and you can stop 'em, then you ought to have a go. That's all. There's no mystery. Now, let's get out of here. I got to be at work in two hours!" He marched out the door, taking the lantern with him. Charlie ran to keep up. Peter was right: Tobias was a good liar. But she hadn't believed a word.

She raced through the Castle, cursing the long, heavy skirts of her new dress and the shiny black boots that skittered on the floor and sent her sliding out of control whenever she rounded a corner. She was looking for Nell, and she only had half an hour before she was due in the Prime Minister's office for her first lesson in Statecraft. The idea of meeting Windlass again terrified her: how could she look him in the eyes and pretend she didn't know what he had done? But she didn't have time to worry about it now.

She was pelting along a second-floor corridor when a voice rang out. "Do that again, Alfie Postlethwaite, and I'll break your nose for you!" She had found Nell Sorrell. Charlie heard the sound of a hand striking flesh and a gasp of pain. She pushed through a half-open door and was confronted with the spectacle of the gawky footman cowering and cringing as Nell boxed his ears, delivering a ringing slap to one side of his head and then the other.

"Leave off, Nell, do!" he moaned, dancing away and rubbing his ears with large, red-knuckled hands. "It were only a little kiss."

"Well you can go and kiss the Castle hounds! But don't you dare kiss me again, you great lummox, or I'll give you worse than that!" Nell's cap was askew, her brown hair tumbled about her flushed face, and her eyes flashed golden sparks.

Charlie jumped up and down in delight. "Hit him again!"

Both servants turned, both dropped their mouths open. Nell grinned, but Alfred blushed until his spots turned purple.

"Go away, Alfie," Nell said. "You got no business here."

"Nor has she!" Alfred muttered, scowling. But he left.

"Well, Charlie?" Nell walked to the dressing table and stood, tucking her hair in her cap and straightening her apron. "Is Tobias with us?"

"Yes. That's what I came to tell you. We're going to search Windlass's office tonight. See what we can find out about the weapon."

"Both of you?" Nell turned from the mirror, frowning. "I don't like it. You shouldn't be involved in all this sneaking about and spying. It isn't safe. I better go instead."

"I'm going. I may not know much about my mother's research, but I know more than you or Tobias."

"You're just a kid."

"Tobias is only a year older!"

"Yes. But he's a Petch."

"I'm going, and you can't stop me."

Nell sighed. "All right. No point all three of us clumping around in the dark. Just promise to be careful. And let me know what you find out. We'll need to set up regular meeting times. Tuesdays and Thursdays, after your lessons, starting tomorrow. I'll be waiting in the room next to the schoolroom. If anyone asks where you've been, you can say the Professor kept you late. Now get out of here. O'Dair is particular about her bedroom."

Nell picked up a feather duster and began dabbing at the ornaments on the marble overmantel. Charlie disliked the Rosamund suite, with its pink and gilt wallpaper and thick cream carpet patterned with roses. O'Dair was welcome to it. At the thought of the housekeeper, the scent of oil of cloves and mothballs wafted through the room. Charlie shuddered and turned to go.

Mrs. O'Dair stood in the open door, Alfie quivering behind her like a skinny shadow. At Charlie's gasp, Nell turned from the fireplace and curtsied. "Sorry, ma'am," she said. "Nearly done."

O'Dair advanced into the room. A muscular hand swooped out and caught Charlie by the wrist. The hand twisted, and Charlie winced. She glared up at the housekeeper, determined not to make a sound, not even if O'Dair broke her arm. "What is this creature doing in my bedroom?" O'Dair shoved Charlie towards Nell.

Nell looked through Charlie as though she was invisible. "If you mean Princess Charlotte, ma'am, she wandered in here a few minutes ago. I couldn't say why. Didn't feel it was my place to ask. Perhaps she was searching for you? With her mother gone away and all, I expect the poor child looks to you for comfort and guidance. 'Twould only be natural." Nell smiled at Mrs. O'Dair, seeming not to notice the housekeeper's face turning the colour of stewed plum pudding.

"And I see that you are as thick-witted as that

seamstress aunt of yours! Stupidity must run in your family!" spat O'Dair. She grabbed Charlie's shoulders and began to shake her. "Why are you in my bedroom? Tell me the truth!"

Charlie stared up at the housekeeper. She didn't dare look at Nell. Her tongue was stuck to the roof of her mouth, and her brain seemed to have stopped. What possible reason could she have for being here? "I . . . I d-don't—"

"Check her pockets, ma'am!" hissed Alfie, wriggling from one skinny, black-clad leg to the other in his excitement. "She put manure in my boots. She's up to some such mischief, I'll be bound!"

Charlie looked from O'Dair's furious face to Alfie's spiteful one. She could have kissed him. "I wouldn't!" She cringed with pretended guilt. "I never would, Mrs. O'Dair. It isn't true!"

Mrs. O'Dair's great prow of a nose sniffed. The nostrils flared. "Not manure, no." Her thick fingers felt in Charlie's pockets. She pulled out a crusty handkerchief, an ancient apple core, a withered conker, a pencil stub and a silver thruppence. O'Dair scowled at the things nestling in the bowl of her palm. She plucked out the thruppence and shoved the rest at Charlie. "Nothing," she growled. "But I've no doubt you had mischief in mind. Not this time, my girl! No fancy dinner in the dining room for you tonight. You'll have bread and water in your bedroom. I shall instruct the kitchen. Go!"

Charlie was five minutes late for her lesson with the Prime Minister. She stood outside his office door, waiting while the guard announced her, and felt sick. He would take one look at her face and know that she hated him. Her palms and armpits prickled with sweat.

She kept her head down as she entered. Her heart was thumping. She took a deep breath and tried to calm herself. Her boots clattered across the floor as she scurried to the chair in front of Windlass's desk. She was aware of his eyes on her the whole time.

"Are you quite well, Charlie? You seem out of breath, and you look pale."

How dare he pretend to be some sort of adopted uncle, full of concern and kindness, when he was responsible for her mother's disappearance and her father's illness? Hatred swallowed her fear. She would pay him out if it took the rest of her life!

"I'm sorry," she said, lifting her head, making herself look him in the eyes. "I was running because I was late."

"And why were you late?"

"The Professor was explaining Latin declensions. It was so interesting that we forgot the time."

He raised an eyebrow. "I'm pleased you find Latin grammar so fascinating."

"Thank you," she said.

"And I'm pleased to see you suitably dressed. Do you like your new clothes?"

She hated her new clothes. There were too many layers and too many buttons. Her dress was made of thick moss-green wool with a scratchy lace collar and cuffs. It had taken her twenty minutes to button her new boots. She also hated being tidy and clean. Her scalp ached from tugging her hairbrush through tangles, and she had scraped and scrubbed her fingernails until the ends were as white as Mr. Moleglass's handkerchief. She had been rubbing them against her dress all morning, trying to wear away the naked feeling.

"Well?" Windlass sat on the end of his desk, his arms crossed. His face was serious, but she thought he was probably laughing inside.

Very well. She would tell him the truth. Perhaps it would amuse him even further. All the safer for her if he thought her a figure of fun. "It isn't fair!" she said.

"Many things are not," he agreed. "Which one did you have in mind? I'm not particularly fond of boiled tongue myself. But the cook keeps sending it."

He was laughing at her. Indignation surged through her. She didn't have to pretend now. "Not that. That's stupid! Clothes! Girls' clothes! Would you like to have to wear long skirts? With petticoats?"

His eyes widened in surprise. He put a hand over his mouth and gazed down at his trousers of soft grey wool, chalk-striped with palest blue. "No," he said. "No, I can't say I would."

"Well?" she snapped. "Why should I have to just because I'm a girl? You can't run or climb properly in skirts. Trousers are much more practical."

Windlass stared at her over his hand. "I have to agree with you," he said. "However." He removed his hand, and his face was even more solemn. "We do not live in a logical world. We are bound by custom and prejudice and . . ." He smiled at her: ". . . etiquette. I think it most sensible of you to wish to wear trousers, Your Highness. However, that wish must remain unfulfilled. And no, it isn't fair. If it's any comfort, you look charming."

"That's no comfort at all," Charlie snapped. "In fact, it makes it worse."

"Spoken like your mother's child," said Alistair Windlass. He leapt to his feet and picked up the hamper resting beside his desk. "I think we'll picnic in the library today." He strode to the door and flung it open. "Come along!" He disappeared without a backward glance. Charlie took a last look around the room she hoped to break into that very night, jumped off her chair, and followed.

"What do you know about Esceania?"

Deeply embedded in the squashy cushions of one of the library sofas, Charlie peered over her ham sandwich at the Prime Minister. The bite of ham and bread seemed to swell in her mouth until she could barely chew, let alone speak. Windlass was leaning against one of the library tables, twirling the globe that stood upon it. He waited for her to answer his question. She sensed his impatience, although his expression did not change, and his fingers continued to stroke the globe.

She swallowed the lump of sandwich, trying to remember everything Professor Meadowsweet had told her about Esceania. "Um . . ." she said. Windlass's eyes narrowed slightly, and she felt a chill slide down her back. The gently teasing man of fifteen minutes ago had vanished. This Alistair Windlass expected clever answers to his questions. He expected her to be her mother's daughter and, much as she hated him, part of her wanted to prove that she was. "I-it's our nearest neighbour," she stammered. "Our ally in the Lascauxian Alliance, along with the Durch Principalities. We conquered the Western Hemisphere in the Saltpetre War of 17..." Her voice trailed off. She had forgotten the year.

"Of 1773. Good as far as it goes, which isn't very far. What do you actually *know* of Esceania?" His silver eyes glinted at her.

"I know that Esceania is the greatest imperial power in the world. That our alliance is one of convenience. I think..." She paused. This was getting into dangerous territory. "I think we shouldn't trust them."

"Why not?" he snapped.

"Because... because their empire is expanding. Ours is shrinking. They're growing stronger than us. And if we let them get too strong..." She hesitated, looked into Windlass's eyes. "They'll invade."

He smiled, gave the globe a vicious twist that set it whirling and rattling on its stand, then clamped his fingers on its painted face and stopped it dead. "Excellent.

You're not just Meadowsweet's parrot—you can think! You're right. Esceania seeks to dominate the world. Our job is to prevent that. How?"

Her mouth fell open. "I-I don't know! We need to build up our army, our navy. Form new alliances with other countries—"

"Too late! The past five years of recession mean that our resources are stretched beyond what the country can bear. All our old allies are either already in Esceania's thrall or too frightened to offer even a show of resistance. We're on our own, and the threat grows ever nearer." Windlass leant forward. "What we need, Charlie, is a scientific breakthrough. We need a new technology of war."

Her heart was hammering in her chest. This was it. This was what her mother had created and ran from. This was what the Resistance wanted. She swallowed and prayed her voice wouldn't wobble. "And do you have one?"

He smiled at her. "Not yet. But I shall. I don't intend to fail."

# Thirteen

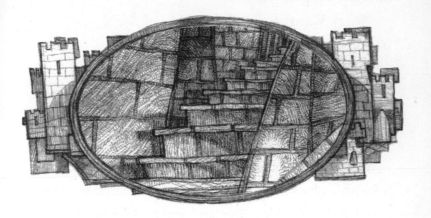

At twenty minutes past midnight, Charlie opened the door to the library and slid inside. The flame of her candle quivered, then steadied. "Tobias?" she whispered. "Tobias, are you here?"

A snore answered her. Then another. She tiptoed towards the sound until her puddle of candlelight revealed the gardener's boy sprawled on his back on a sofa. "Wake up!" He didn't move. She reached out and shook his shoulder. "Wake up!" she hissed. His hand snaked up and grabbed hers. "Ow! Stop it, Tobias!" His eyes opened, and he stared up at her blankly. He looked at his fist twisting hers and threw her hand away as if it burnt him. He hunched upwards, shaking his head as though to clear it.

"Sorry. Wasn't awake. I thought . . ."

"What did you think? That hurt!"

"Sorry!" His voice was rough. He jumped to his feet. He didn't look at her. "Come on. Let's get this over." Pushed past her and out the door. She ran to catch up. "Put that candle out," he snapped. "No use advertising."

She bit back her retort. Blew out the candle. Something had rattled him. She was too tired to think about it now. Exhaustion and excitement fought for her attention. Excitement won. It was like fire burning through her veins, and she thought she might explode with it.

The ground-floor corridors were ghostly in the moonlight. Soon, they slipped past the door to the dining room and reached a thick stone wall with a heavy oak door set deep inside it. Beyond lay several reception rooms and the throne room. Beyond these lay the ministerial wing. The internal doors of the domestic areas of the Castle were unsecured, allowing Watch to roam freely on his rounds. But from now on, every door would be locked, starting with this one. Tobias set to work.

A few seconds with his hands pressed against the keyhole, manipulating the shiny set of lockpicks he'd brought, and the locks clicked open, one after the other. He didn't even want a candle. "Save 'em for searching the office. You do locks by touch, see? Feel things better with your eyes shut."

His success seemed to cheer him. "Proper tools don't half help!" He grinned at her, shaking the set of lockpicks. "Nipped off at lunchtime and bought these off a bloke I know in Flearside. Got 'em cheap, too, 'cause these are quality. I'll have to keep 'em out of me mum's sight. She'd have a fit!"

He made it look so easy. If she learnt the trick of it, O'Dair would no longer be able to lock her in her room. It was worth asking him again. "Teach me?" But he just smiled and shook his head, trotting down the corridor towards the next door.

"Nearly there. Mind now, we got to be quiet!" he whispered. "Not a sound! The guards' hut is only a few feet away, and I don't fancy playing tig with a bullet!"

Charlie felt her heart lurch. Until a second ago,

her greatest fear had been being caught by Watch and hauled before the Prime Minister. It had never crossed her mind that she risked being shot dead by the Castle Guard.

They approached the door to the great hall of the ministry, with its marble floor and glass-domed ceiling. A bead of light shone at the bottom of the door. Both of them spotted it at the same moment. They looked at each other, then Tobias crept to the door, crouched down. She heard a faint click, and he eased the door open an inch and put his eye to the gap. He pulled back, looked at her, put his finger to his lips in warning and nodded at the door.

She edged past him to look in her turn. As she had guessed, the gas was lit, the great hall as bright as day, and a guard stood to attention beside the door to the Prime Minister's office. They would not be breaking in there tonight—or any other night.

"How was I to know?" Charlie asked for the third time. Tobias muttered curse after curse as he relocked door after door.

"No sleep for two nights!" he growled. "It's flipping

two in the morning, and I've got to be at work at seven! Rot Windlass! Who'd have thought he'd post a guard on his office door when there's two more standing outside in the hut barely five feet away? Blast him!" Tobias subsided into muttered curses once more.

By the time they got back to the east wing and Toby bent to relock the last door, Charlie was exhausted. They were so intent on the workings of the lockpick that neither noticed a light glimmering around the corner.

"Oi!" roared Watch. "Who's there? What're you up to?"

For a frozen second, Charlie and Tobias stared at each other. "Run for it!" he hissed in her ear and was off. Charlie pelted after him.

"Here! You! Stop!"

Tobias's footsteps clattered ahead of her, spun off sideways and disappeared down invisible stairs. Charlie flung herself headlong into darkness. Tobias had gone to earth like a fox. She would go up. Lose Watch in the maze of rooms, staircases and cupboards on the upper floors. She felt round a corner. The stairs waited, just ahead. She tugged off her boots and stood holding them, straining to listen above the banging of her heart. Would he follow Tobias? Or her?

The shuddering, swaying light of a lantern appeared. It was her. Charlie groped for the stairs. When her feet found them she flew up soundlessly. Fingers of light hesitated on the landing below, searched upwards. But she was beyond their reach, racing blindly for the servants' stair to the attics.

She flung herself through her bedroom door and pulled it shut behind her. She didn't know how much time she would have. Not much. Frantically, she changed into her nightclothes. Fumbling in the dark, she hid the candles and put her boots and clothes away in the wardrobe before crawling into bed. Now there was no evidence other than the thudding of her heart. She closed her eyes and made herself lie still and breathe deeply.

She did not have long to wait. She recognised O'Dair's approach even without the warning groan of corsets. Footsteps stumped to her door. It was flung open, and candlelight speared into the room. Charlie lay as if she were dead.

O'Dair advanced. Her breathing was harsh and

rapid, like the panting of a bear. "Open your eyes!" she growled. "Don't you pretend with me."

Charlie gave a sleepy sigh and turned over.

"Enough of that!" roared O'Dair. She took hold of the side of the bed and shook it until it rocked.

Charlie screamed and sat up. "What is it? What's the matter?"

O'Dair was a pillar of red in a flannel dressing gown. Her hair dangled in long black plaits. Her face was as scarlet as her gown. It convulsed with fury. "You were out of your room!" she panted. "Sneaking about where you'd no business. What were you after? Tell me, or it'll be the worse for you!"

"What are you talking about?" Charlie cried. "I've been asleep."

"Don't lie to me!" O'Dair snarled. "Watch saw two people near the dining room. *Small* people. You were one. I know it. Now tell me what you were doing sneaking round the Castle!"

"I wasn't! Whatever Watch saw, it was nothing to do with me. I can't think of anything worse than wandering around the Castle in the dark." She shuddered.

Mrs. O'Dair glared at her through narrowed eyes.

"I want the truth from you! Perhaps you'll remember what the truth is after a few days locked in your room."

"I'm telling the truth! And I don't think the Prime Minister will be very pleased if you lock me in my room. He's presenting me to Parliament tomorrow."

She watched with satisfaction as Mrs. O'Dair took in the news. "Parliament!" she spluttered. Even in the candlelight, Charlie could see her face flush purple. "The fool!" she hissed. Her eyes narrowed, and she glared down at Charlie with hatred so fierce it was like being hit in the face. Charlie gasped.

"Think you've got him round your little finger, don't you?" Mrs. O'Dair whispered. "Like your mother before you. Well, be warned! I'm not going to let you spoil everything I've worked for here! Remember what happened to your mother, little girl, and be careful, lest you disappear too!"

In the flickering light of the candle, the housekeeper's eyes were empty holes. She stared at Charlie for a long time, then turned in a swirl of red flannel and disappeared out the door. Charlie began to shake. A chill had seized her and was seeping through her body and into her heart. The hatred in Mrs. O'Dair's eyes had been heavy and poisonous. For the first time in five years, Charlie felt doubt creep into her mind. Was it possible that her mother was dead?

She pulled the eiderdown up to her chin and stared into darkness, until exhaustion swept up from the depths like a lurking crocodile, scooped her into its jaws and pulled her down into deepest sleep.

# Fourteen

The dress was made of silk the colour of cool water. Inside it, Charlie sweated beneath three petticoats and a crinoline that scratched whenever she moved. She had washed her hair and spent long painful minutes combing out the tangles. Her fingernails were scraped to spotless perfection. Her feet, looking strangely vulnerable in a pair of satin slippers instead of boots, were the only bits of her that were comfortable. She glared at herself in the mirror and stuck out her tongue.

The large corporal opened his eyes wide and swept

his moustaches low in a deep bow as she padded down the grand staircase, holding tight to the railing because the slippers did exactly that.

"Her Royal Highness, the Princess Charlotte Augusta Joanna Hortense!" the corporal boomed as he opened the door for her.

The Prime Minister greeted her transformation with an approving smile. "Well done," he said and stood. He had never got to his feet for her before. Just because of a fancy dress and clean fingernails! She forgot herself for a second and glared her contempt at him.

Amusement gathered in his eyes. "Is it so very uncomfortable, Your Highness?"

"Yes," she hissed, a blush spreading up from her neck.

"And you resent the fact that appearances matter." He raised an eyebrow. "But they do, Charlie. After all, you are only a princess because that is the story we have all told ourselves. We have agreed that you shall be Princess of Quale, just as our ancestors agreed that your ancestors would be Kings and Queens of Quale. It is a fairy tale, Charlie. In reality you are no different than any other eleven-year-old girl in the Kingdom. More stubborn and intelligent than some, perhaps. But you take my point. It suits us all to pretend to believe the fantasy, and your job is to make that belief easy. Therefore, like any actor, you must dress the part."

She stared at him, shocked and intrigued. "Then you are only an actor too!"

He shook his head. "No, Charlie. No one made me Prime Minister. I did that myself." He smiled. "But, I must confess that, unlike you, I rather enjoy dressing the part."

Looking at him, she could not doubt it. He was resplendent in a black cutaway frock coat, pale grey trousers and a silver and blue-figured silk waistcoat. The collar of his white shirt was fashionably high and his dark blue cravat tied in an intricate knot. He might have strolled out of the fashion pages of the latest *Gazetteer,* but no one meeting his gaze would mistake him for a mere dandy. Charlie stared up at him, fascination and hatred mingling.

"And now, Your Highness, to complete your costume!" He strode across to the coat stand beside the door, plucked down a garment and held it out to her. It was a cloak made of thick purple velvet so dark it was nearly black, the body and hood lined in silk the colour of asparagus. Charlie reached out a finger, stroked the velvet. It was softer than rabbit's fur. She looked up at Windlass, her eyes wide with wonder, and he smiled at her.

"Enjoy it, Charlie. It is yours. As are these." He re-hung the cloak and produced a pair of gloves made of the same pale green silk. He held one out. She slid her hand inside and stared, disbelieving, at its sudden elegance. "You have narrow wrists," he said, "like your mother."

"And my father!"

His eyebrows shot up. She dropped her gaze. She must be more careful. "And your father," he agreed. He helped her on with the second glove, then turned abruptly and walked to his desk. Had he seen her hatred?

But he merely picked up a narrow velvet box. "This was last worn by your father's mother," he said. "You may wear it today, but you must return it to me. It belongs to the Crown and must stay safely in the Royal Armoury when not in use."

Charlie took the box in trembling hands. The velvet was old and worn, the hinges stiff, but she managed to pry it open. She gasped at the lustrous beauty of the pearls: a single strand with a simple diamond clasp.

"Suitable for a girl of your years," Windlass said. "You should be seen in at least one piece of Crown jewellery. It's quite old. The women in your family have worn it for five centuries. Here . . ." His gloved hands plucked the necklace from the case and, before she could move, he had fastened it round her neck and stepped back.

Their weight was heavier than she had expected. She reached up a hand to touch the smoothness of the pearls, was foiled by her glove, and a wave of almost unbearable claustrophobia washed over her. She wanted to yank the necklace from around her throat, strip off the deadening gloves. Instead, she stood like a girl turned to marble as Windlass draped the cloak around her shoulders and tied its satin ribbons in a perfect bow.

"And now, Princess Charlotte," he said, collecting his top hat and a slender ebony and silver cane from the coat stand. "Your father's subjects are about to be introduced to his daughter. It is time for you to take centre stage."

Something seemed to be squeezing her round the middle, making her breathless. Charlie wondered if this was what it felt like to wear a corset. If so, she would rather look fat. She perched on the deeply buttoned leather cushions, trying to relax.

It was a fairy-tale coach. She hadn't believed such things existed outside the pages of storybooks. Despite the cold November wind, Windlass had chosen the open landau carriage. It was painted dark blue, with the Royal crest emblazed in crimson and gold on the side panels. Even the spokes of the great red wheels were picked out in gold paint.

He settled himself opposite her, facing backwards, his magnificence concealed beneath a black cloak. Charlie hardly noticed him. There were too many other things to see, smell and hear. The four horses were matched greys. They stamped, shifted, snorted. Harnesses clinked. The landau lurched as the coachman mounted the box behind her. A groom swung himself onto the back of the lead outside horse, which whinnied. Windlass nodded to the coachman, there was the crack of a whip, and they were off, grinding down the drive in a clomping trot.

She sat stiffly, her hands clutching the seat either side of her, watching the Castle gates speed towards her. Despite her beautiful new cloak, she was shivering. And then—through the gates and out! Out into the City of Quale. But there was no time to look, no time to think. Noise attacked her. They drove into a wall of sound: shouts, cheers, screams. Every inch of space seemed crammed with people. They surged between the buildings either side of the street, pushing, shoving, shouting, waving the red and white flag of Quale. Banners with the royal crest hung from balconies. Red and white bunting looped between the lampposts.

The carriage slowed to a walk, ploughing steadily through the sea of people. Charlie thought of ants pouring out of an anthill. She thought of wasps swarming over jammy bread. She thought of the Pied Piper of Hamelin, and the rats flooding the city streets on their journey to death by drowning. She thought of the thronging citizens of Oppiet following their king's tumbrel to the guillotine.

The crowd pushed towards the carriage, was shoved back by the guards lining the street. People shouted, gestured, screamed. At her. What did they want? Was this what it meant to be a princess? It was terrifying! There were too many people, and she had nothing to give them. Charlie pressed back into her seat and squeezed her eyes shut.

*"Wave, Charlie. Look at them, and wave!"* She opened her eyes and saw Windlass, leaning towards her. His voice cut through the tumult; his eyes were fierce blue

stars. They held her, and she found that she could sit up, could smile, could look out at the mass of people shouting at her and raise her hand and move it slowly back and forth.

A cheer rose and undulated after them, circling round the carriage. The faces were smiling now. Was this all they wanted? This meaningless gesture? Her eyes scanned the crowd and were caught by the stillness of a single figure. A rock lapped by a seething tide, a woman stood, watching her. For a second, their eyes met. The crowd surged; the woman disappeared.

It wasn't her. Charlie knew it, but her heart was pounding. The woman in the crowd had brown hair plaited round her head; she wore spectacles; her face was thin, her clothes shabby. *Not mine. Someone else's mother.*

She glanced at the Prime Minister. He was watching her, a slight smile on his lips. She shivered and turned back to the people of Quale.


A cloud of cigar and pipe smoke partially obscured the room and the two dozen or so men arrayed on the benches lining the two longest walls. They stared as she entered. They tottered to their feet. All the men were terribly old. Those who had hair had white hair. Some of them prised themselves upright with their canes and swayed alarmingly before finding an uneasy balance.

The House of Lords was too small. It was a large room, of course, but not nearly as large as in her imagination. It was also drier and dustier and dingier.

The tall Georgian windows at the top of the two long walls needed cleaning. The Royal portraits lining the walls of the gallery were dark with age and tobacco smoke. The Wool Sack looked tired. Its fabric was fading where the sun struck it, and Charlie fancied she saw a few moth holes. Even the gold leaf on the throne needed regilding. Parliament was a little faded, a little tired. Elderly. Like the men who stood before their benches, staring at her.

The Prime Minister did not seem to notice. He positioned himself in front of the Wool Sack. "Gentlemen!" His voice echoed around the gallery. "May I present to Parliament Her Royal Highness, the Princess Charlotte Augusta Joanna Hortense of Quale!" He smiled at Charlie and gestured for her to come and stand beside him. But before she could move, someone answered the Prime Minister's question:

"No!" A short, fat old man wearing ancient morning dress and a curly white wig heaved himself forward. "You jolly well may not!" he roared.

Silence drifted through the room with the cigar smoke. Charlie stared at the old man and then turned to look at the Prime Minister. She wished she hadn't. His face was not a comfortable sight. It was as hard and smooth as metal, and his pale eyes glittered.

"And will Lord Topplesham be so kind as to tell us why he does not wish Her Royal Highness be presented to Parliament?" Windlass asked in a soft and deadly voice.

Lord Topplesham glared at his colleagues. He glared at the Prime Minister, and he glared at Charlie. The Parliamentarians took sudden interest in their fingernails or the toes of their boots.

Charlie looked back at him, into his piggy little eyes. He looked hot and cross and stared at her as though she were something unpleasant on the bottom of his boot. Charlie blushed.

"Aye, I'll tell ye," the fat gentleman barked. "Because that girl is *not* the Princess!"

# Fifteen

Silence crashed into the room like a felled tree. Two dozen pairs of elderly eyes widened in shock and turned to stare at Charlie. Surprise made her breathe in too quickly and cigar smoke made her cough. One of the old men who had been dozing in a corner woke up with a start. "What's that?" he cried. "What did 'e say?"

"I said the chit's not Princess Charlotte!" snapped Topplesham. "And get her some water, Mumps, before she chokes to death!"

A footman who looked like a chicken in a wig scurried forward and handed a glass of water to Charlie.

She sipped it slowly while she got over her surprise. She wasn't frightened. No one could be frightened by these creaky, flustered old men. The only person in the room who scared her was Windlass, and she was careful not to look at him. His silence meant he was leaving her to deal with Topplesham. Another test.

"Thank you," she said and handed the glass back to Mumps. She remembered what Windlass had said about acting a part. She marched to the Wool Sack and sat on it, perching upright in her best princess manner: back straight and hands folded in her lap. She looked at all the startled old men. "You may be seated."

They sat, all except for Lord Topplesham, who folded his arms over his barrel of a belly and glared at her even more fiercely. "Thank you for the water, Lord Topplesham," she said. "When I next visit Parliament I would appreciate it if the gentlemen of the Lords and Commons would leave their cigars and pipes unlit. Tobacco smoke is bad for children. My mother made my father give up smoking when I was born."

Topplesham's scowl stuttered. "So she did," he gasped. "The King complained of it to me more than once."

"Please, Lord Topplesham," Charlie said, "tell me why you don't think I'm me."

He threw a dark glance towards the Prime Minister. "I'll tell ye," he said. "And I'll not mince words. There's been too much of that for too long!" He scowled at the old men scattered along the benches. The old men coughed and stared at the ceiling.

"When the Queen disappeared no one was allowed near the King. That one," he jabbed his thumb at the Prime Minister, "banned everyone from the King's presence. Medical reasons. Ha!"

Topplesham glowered at Windlass. "And no one's seen the Princess, bless her, since then either. Perhaps her mum took her with her when she disappeared. Perhaps she's took ill and died. Perhaps," he glanced darkly around the room, "*someone* did away with the mite. I don't know what happened to Princess Charlotte. But I know that man," he pointed a podgy finger at the Prime Minister, "serves no one but himself!"

Topplesham turned his glare on Charlie. "He brings you here, missy, and says you're Princess Charlotte. Well, where's the proof? No one's seen the child for years. Are we to take his word for it? What's in it for him? That's what we ought to ask. What's in it for him?"

Charlie drew a deep breath. She didn't dare look at

Windlass. Instead, she gazed at the old men scattered around the benches. They were waiting for her to prove her identity . . . or to fail. She looked up, and the past monarchs of Quale stared down at her dubiously. Her eyes paused on the last of the portraits.

Charlie stood, hardly noticing that half the Parliamentarians tottered to their feet while half remained seated. She strode down the central aisle, her silk skirts rustling. She mounted the stairs to the gallery and paced along it until she stood directly beneath the portrait of her father in his coronation robes, aged fifteen.

She turned to face Parliament, knowing now the truth of what Windlass had said about appearances, wishing she had a diadem to glitter on her head, a sceptre to hold. She put up a gloved hand, adjusted the necklace. Windlass had said she was nothing but an actress. Then she would give them theatre! She gazed down at Lord Topplesham and the dregs of the Qualian Parliament.

"Gentlemen!" Her voice rang round the room and echoed from the walls. "I stand below the portrait of my father, King Henry Julius Stephen Charles Xavier of Quale. I challenge anyone to look at me and look at my father's portrait and doubt my lineage!"

The old men craned their necks, stared up at the painting, took out their spectacles and squinted through them. They began to mutter and nod.

Charlie waited. Her blood was singing, thrilling in her veins. All at once she felt invincible, capable of anything—even besting Alistair Windlass!

She lifted her chin, wishing she was taller. "I am Her Royal Highness, the Princess Charlotte Augusta Joanna Hortense of Quale! If any of you still doubt my identity, I am sure the Prime Minister would be only too happy to arrange an interview with my father so that he can confirm that I am, indeed, his daughter. My father is indisposed, but he is not so ill that he does not know his own child!"

She waited a few seconds, each one as long as a minute, then marched back down the stairs. She did not dare look at Windlass. All her confidence had gone as quickly as it had come. What if it hadn't worked? She strode to the Wool Sack, turned to face Parliament, and glanced at Topplesham's face. The confusion she saw there made her almost sorry for him.

"Well, Lord Topplesham, are you satisfied as to the young lady's identity?" Something in Windlass's voice made Charlie shudder.

Topplesham turned so red in the face his white wig looked in danger of bursting into flames. But he managed to give a curt nod. "I completely, and without reservation, retract my previous statement about the young lady who honours us with her presence. I was hasty in my accusation. She is the image of her father in his youth. I ask Her Highness's pardon for doubting her."

"Well, of course—" Charlie began.

"As to that," the Prime Minister interrupted, "things are not so simple. Your outrageous accusation, Lord Topplesham, might well be considered treasonable."

All the colour drained from Topplesham's face, leaving it as white as his wig. The old man gasped in dismay and began to shake with fear.

"But surely not," Charlie cried, daring to glance into Windlass's eyes at last. "It was just a mistake."

There was no warmth in the look he gave her. "These matters are best left to Parliament, ma'am." His voice was dangerously smooth. He expected obedience.

Charlie felt her face grow hot. She dropped her eyes to the floor. What could she do? Windlass thought her a compliant puppet, a gullible little girl who believed every word he said. To challenge him now would be a declaration of independence. She couldn't save Topplesham. It would be madness to try.

She glanced up at the old man. He stood with his head sunk on his chest. All the other Parliamentarians looked away, shuffled papers, hummed, stared at the ceiling. With a sinking heart, Charlie knew she had to do something.

"I don't understand," she said. To her relief, her voice didn't wobble. She forced herself to turn and look at Windlass again. Forced herself to smile at him: a trusting, naive smile. "I'm only the daughter of the King, Prime Minister," she said. "Questioning my identity was silly, but surely it cannot be called treason! Lord Topplesham did not question my father's right to the throne."

Windlass studied her. After a moment, one side of his mouth quirked in an unreadable smile. "Well done, ma'am," he said. "You put your argument succinctly. But I regret to inform you that questioning the legitimate succession to the throne is also a treasonable matter."

Topplesham gave a dusty sigh, like a deflating bag-pipe. Charlie felt sick. She had gambled and lost. She didn't dare look at Windlass again, so she stared at the floor, trying to stop shivering. He would call the Guard, and they would drag poor, foolish Topplesham away to prison.

Why had she done it? If she lost Windlass's trust, she would never find out about the weapon. Her useful-ness to the Resistance would be over. They might stop searching for Bettina. The Prime Minister would wash his hands of her, and O'Dair would once more have complete power over her. Charlie wished for the glass of water back: her mouth felt as dry as dust.

"However," Windlass said and paused. Charlie glanced up. His eyes gleamed at her, and she couldn't look away. "Lord Topplesham has been foolish and im-polite, but your own generosity of spirit in overlooking his rudeness is persuasive. Perhaps he did not intend treason. Perhaps he should be given the benefit of the doubt." Charlie blinked. Her mouth fell open, and she quickly shut it again.

"On the other hand." The smooth voice grew as cold

and pointed as an icicle. "Lord Topplesham would do well to consider whether his foolishness is not in itself a resigning matter."

"I resign at once!" Topplesham gathered his belongings and stumbled from his seat to stand, plump and quivering, in front of Charlie, his armful of papers and portfolios threatening to spew onto the floor at any second. "Your eternal servant, ma'am." He swept himself and his belongings into such a deep bow that he only stood again with difficulty. Then, without a backward glance, he turned and hobbled from the room.

"You seem to have a talent for inspiring devotion," Windlass said, as he and Charlie sat on the Wool Sack in a chamber empty of all traces of Parliamentarians except for the lingering stink of tobacco smoke.

Charlie smoothed the skirt of her dress. Inside the gloves, her hands were clammy with sweat. "Isn't that what you wanted me to do?" she asked innocently. "That man is rather a fool, I'm afraid," she added, as though she had only just thought of it.

He stared at her and then threw his head back and roared with laughter. Charlie jumped. She didn't know whether to be pleased or frightened.

"Well that, at least, cannot be said of you." The Prime Minister got to his feet. He towered over her, seeming taller than ever in his elegant clothes. A jewel shone moonlike from the folds of his cravat, reflecting the colour of his eyes.

"Have we finished?" she asked.

"Only just begun, Your Highness." He smiled down at her. She knew then that she had not fooled him for a moment.

# Sixteen

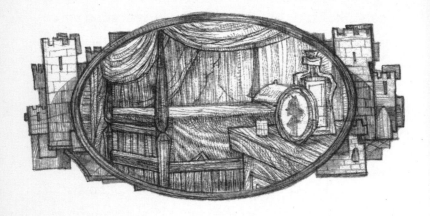

When Charlie slipped into the next door room after her lessons the following morning, the first person she saw was Tobias, standing with his back to her, gazing out the window. Outside, rain slanted sideways on the wind. Nell sat hunched on a wooden box in the corner, staring at the floor. Tobias turned at the sound of her footsteps, leant against the wall, crossed his arms. Nell glanced up. Neither said anything.

"Is there any news about Bettina?" The other two looked as gloomy as the weather, so she wasn't surprised when Nell shook her head, but the disappointment cut deep. "Nothing at all?" she cried.

Nell sighed. "No hint of the woman in Quale. So Peter's sent people to Durchland, but nothing yet."

Charlie crossed her arms to hold in her frustration and began to pace. "What are we going to do now?" she said at last. She wanted to break the silence so she could stop thinking about Bettina. Besides, she had lain awake half the night asking herself that question. Silence. She tried again: "Why aren't you working, Tobias?"

He jerked his head at the window. "Even Fossy can't garden in that. I've been cleaning pots all morning in the glass house. He's gone off home till tomorrow. So I'm taking the afternoon off." He tilted his head, raised an eyebrow. "Guess we ought to be bowing and scraping, Your Highness. The City's full of talk about your procession to Parliament. Missed it, myself: I was shovelling muck. Did you get to wear a pretty dress, then?"

Charlie felt herself blushing. "None of that matters . . . except . . ." She looked at Nell, who frowned.

"Something happened? What?"

"One of the Lords, Topplesham, he accused me of being an imposter brought in by the Prime Minister."

"What an idiot!" Tobias grinned. "One look at that red hair of yours—"

"Oh shut up! The point is, when he'd finished making a fool of himself, Windlass said he'd committed treason, and I couldn't just . . . I . . ."

"Oh, Charlie!" said Nell.

"I'm sorry! Anyway, I think Windlass knows I suspect him. I . . . I'm not sure."

Tobias groaned. "Can't you learn to think before you open your mouth? Well, that's torn it. Because there's no way we're gonna get in his office. Not with a guard beside the door all night long. We've had it. It's up to your lot now, Nell." He frowned at Charlie. "Maybe you *would* be better off out of the Castle."

"Giving up so soon, Toby?" Nell's voice was soft, but her eyes were hard brown pebbles. "Guess you ain't a Petch—just like you always say."

Stillness fell over Tobias. Then he shrugged and smiled. "I ain't a quitter!" he said. "But I ain't stupid either. There's no percentage in trying to do the impossible. If you're so clever, you tell us what we ought to do next."

"I will," Nell said. "There's the rest of the ministerial wing. What about Windlass's secretary? He must keep a diary. Peter wants to know Windlass's movements around the City. Who he's meeting, where he's going and when."

Charlie frowned at her. "Why does Peter want to know that?"

Nell met her eyes for a moment, then glanced away. "He just does."

"Peter was right," Charlie said. "You're a rotten liar. He's going to try to kill him, isn't he? He wants to assassinate the Prime Minister!"

Nell began to pace up and down the room, not looking at either of them. She rubbed her hands across her eyes, shook her head. Finally, she turned and glared at Charlie. "I don't like it!" she cried. "I don't like it any more than you do. But . . . if we can't stop him any other way—"

"It's murder!"

"And what about your mother, girl?" Nell's voice whipped back. "She's gone, and it's Windlass's doing. Your daddy's mad and playing with toys in his nursery, and that's Windlass's doing too. He's made himself King in all but name, living high while he let O'Dair half-starve you and dress you in rags!"

"He didn't know about Mrs. O'Dair."

"He should have done! If he didn't, it was because

you weren't important enough for him to bother with. Now he thinks different and you're all dressed in silk and ribbons and riding in coaches to Parliament. No wonder you don't want him killed!"

"That's a lie!"

"Shut up, Nell!" Tobias said. "Charlie's right. I'll help put that man in prison. But I won't help murder him. Count me out."

"We'll find out whatever we can," Charlie said. "Anything that will help. But not that."

"Then you'd better think on this, Charlie." Nell's voice trembled with fury and frustration. "You'd better decide who you want to live: Alistair Windlass or your father. If you change your mind, you know where to find me." And she whirled away out the door.

Charlie stared after her, then turned to look at Tobias. "What did she mean?"

His eyes flickered; he glanced away. "I don't know. She don't mean nothing. Don't worry about it."

"You're losing your touch, Tobias Petch!" she spat, fear spinning, as it always did, into anger. "You used to be a halfway decent liar!" And she turned and ran from the room.

———

If her mother were dead, her ghost did not haunt her bedroom. Charlie had never felt such an empty room. Everything shouted of absence: the windows staring over the remains of the rose garden; the hangings of the four-poster bed, tidied into prim folds; the dressing table, with its pots of rancid cream and bottles of stale scent.

Worst of all was her mother's dressing room. Most of the cupboards empty, the clothes gone, presumably stolen by O'Dair and sold. The rails that had once held rows of dresses, riding habits and ball gowns were empty except for dangling bunches of lavender that disintegrated at a touch. Charlie couldn't stand the scent of lavender: it smelt of loss. She had not come here for years.

Braving this room was an act of sheer desperation. She knew it. But this was the last place in the Castle she could think of to search for clues to Bettina's identity. There might just be a secret cache of letters hidden at the back of a drawer, under her mother's mattress, in a hatbox tucked high in a cupboard. But all the drawers were empty, and the hatboxes had been stolen along with the hats.

She made herself look in every drawer. She felt beneath the mattress. She checked behind the mirrors and lifted the pictures from the wall to search their canvas backs. Her mother's jewel case was empty. Charlie's heart hammered at the sight of it. She imagined the O'Dair's thick fingers plucking pearls, emeralds and diamonds from their resting places.

There was nothing of her mother left. Not so much as a single hair tangled in a hairbrush. Only, under her mother's pillow, Charlie's fingers touched a familiar shape. A playing card. The queen of hearts. She pushed it back with a shaking hand.

She closed the door behind her. She hadn't expected to find anything. Windlass would have had the room searched when her mother first disappeared. If there had been anything to find, he would have found it. It had been stupid to hope, but miracles happen sometimes. Only not today. She raised her head and found herself staring at the only other door in the corridor.

Charlie could not remember ever having been in her father's bedroom before. It surprised her. Somehow, she had not expected it to be so tidy. No. Not tidy. Barren. It was much smaller than her mother's room. A four-poster bed stood alone in the middle of the floor. Not a modern one, like her mother's. This was an old bed. Dark. With figures of people and animals carved into the headboard and up the thick columns. They were crudely carved, with heads too large for their bodies and round, staring eyes. The eyes were old and cruel. She shivered and turned away.

The only other furniture was a narrow dressing table. There was no mirror and only one picture. It was small and set in a heavy golden frame that made it seem smaller still. It was a portrait of her mother.

The painted face was stiff, like a doll's. But the artist had managed to capture her mother's hair exactly: golden wires, tendrils and curls no comb could tidy. Hair exploded away from the painted face like fireworks. Charlie remembered the woman in the crowd. No, it had not been her.

It was time to leave. As she passed the dressing table, she noticed a little brown bottle and teaspoon on a small silver tray. Her father's medicine. She had seen him take it dozens of times. She stared at it. Slowly, Charlie approached the table, picked up the bottle and slid it into the pocket of her skirt.

Tobias dropped the packet of broad bean seeds. Large wrinkled beans scattered across the rusty soil. "Blistering heck!" He knelt down to pick them up, and the pebble sailed over his head. Charlie cursed too, but silently, and fished another pebble from her pocket.

She blew on her fingers to warm them. Accuracy was important. Just a few rows in front of Tobias, old Foss was hoeing leeks. Charlie clung to the top of the kitchen garden wall, holding herself up with her right arm, her toes gripping the crumbling bricks. It made throwing difficult. But she had to speak to Tobias. She had stalked him through the Castle garden since early morning, and she would have to go to her lessons soon. Foss might have been Tobias's jailer, so jealously did he watch over his every movement.

She cocked her left arm back, aimed, threw. *Clunk!*

"Ow!" Tobias clamped his hand to his head, and Charlie winced. She had thrown harder than she meant to. Tobias whirled round, scowling. His mouth dropped open as he spotted her. He shot a glance at Foss, but the gardener was bent over his hoe. Tobias turned back and jerked his head at her with unmistakeable meaning, warning bright in his eyes.

Charlie slid from the top of the wall and dropped to the ground. An overgrown hydrangea slumped nearby, its brown mop heads bent beneath a net of bindweed. She crouched behind it, waiting.

Fifteen minutes later, Tobias sauntered out of the kitchen garden, whistling loudly, hoe and spade slung over his shoulder. Without breaking stride or looking to see where she was hiding, he motioned for her to follow and strode on in the direction of the green-houses.

When she caught up with him, he was standing out-side the tool shed, scraping mud from his spade. He straightened as she approached. "Well?" he said. She could tell he wasn't pleased to see her. "What is it? This isn't a good time. Fossy's on the warpath today. I can't do nothing right for him."

"I need to talk to you!"

"Oh well. What's one more ticking off?" He put the spade and hoe in the shed. "Come on," he said. "We'd best go somewhere private. He'll be along here in five minutes." He strode off, rubbing the back of his head. "Next time," he said without turning around, "throw gentle! I got a lump the size of a hen's egg."

She knelt between the roots of the largest yew tree in the Castle grounds. The giant stretched sixty feet into the sky; its lower branches swept the ground, forming a cave. It was dry under the tree, and the winter sunshine filtered through the branches and lit the cavern with an emerald glow.

"It's nice here," Charlie said. "It feels safe."

Tobias nodded. "Foss won't find us here. But I can't stay too long. He'll be looking, and he won't stop till I show up. Doubtless I'll be shovelling muck all day tomorrow." He was sitting on the thick root that burrowed into the ground beside her. There was no complaint in his voice, only a sort of bleakness.

She looked at him. "You really hate gardening, don't you?"

"Yes." He smiled. "But that ain't why you're here. What's up? I gotta get back to work."

She fished the bottle of medicine from her pocket and handed it to him. "This," she said. "I need to know what it is. Would you ask Maria if she can figure out what's in it? She knows about herbs and medicines."

"Why don't you ask her yourself?"

"Because she likes you better. She'll do it for you no matter what. With me it's chancy."

"Fair enough. Where'd you get it?"

She hesitated. "I'd rather not say. Not yet. Do you mind?"

He frowned, shrugged again. "All right, Charlie. You

don't have to tell me. I'll take it to Maria." He shoved the bottle in his pocket.

"Thanks." She smiled at him.

"She's a brick, Maria."

"Watch certainly seems to think so."

Tobias's eyes darted to her face. "What d'you mean by that?"

"Nothing. Only wondered if you'd written any love letters lately."

Even under his tanned skin and the smudges of dirt it wore, she saw his face flush bright red. His mouth fell open. He shut it. "Peter certainly got his end of the bargain! You're a born spy. Just don't let Watch catch you. Not these days, with O'Dair on the rampage."

"You seem friendly enough with him."

"He's all right, Watch. When he ain't drunk too much. We're old mates. But he ain't altogether to be trusted. So don't go wandering around the Castle at night on your own."

"It's none of your business, Tobias Petch! I don't tell you what to do!"

"Charlie . . ." He paused, shook his head. "This isn't a game. People can get hurt. *You* could get hurt. O'Dair hates you, in case you hadn't noticed!"

"I don't know why. I never did anything to her."

"That's the way some people are when they do someone down. They can't be an honest villain, so they blame the person they're hurting. Now . . . breaking into the secretary's office. Can you do tonight? Nell's agitating."

"But you said—"

"There's other stuff we can look for. Proof that Windlass is working with the Esceanians. We could give Peter names, contacts. The secretary's bound to have a record of his meetings and correspondence in a tidy little file somewhere. It's worth the effort, I reckon. Meet me in the library?"

"What time?" asked Charlie. "Midnight."

# Seventeen

Tobias was late. Charlie pressed her lips together and examined her candle. Fifteen minutes left at best. She curled into a chair, blew out the flame and waited for her eyes to adjust. The moon was bright tonight. The leaded windows sliced the floor into diamonds. She would have to wait.

Her eyes snapped open. She must have dozed off. She heard it again: a muffled footstep. The door hinges creaked. She was too stiff with cold to move. Her eyes strained, big as gobstoppers. Someone was in the room. She could hear them panting.

"Hey! You there?" It was Tobias. He stepped into the moonlight, and the diamonds cut him into a dozen pieces.

"What's wrong?"

"Come on! We gotta get out of here. Watch is after me! He's got a gun!"

She must have misheard. Sleep, cold and shock had frozen her. Tobias lurched forward and grabbed her arm. "Come *on!*" He pulled her from the chair. The candle fell onto the floor, and she tried to pick it up, but Tobias's hand was like an iron band around her wrist. He pulled her to the door and out. Charlie's legs began to work. Out of the corner of her eye, she thought she saw light swaying towards them down the corridor. She ran faster.

After five minutes, Charlie realised that Tobias was lost. Her breath tore through her in great sobs. There wasn't enough left over for talking. She grabbed his arm with her free hand and pulled. It was like trying to stop a runaway horse. She pulled again and braced her feet. She toppled over and pulled him down with her. His foot kicked her in the side, and she curled up, gasping for air.

"Dolt!" Tobias scrambled up. His voice was thick

with fear. "He's right behind us!" Charlie looked. The end of the corridor lurched, lightened.

"Follow me!" she hissed. "I know where to hide."

Tobias yanked her to her feet, and they ran on, Charlie leading this time. Her ankle and ribs hurt, but she gritted her teeth and ran, remembering the look on Tobias's face as he stood in the moonlight.

They had nearly reached the east wing. Charlie flew round the corner and into the grand vestibule. Their feet clattered on cold marble. The noise bounced off the thick stone walls and chased after them. And now she heard other footsteps behind them. Watch was gaining.

Here! It was here. Charlie raced past the lesser dining room at breakneck speed and burst into the serving room. She pulled Tobias in after her, closed the door, and ran across to the dumbwaiter.

It was a dumbwaiter of generous proportions, designed to help feed parties of one hundred or more, but the two of them barely managed to squash inside. She could not reach to work the cables even if she had dared. She crouched, squeezed on three sides by the dumbwaiter's walls, and on the other by a gasping, shuddering Tobias. The air inside was thick and sweaty. She felt panic rising and forced herself to breathe slowly. She closed her eyes so that she would not have to see the dark.

She felt Tobias stiffen. Her eyes popped open. Light showed around the edges of the dumbwaiter's door. Watch was here.

Four hands grabbed hold of the metal bar that worked the latch and pulled backwards with all the strength four arms, four shoulders and two backs could muster. Charlie braced herself. Footsteps shuffled towards them. The light grew brighter. Charlie pulled backwards so hard she could feel her ears popping.

The tug, when it came, was piffling. One brief, exploratory yank. On the other side of the door, Watch grunted. Charlie thought her heart would explode as the light lessened and went out altogether. A door slammed shut.

"Thank you, God," Tobias groaned, "for inventing good-for-nothing slackers with brains the size of rotten walnuts."

"Shut up," Charlie found enough breath to say, "and open the door."

"I don't believe you!"

"I saw it. Plain as I'm seeing you now. He's got a gun!

A ruddy great pistol. One of them fancy new revolving types that'll shoot six bullets without reloading. He was waving it about, shouting: 'Come out, or I'll shoot!' I never run so fast in me life! I'm not likely to be mistaken about it."

"But why? Who would give Watch a gun? It's crazy! He's not safe as it is, drunk half the time."

"Watch belongs to O'Dair. You know that."

"But that means . . ." Charlie stared at Tobias. They were sitting in the schoolroom, the door locked from the inside. She shook her head in disbelief. "The Prime Minister wouldn't let her."

"I don't expect she's told him, do you? You can have the joy of doing that."

"Oh yes? And shall I tell him how I found out? Creeping round the Castle at night? I might as well tell him straight out that I'm spying on him!"

"You'd rather Watch shot you? 'Cause that's what O'Dair's after. She's out to kill you, girl! And she won't shed no tears if I get plugged as well."

"She doesn't know you're helping me."

Tobias sighed. "Don't be daft. Watch saw us, the other night. Enough to judge size, anyway. Ain't no other kids in the Castle, is there? She knows, all right."

"But . . . surely Watch wouldn't shoot you? You're friends. He couldn't have known it was you!"

Tobias stared at the floor. "I don't know. I didn't much feel like staying to find out." He looked up at her. "So," he said, after a moment. "What're we gonna do about it?"

"I'm not giving up," Charlie said.

For the first time that night, he grinned. "No," he said. "I didn't reckon you would." The grin faded. "Look, Charlie, this ain't a lark no more." His eyes fastened on hers. "You could get killed. I ain't gonna help you do that. You're out of this from now on."

"You can't tell me what to do!"

He shook his head. "You're only a kid, Charlie! A snarky little eleven-year-old girl! I can't just let you . . ." He trailed off. Sighed. "You're not listening to a flipping word I'm saying, are you?"

"And what about you?" Charlie snapped. "Are you going to give up?"

His mouth fell open. His eyes dropped to the floor. "That's different," he muttered.

"Why?" A smile spread across her face. She didn't often win arguments with Tobias. It felt good.

He scowled at her. "It just is! I'm older."

"One year! What you mean is: you're a boy."

"Well of course. Girls isn't supposed to . . ." He stopped, sighed. "Oh, sweet Betty! All right! You win."

"Good. Because we're going to the secretary's office right now. It's the last thing Watch will be expecting."

The moon hung low in the sky, illuminating the ministerial wing of the Castle. A shaft of light fell through the window and across the floor of the secretary's office. It looked solid, as though she ought to be able to touch it—feel it trickling between her fingers like fine sand, cool and silver. Everything since they left the schoolroom—the trip to the ministerial wing, the ease with which they had avoided the guard standing on watch just a few yards away, and the way the door of the secretary's office had opened as though it wasn't even locked—had all felt charmed, like the moonlight. Watch was vanquished. Nothing could go wrong.

Tobias squatted on the floor in the wash of light. She heard the scratch of a match; the smell of sulphur pricked her nose, and there was a sudden flare of light from the strange one-eyed lantern he had collected from the corridor where he'd dropped it. "What is that thing?" she whispered.

"Dark lantern," he said. He looked up at her with a sardonic smile. "We're thieves now, Charlie. Might as well use the proper gear. This don't leave no telltale drops of wax behind, and we want our little visit kept secret."

"What about the window?" She had noticed at once that it had neither curtains nor shutters. Anyone outside in the grounds would be able to see their light.

Tobias glanced at it, shook his head. "We'll have to risk it. I'll keep watch at the window, look for any sign of the patrol. See that sliding door on the lantern, next to the bull's-eye? If I say, you pull that across; it'll shut off the light."

Charlie balanced the lantern on a chair and directed its beam towards the filing cabinet. She had never met the Prime Minister's secretary, but he seemed highly organised. She supposed Windlass would not tolerate anything less.

Correspondence was filed alphabetically by sender, and Charlie soon realised there was far more here than she could hope to search through tonight. She scribbled down names, subject matter and dates. After about forty minutes, her fingers began to ache. She decided to try the appointments diary. Tobias grunted as she stood up, but said nothing. She adjusted the lantern so that it shone onto the desk.

The diary was in the top right-hand drawer. She noted down visitors to the Castle over the last month and Windlass's movements both in and outside the City. Then she flicked over the page and saw the list of Windlass's meetings for the next week. Several were in the City, the location, date and time clearly noted.

Her heart lurched. All she had to do was give this information to Peter, and Windlass would have an appointment with death. *She* wouldn't have killed him— that would be the Resistance leader's responsibility; his crime . . . if it was a crime. But how could it be a crime to kill someone in order to prevent them doing evil? And Nell was right: she had to protect her father. Windlass deserved to die for what he had done to her parents.

Charlie glanced behind her. Tobias stood motionless beside the window, staring out into the night. She flipped to the back of her notebook and scribbled down the appointments, then, heart thumping, rose from the chair on wobbly legs. "I'm done," she whispered. "We can go now."

———

"Did you find anything useful?" Tobias's face was striped black and grey by the moonlight seeping through the slatted door. Charlie was too busy shivering to reply. They were inside the enormous airing cupboard in the east wing, drawn to its warmth like moths to candlelight. The cloudless night had grown bitterly cold.

She pushed her back against the giant cylinder of hot water and gave a violent shudder as its warmth penetrated her clothes and eased into her bones. The cupboard had been designed to keep hundreds of sheets, towels and pillowcases free of damp, and the cylinder had supplied hot water for the baths of the guests and dignitaries who no longer visited the Castle. The hundreds of sheets were now merely dozens, and there was plenty of room for two freezing children.

"I don't know. Names mostly. Peter can figure out what to do with it. They wanted a list of contacts. I'll give it to Nell tomorrow."

"No," said Tobias. "Nell can't get out the Castle any easier than you. O'Dair gave her the one day off already; she won't do more—she ain't the charitable sort."

"Are you going to take it to Peter then?"

"Nope. He don't want that." Tobias grinned a stripy

grin. "Don't think he trusts me overmuch. He does have a point: Windlass has got more spies in the City than fleas on a beggar. You never know who's watching. No, Nell's got a better idea."

"What?"

"The messenger tubes."

"But they only work inside the Castle."

"Not all of them. A few are direct lines into the City. The one in Windlass's office, for example. And the one in your mum's laboratory."

"How do you know that?"

"Nell's been doing her own bit of spying. Well, she asked Mr. Moleglass. But she thought to, and we didn't. Apparently, your mum used the pneumatic messenger in her laboratory to chat with other scientists in the City. It's a direct line to the Exchange. Peter's had someone working in the Exchange for years. His bloke will divert any message coming from your mother's laboratory from now on, and take it straight to the Resistance. So all we have to do is get back in the lab."

"Tonight?"

"Come on, Charlie. I gotta get some sleep. Tomorrow after lunch, like we done before."

He had opened the airing cupboard door and was climbing through when she remembered. "Wait! That bottle I gave you. Did you give it to Maria?"

"Oh," he said, turning round and fishing in his pocket. "I nearly forgot. Yeah, I gave it to her. Here it is if you want it back." He dropped it into her hand.

"Well? Come on. What did she say? What is it?"

Tobias sighed, deep and slow. "Where'd you get this stuff from, anyway?"

"Never mind that! What's in it?"

"Do you want to know what Maria said or don't you?" Exhaustion underlined every word, but so did stubbornness. She gave up.

"All right. It's my father's medicine. The stuff O'Dair makes him take." In the slatted moonlight, she saw him wince. "What is it?" she cried.

"It's not good," he said slowly. "That stuff—it does things to your brain. Makes you dreamy. So you don't care about nothing. She's drugging him, Charlie. I'm sorry."

"Charlie?" The voice came again, from a long way away. Charlie stared ahead of her. Not looking. Not listening. She felt like she was carved from a block of wood. Only her heart pounding in her ears told her she was not. She would destroy Alistair Windlass for this. And she had the means to do it right here in her notebook.

"Charlie?"

"Go away."

"I'm not going till you're all right."

"Go away!" The numbness was fading, and she was beginning to hurt. She didn't want him here. She didn't want anyone.

"Charlie?" His voice was gentle. He reached out and touched her shoulder. She hit him. She punched out with her left fist and hit him somewhere in the face. It hurt her hand, and she heard him cry out. Felt him jerk back.

"Dammit, girl! You . . ." He paused.

"Go away." Her voice was a stone in the silence.

He went.

She sat and waited for tears to come. She wanted to cry because she had hit Tobias when he was trying to be kind. She wanted to cry for herself. Most of all, she wanted to cry for her father. But the pain was too fierce for tears. It burnt them to ash.

After a while, she crawled out of the airing cupboard and began the journey up the long winding staircase to her bedroom.

# Eighteen

Charlie woke early. She felt numb, inside and out. She looked at herself in the mirror as she brushed her hair. Her face looked strangely stiff. She needed to see Mr. Moleglass. Now. Before lessons.

It was still dark as she descended the endless stairs. The Castle clock chimed seven as she climbed inside the dumbwaiter. She hardly noticed the journey into deeper darkness. The butler would be awake: he still woke at five every morning, even though he had no work waiting for him. But he would not be expecting her. She knocked on his door, and it opened at once. This was so unusual that Charlie's numbness was pierced with a brief jolt of surprise.

Mr. Moleglass stood aside for her to enter. The first thing she saw was Tobias. His right eye was bruised purple and red and swollen half-shut. She winced at the sight and turned back towards the door, the dust, the journey up through darkness. But before she could leave, Mr. Moleglass's arms folded round her.

He held her gently, as though she were a child of three who had fallen and hurt herself. The numbness shattered, and she began to cry. She cried for a long time, and when she had finished, he pulled the pristine white handkerchief from his breast pocket and handed it to her.

"I am so sorry, Charlie," he said. She looked up and saw that his seal's eyes were sadder than they had ever been. His face looked thinner, older. "Tobias has told me about the drug which is given to your father. I can only beg your forgiveness."

She stared at him. She must have misunderstood. She looked at Tobias, but he was frowning at the floor. "I don't understand," she said, looking back at Moleglass. "It's nothing to do with you."

A look of pain crossed his face. "But I am responsible. Oh no," he said, as she gasped in disbelief, "not for the drug in the medicine. No. I am responsible for Mrs. O'Dair."

Charlie gazed at him, speechless. What could he mean?

"Forgive me, Charlie. It's my fault she is here. Perhaps it is even my fault that she has grown so dark inside. I ask myself that question every day. She was different when I first knew her." He looked at Charlie and shook his head at her incomprehension. He groaned. "She is my wife, Charlie. She married me because I was the butler here. She married me and persuaded me to give her the job as housekeeper."

"B-but . . . her name isn't Moleglass," Charlie said, as though this fact would wash away what she had just heard.

He smiled at her sadly. "It is the custom, in the case of servants marrying each other, for the woman to keep her maiden name. Particularly if she holds a position of authority. She is indeed my wife, Charlie, although we have not lived as man and wife since I first became aware of her scheming.

"But even so, I was not strong enough to cast her

off completely, to repudiate her and leave the Castle for a dangerous and hungry world. I'm far too fond of my own comfort for that! And I added to my store of comfort by telling myself that I could not abandon you. That I might prove to be of some small use. But I deluded myself. I have never been able to influence her treatment of you in the slightest, although I have pleaded and argued with her countless times over the years. All I was ever able to do was feed you occasionally, and teach you chess. It is pitiful!" He groaned again, staring in front of him, his face pale and set. "But this . . . this I will not tolerate!"

"What do you mean?" she asked. The numbness had come back, and her head was singing, but it seemed important to find out.

"Tobias has told me about the pistol," Mr. Moleglass said. "You should have come to me at once instead of waiting till morning! And now I discover that she has been drugging the King! I will visit her. Force her to listen to reason!"

"How can you stop her? She won't pay you any mind." Charlie heard the contempt in her voice and watched Moleglass wince.

"I will threaten to leave," said Mr. Moleglass, looking

at his hands and smoothing his gloves with the tip of a finger. His hands shook. "Surprisingly, perhaps, she does not want that. She has always hoped our estrangement would be temporary. She is … fond of me, as some women are of their lap dogs." He shuddered.

As soon as Mr. Moleglass's door closed behind them, Tobias caught hold of her arm. "There's no point in blaming him, Charlie."

They stood in the dust of the cellars, in a puddle of early morning light that had struggled through one of the grimy windows at the top of the wall. "I don't," she said.

"Tell that to your mirror. Your face is a study."

She yanked her arm away. "And how long have you known … about him and O'Dair?"

"Don't you go blaming me, neither. What's between Mr. M and me is none of your business. He's a good man, Charlie. He cares for us both, and he's done the best he can by us. You can't ask no more." He paused. "It's more than some get from their own fathers."

Charlie gasped. She stared at him in disbelief. She couldn't believe he had said it. And she couldn't believe how much it hurt. "How dare you!" she whispered. "How dare you say such a rotten, horrible . . . when you know it's not even his fault! I'm glad I gave you a black eye! I'd like to give you another. I hate you, Tobias Petch!" She whirled around to leave, slipped in the dust and fell onto her hands and knees.

*"You self-centred little idiot!"*

Charlie stared up at him in surprise. Tobias was shaking. His eyes blazed in his white face. She realised she had finally achieved one of her life's ambitions. She had made Toby Petch lose his temper.

"You think everything is about you, don't you?" he shouted, his face twisted with fury. "I wasn't talking about *your* father. What sort of person do you think I am? I was talking about *mine!*"

Too shocked to make a sound, she watched him turn his back and stalk away into the dust.


The spade coughed as it bit through the frozen sod. *Hack! Hack! Hack!* The noise echoed through the garden. She followed the sound and found him standing in a hole up to his knees, double digging the trench for next year's runner beans.

"What are you doing out here?" Tobias growled up at her. It was only a few hours since she had seen him, but it might have been years. His voice was cold. His black eye glowed in the sunlight. "Foss is disinfecting the greenhouse, but he'll be checking up on me soon enough."

"I've got to talk to you," she said.

"Well, I don't want to talk to you." He turned back to his trench, stabbed at a lump of rusty earth. "Go on. Get out of here before you get caught. We've got enough trouble already."

"But I want to say I'm sorry! For hitting you and . . . for what I said. I'm sorry your stepfather was rotten to you."

He stopped shovelling but didn't look at her. "He's dead. It don't matter."

"What happened to him?"

"Someone stuck a knife in him and tipped him in the canals."

Charlie gasped. "Why?"

Tobias shrugged. This time he did turn to face her. "He was a thief. Fell out with someone he did a job with. Trusted the wrong person. That makes him a fool.

A dead fool." His voice was as bitter as the frost. "Now get out of here. Don't worry; I'll be along later just like we planned."

He turned his back, stabbed the earth again. Charlie watched him for a moment. Had he accepted her apology? She was surprised how much it meant to her that he should.

A creaky voice shouted for Tobias. Fossy was coming. Charlie turned and ran.

Her mother's laboratory still bore traces of their previous visit: footprints scuffed the dusty floor, tracked around the room. Charlie ignored them, going straight to the pneumatic messenger. She had written two messages to Peter this morning. One contained the list of Windlass's appointments. She would send it if she could, but she didn't dare let Tobias see it. He might stop her, and she couldn't take that chance.

He hadn't spoken to her the whole journey from the scullery to the north attics. The idea of Tobias hating her made her oddly miserable. She clattered open a message capsule, stuffed a folded paper inside.

"Here. Let me have a look at that." He plucked the

tube from her hands, pulled out the paper and read it. His black eye was turning purple and yellow, the colour of rotten bananas. Charlie winced. "All right." He slid the paper back inside the tube and handed it to her. "Send it."

There wasn't going to be a chance to send Windlass's appointments to Peter. Not unless she could get rid of Tobias. She slotted the brass capsule into the messenger tube, and he reached up and pulled the lever. There was a hiss, a whoosh, a faint clatter, and the capsule was sucked along twisty rubber tubes towards the City and the Exchange.

"Right. I'll be off now then." Tobias turned to go.

"Go ahead. I want to stay for a while," Charlie said. "Study some of the research papers that are still here. I didn't have a chance to more than glance at them last time. There might be clues to what my mother was working on."

"Windlass'll have snaffled anything useful and taken it away years ago. If your mum was daft enough to leave anything behind, which I doubt."

"I know. But at least I can find out more about her science generally. She was studying synthesis. I don't even know what that means."

He sighed in exasperation. "Then I gotta stay too! You can't relock the door."

"Just go! The door doesn't matter!"

"Don't be an idiot!"

"Well, I'm staying here! Do what you want." She turned her back and marched to the filing cabinet. Tobias would just have to have one more reason to hate her. With any luck, he'd soon get fed up and leave.

She settled down on the floor to read, ignoring the angry scuffing noises he made as he stalked around the laboratory. When she looked up, a long while later, he was sitting with his back against the electricity generator, doodling in the dust of the floor with his finger. She groaned, rubbed her neck, and put the paper she had been reading back in the filing cabinet. Trying to make sense of all the strange words was hard work.

"Well? Found anything? Only it must have been over half an hour. I gotta go!"

"Fine!" she snapped. "I'm staying here."

They both heard it: the squeak of the stairwell door. Charlie leapt to her feet, knowing, even as her eyes scanned the room, that there was nowhere to hide. Footsteps now, in the corridor. Tobias gestured for her to join him. She darted across the room and squatted beside him. She peered around the side of the generator but jerked back at once and hunched herself as small as possible. She was shivering with shock. She had just seen the laboratory door open and Alistair Windlass stride into the room, an unsheathed swordstick in his hand.

# Nineteen

"Come out from your hiding placc! If I'm forced to come and find you, you will regret it." Windlass's voice echoed through the silence.

The skylights chequered the dusty floor with cheery patches of sunlight. Charlie stared at the tarnished brass of the generator three inches from her nose. This room had seemed so safe and dull a few moments ago. This couldn't be happening. But it was.

How did Windlass know they were here? Her heart was thudding in her ears. In a minute he would find them. She could hear Tobias, breathing heavily beside her. He smelt of fear. Her own armpits were damp. She clenched her teeth to keep from screaming.

"Come out from behind the generator at once, or I will come after you. And I am armed!"

Charlie felt sick. This was it. But Tobias squeezed her arm in fierce warning. "Stay hid!" he mouthed. "Do it!" He pushed her further down, shoving her against the generator. Before she could stop him, he had gone. For a moment, she was frozen. What should she do? He had told her to stay hidden. But she couldn't leave him to face the Prime Minister alone! She crouched, uncertain, her heart pounding.

"You!" exclaimed Windlass. "Damn you, boy! What are you doing here?"

"Just having a snoop round. Thieving runs in my family, Mr. Prime Minister, and times are hard. I was looking for something I could nick."

"Don't be ridiculous."

"How did you know I was here?" Tobias asked.

"Someone sent a message from this room twenty-five minutes ago. Once I was notified of that fact, I came to investigate."

"You've got a spy in the Exchange!"

"Of course. I assume it was you who sent this message?"

There was a rustle of paper, and Charlie heard Tobias's intake of breath. "Never seen it before." Tobias had recovered. His voice was as bland as if he were discussing last night's dinner. He was a champion liar! She squeezed her eyes shut, squeezed herself into a tiny ball. She was shivering. It was the hardest thing she had ever done, crouching there listening to Tobias sacrificing himself, even though it wouldn't help anyone if she were caught too. But she also knew that she wouldn't stay hidden and let Windlass kill him.

"No doubt your message was intended for Mr. Peter Magorian, second-rate actor and sometime leader of an organisation that chooses to style itself the Resistance. Mr. Magorian's days at liberty are numbered. And you are a very foolish boy. You need to learn to pick the winning side, Mr. Petch."

"That's you, is it?"

"It is."

"Then I reckon I'll stay on the losing side."

"That is no longer your decision."

Charlie tensed. Silence grew through long seconds.

"So," said Tobias. "What you gonna do? Throw me in prison? Or maybe just kill me? You got a pretty little sword there. Dinky, ain't it? But it looks right sharp. You gonna do the job yourself?" His voice was shaking wildly. "Or hire someone in?"

What was he doing? *Trying* to get himself killed? Charlie tensed her leg muscles, preparing.

"Do you really think I would murder you in cold blood?"

"I think you'd do anything it takes to get what you want, Mr. Prime Minister. No matter who you hurt along the way. I'm nothing. What do I matter? A gardener's boy? You wouldn't lose five minutes' sleep over me." Tobias's voice shimmered with hatred.

Silence.

"Get out." Windlass spoke at last with a voice like ice. She heard the sound of metal hissing on wood. Relief made her giddy, and she rested her forehead against the cold metal of the generator. He had sheathed his swordstick. "Go on, boy! Run to your friends in the Resistance. Tell them they'll have to find another spy. Let them take you in if they will. But don't dare to show your face in the Castle again, or you'll find yourself on the next convict ship to the colonies. You have ten minutes to get out of the Castle grounds before I unleash the Guard, and heaven help you then, boy, because no one else will! Go!"

Charlie heard the sound of someone walking, then running away. Then a sigh, so deep and full of pain that her eyes sprung wide in surprise. She heard Alistair Windlass stride out of the room and down the corridor. There was a squeak from the stairwell door. And then silence.

She waylaid Nell in the withdrawing room, a long room full of gold and green furniture, pale walls and vast oriental rugs. Cold radiated from the walls and the smell of beeswax and turpentine hung in the air. The maid was kneeling in front of one of the upholstered side chairs, polishing its gilded wooden legs. As Charlie ran in, Nell jumped to her feet. "What's happened?"

"Tobias!" Charlie flopped into the chair, gasping, struggling for enough breath to speak. She had run all the way from the laboratory.

"What? Tell me!" Nell grabbed her shoulders and shook her.

Charlie pushed her away. "Give me a moment." She gasped several deep breaths, then looked up at the maid. Nell Sorrell had gone greyish-white, like suet pastry. "We were in the laboratory in the north attics. We sent the message to Peter, like you said . . ."

Nell nodded. She had wrapped her arms around herself as though trying to hold in her shivers.

"Only Windlass has someone in the Exchange too. His spy intercepted our message, sent it straight to the Prime Minister. He came to the laboratory. He found us. H-he had a sword."

Nell looked like she was going to faint. "Toby! Is he . . ."

"Windlass didn't kill him. But he's banished him from the Castle! He knew the message was for Peter."

"Then why didn't he hand him over to the Guard? Throw him in prison?"

"I don't know. He let him go. But he said that if Tobias ever came back he'd be arrested and shipped to a penal colony."

Nell clutched her head, paced in circles of frustration. She stopped in mid-stride. "So why are you running around free?"

"Windlass didn't know I was there. We hid, but he guessed someone was still there. And . . ." Tears began trickling down Charlie's cheeks. She rubbed them away angrily. "Tobias gave himself up to save me." Guilt was a horrible feeling. If she hadn't insisted on staying longer, Windlass would never have caught them. It was her fault.

"Oh, Charlie." Nell shook her head. "Don't blame yourself. I should never have asked Toby to get involved. You're both too young. He'll be all right—stop fretting. Peter'll hide him away if Windlass comes looking. What a mess! I don't know how Aunt Rose will manage without Toby's wages . . ." Nell groaned. "She'll never forgive me for getting him mixed up in this." She began to pace once more. "I have to think! That message—Peter never got it?"

Charlie shook her head. "But I can make a copy," she said. "The notes are hidden in my room."

"Good. Do it and get back here as quick as you can—no!"

Charlie was halfway to the door. She whirled round.

"It's no good." Nell had gone pale again. She looked terrified. "I've got to get out! It must be fifteen minutes gone since Windlass caught Toby. I can't wait. O'Dair knows I'm Toby's cousin; odds are Windlass knows it too. He's no fool. He'll be after me. And it's not just prison, Charlie. I've heard stories of what his men do to folks to make them talk."

Charlie stared at her in horror, and Nell reached out and gave her a fierce hug. "Be careful, child. Don't try nothing on your own. Stay away from that man. Someone will be in touch. Don't worry about Toby. I'll see him safe. Goodbye." She turned towards the door, but Charlie grabbed her arm.

"Take this." Charlie pulled a crumpled paper from her pocket. "It's Windlass's appointments in the City."

Nell's eyes widened. She put out a hand to take the paper, hesitated. "Are you sure?"

"Yes! Give it to Peter."

Nell took it. Her face was solemn. "Thank you. You may just have saved a great many people's lives."

Not Alistair Windlass's, Charlie thought, and shivered.

She sat next to the hob and sipped her tea. Moleglass sat beside her in his armchair. He placed his teacup in his saucer and looked at her. "Feeling better?" he asked.

She blinked and stared into her cup. "Nell and

Tobias are in trouble, and it's my fault. What if the Prime Minister changes his mind and decides to arrest Tobias after all? He's bound to set spies watching him in the hope that he'll lead him to Peter."

"Do you think Tobias doesn't know all that himself?" Moleglass asked gently. "He will have gone into hiding already. As will Nell. He must just keep out of the way for a while. Try not to worry. He will be fine. Now, in order to take our minds off these unfortunate events, I will obliterate you at chess."

Sometime later, he put his hand out to make a move. Paused and looked up at her with his seal's eyes. "Have you forgiven me, Charlie?" he asked. She knew at once what he meant: Mrs. O'Dair.

"I wish you had told me. Tobias knew." She couldn't keep the bitterness out of her words.

"I am not as brave as you." His voice was low. "Your regard means much to me. I feared to lose it." His brown eyes were wistful.

"Silly! Of course you haven't lost it."

"No." He beamed at her; swooped his bishop across the board and took her queen. "But you have, my dear. Checkmate!"

The next morning Professor Meadowsweet had only just begun Latin declensions when the pneumatic messenger on the wall behind him gave a shrill whistle and a capsule clanked into the catch basket. The Professor dropped his chalk.

"Oh dear!" he gasped, craning his neck around the blackboard to identify the source of the noise. "What is that machine? Drat this new-fangled technology! Never a moment's peace. Now . . ." He advanced on the messenger. "Hmmm." He poked at the basket. "Do you know how to work this contraption, Your Highness? You do? Excellent! Would you be so kind?"

She was shaking as she took the capsule out of the catch basket. Wild thoughts sprang into her mind. The message was from Peter, saying that Tobias had been shot dead by the Guard. It was from the Prime Minister, telling her she was under arrest for treason. She pulled out the paper and handed it to Professor Meadowsweet. He unfolded the message and read it.

"How very annoying!" he exclaimed, frowning at the paper. "Ambassadorial Etiquette is next week's lesson. Never mind, you are making progress in Deportment.

It will have to suffice." He peered at her over his spectacles. "Very well. Off you go, Your Highness."

"Where?"

"You must go put on your nicest frock and tidy yourself. The Prime Minister says that you are lunching with the Esceanian Ambassador today. You are to be waiting in the great parlour at precisely eleven o'clock. There will be an informal reception followed by luncheon in the state dining room. Now, run along. And do not forget your Geography revision for the morning: chapters seven and eight. There will be a written examination!"

# Twenty

Charlie stood in the middle of the great parlour, on a cream and pink rug. She smoothed the skirt of her blue silk dress and tried not to be nervous. She had always hated the parlour and its fake cosiness: its pink and gilt decoration, floral upholstery, large paintings of cupids smirking at plumply naked women. It was not a cosy room. It was far too large and the ceilings far too high, and it was always draughty, even when there was a roaring fire in the marble fireplace, as there was today. It was hard to look regal when you were shivering with cold and covered in goosebumps.

Precisely as the Castle clock struck eleven, the door opened and the senior footman swept in, bowed his long nose to the floor and stood back with a flourish. "The Honourable Citizen Oblique, Ambassador to the Court of Quale!" he announced. "And the Prime Minister, Mr. Alistair Windlass!"

A short, thin man with a face like a constipated fish strode into the room. He was dressed all in black, except for a severe white collar that dug into the drooping folds of his chin. His flat hazel eyes were embedded in deep pouches. The eyes fastened on Charlie, and he dipped his head in the most perfunctory of bows. He turned to Alistair Windlass, who had entered the room behind him. "So, this is the Princess Charlotte? She does not resemble her mother. A pity."

Charlie felt her face grow as pink as the rug. She had struggled into three petticoats and a crinoline; it still took her ten minutes to button each boot; she had even brushed her hair and tied it back with a blue satin ribbon. She should have stayed upstairs with the Professor and his declensions! She glared at the Esceanian Ambassador. "If you have any more personal remarks to make, sir, I would prefer you address them to me. I am not a piece of furniture!"

She widened her glare to include the Prime Minister. But Alistair Windlass was wearing his carefully solemn face, the one that meant he was highly amused. His right eyelid dipped, and Charlie's eyes widened in astonishment. He had just winked at her!

A mauve patch blossomed on either cheek of the Ambassador's cod-white face.

"Ah, but you are mistaken, Oblique," Windlass said, moving forward smoothly, taking Charlie by the arm and guiding her to a chair. He all but pushed her into it, then took her hand in his and bowed. When he looked up, his eyes held a clear warning. She was to behave! "Her Highness shows every sign of having inherited a fair portion of her mother's intelligence," he continued. "It would be a mistake to underestimate her, as I have learnt to my cost."

Charlie felt her face go wooden as alarm shot through her. Did he know that the Resistance still had one spy at large in the Castle? But Windlass had turned to motion the Ambassador to a comfortable chair before settling himself in another. When he looked at her again, his face was bland and unreadable.

Charlie felt a strange recklessness seize her. Tobias

and Nell were gone, and she was alone with her enemy. Alistair Windlass thought she was merely an actor in a play he was directing: a puppet to his puppet master. But she was going to pay him back for what he had done to her father, starting right now. She turned to the Ambassador with her sweetest smile. She hoped it poisoned him. "Did you know my mother, Mr. Ambassador?"

"Indeed," he replied. "I have been Ambassador to the Court of Quale for nearly eleven years."

"Ah," she said, "that would explain your talent for diplomacy." Windlass coughed. She avoided his eyes. "Perhaps you are familiar with her scientific research? She was interested in the synthesis of crystals, I believe."

The Ambassador's eyes widened. They looked like a pair of poached eggs with browny-green yolks. He shot a glance at Windlass. Charlie pretended not to notice.

"I am surprised you know anything about it, Your Highness," Oblique said. "You were a mere infant when your mother ran away."

"I was six," Charlie said. "Not quite an infant. My mother often talked to me about her science. And I have a very good memory. But why do you think she ran away? She might have been spirited away—kidnapped. Murdered, even. Many people think my father killed her." She had rattled him now. His mouth dropped open. "Perhaps . . ." She dared a glance at Windlass; he was sitting quite still, watching her with an expressionless face. ". . . someone told you that she had run away?"

"Not at all," snapped the Ambassador. "It is the only sensible suggestion. No one of intelligence could imagine that your father would harm her. I have never seen a man so deeply in love."

They were the first words he had spoken which showed any humanity. Charlie drew in her breath. That had hurt. It had also brought her to her senses. If she wasn't more careful, Windlass would realise that she'd been in her mother's laboratory. Still, she had found out that Oblique knew about her mother's research. Peter was right: Windlass was working for the Esceanians.

"And now," the Prime Minister said, "our luncheon awaits. Your Highness." He rose and walked across the pink rug to stand in front of her. "May I have the honour of escorting you?" His hand captured hers. He tucked it in the crook of his elbow and kept it imprisoned all the way to the dining room.

She behaved herself during lunch, listening politely to the Ambassador's every word. There were a great many of them. Citizen Oblique, she found, was fond of the sound of his own voice. But he seemed very happy to talk about her mother and the glorious days of the Court before her disappearance. He seemed to almost forgive Charlie her plainness as long as he could reminisce about her mother's beauty. Men, she decided, must be very strange creatures.

Throughout lunch, she had managed to avoid Windlass's eye. But when the Ambassador had escorted her back to the parlour and departed, after bestowing upon her a bow at least six inches lower than his first one, Charlie was left alone with the Prime Minister.

"Another conquest, I believe," said Windlass, turning to her with an amused smile. She was not fooled. His eyes were intensely cold, intensely blue. "Rather an unlikely one, in this case. Citizen Oblique is not easily charmed. But you seem to have a talent for charm, when you care to exercise it. *What did you mean by that performance?*"

She jumped. She was standing beside her chair, and

it was all she could do not to dodge behind it. "I don't know what you're talking about." She stared back at him.

"Do you have any idea how important it is to keep the Esceanians pacified just at present?"

"No," she said coolly. "You haven't mentioned it." She was shaking, very slightly.

He stared at her, his eyes slightly narrowed. Then she saw him relax. An amused smile twitched up one corner of his mouth, and Charlie's knees almost gave way. He had decided she was still useful.

"Sit down, Charlie." She sat, numb with relief. "You remember that I said Quale needs a new technology of war." She nodded. "Your mother's research was to provide the basis of that technology. Unfortunately, she disappeared before she completed her work. My scientists are attempting to recreate her research, but we have not yet achieved what we need."

He paused and stared into the fire, seeming to forget her. Then he walked to the adjoining chair and collapsed into it with a sigh. He rested his head on the chair back and closed his eyes. She stared at the hated face, noticing the shadows beneath his eyes. He looked tired to the point of exhaustion. She was glad. Alistair

Windlass was not invulnerable after all. She thought of the paper she had given Nell.

He opened his eyes and looked at her. "You think I am colluding with the Esceanians against Quale." It was not a question. And it was the last thing she had expected him to say. Her mouth dropped open. Windlass smiled, and this time his smile had real warmth. "I like you, Charlie. You have intelligence and determination. You don't give up. Neither do I."

He sat up and rubbed the back of his neck. Sighed. "I'm not a traitor. The Esceanians believe I am selling them Quale because that is what I want them to believe. The Emperor's ambitions do not stop with Quale. They extend to the whole of the Eastern and Western Hemispheres. I intend to stop him. And yes, I will do anything it takes. Quale will not become an Esceanian outpost if I can help it. But they have been capable of dominating us militarily for several years now. I have prevented an invasion through the use of lies and intrigue. Of course they know about your mother's research. I told them myself."

"What?"

"Think! Why else would they hold off—for more than two years—an invasion which would overwhelm us in a matter of months or weeks? Because they want something even more appealing than annexing Quale into their empire. I have promised the Emperor a weapon which would help him achieve his dearest dream.

"That, my dear Princess, is what your mother's research would have given us: a weapon so strong, so powerful, that we would be able to see off the Esceanian threat once and for all! So, I play a double game, gambling that my scientists will break through and recreate your mother's discovery—or that she will return to us—before the Emperor grows tired of waiting.

"Now," he said, leaning forward and gazing into her eyes, "have I regained your trust, Charlie? Because I need you to help me save Quale."

# Twenty-One

Charlie crawled out the window of her attic bedroom onto the narrow balcony. She leant against the stone parapet and looked over the decaying garden towards the City. It was nearly December. The wind blew constantly up here now, and it was cold as death. She didn't dare venture onto the roofs.

Tobias was trapped, somewhere, out there in the City. She was trapped in the Castle. She wished she could talk to him. She could face Tobias's anger at what she had done, but she couldn't bear the thought of telling Mr. Moleglass that she had helped arrange the Prime Minister's assassination.

Today was Thursday. Windlass's first appointment in the City was next Tuesday. She had less than a week to decide whether he lived or died.

Had he been telling her the truth? Could she believe anything he said? Had Nell and Peter got it wrong? Was Windlass trying to save the Kingdom the only way he could?

Oh, why couldn't her mother be here to tell her what to do? Why couldn't her father... The drug Mrs. O'Dair gave him. She had assumed it was on Windlass's orders. But what if it wasn't? What if he didn't know?

Pain and confusion and fear were like stones grinding circles inside her head. Why should she have to decide whether a man lived or died? Why should she have to do all this on her own? It wasn't fair! She didn't know what to do, and the wind, whining over the slates and muttering through the gutters, told her nothing. Defeated, she turned and went inside.

———

Something clamped onto her mouth, holding her down, shocking her out of sleep. For a moment she was frozen with terror, then she convulsed, hands and feet whirling, tangling her bedclothes, hitting, trying to bite, trying to scream.

"Shhhh! It's me, Charlie! It's all right. It's Tobias! Be quiet! Watch is prowling on the floor below!" Tobias's voice was a harsh whisper in her ear. He was half sitting on her. She stopped struggling and lay quite still, her heart pounding, feeling the terror sink to a lower level, but not drain away completely. Why was he here? How had he got in the Castle? Why was Watch lurking on the fifth floor? There was nothing there but dust and empty rooms. What was going on?

"I'm gonna take my hand away now," Tobias whispered. "Promise not to yell?"

She nodded, and the pressure lifted from her mouth, but he was still sitting on her. "Get off!" she hissed at the dark shape hovering above her. The shape removed itself. Charlie sat up and pulled her eiderdown around her for warmth. "What's going on?" she whispered. "Sit down! I can't see you!"

The shape sat on the bed. "Didn't mean to scare you so bad," said Tobias.

"What did you expect?" She was still rattled. "What are you doing here? Why is Watch downstairs? Is he after you?"

"Reckon he might have heard something. The moon's covered in cloud tonight, and I didn't dare use the lantern or even a candle. Bumped into a table or something on the third floor. 'Spect he thinks it's you wandering about. He wouldn't dare shoot you in your bedroom, but if he found you on another floor . . . So he's lying in wait."

Charlie wondered if she might throw up.

"All we gotta do is wait here for a while. It's cold enough to freeze the feathers off a duck. He'll make for his bolt hole and his beer soon enough."

"Fine." She shivered. "But what are you doing here? If Windlass finds you—"

"Well, he won't, will he? There's news—and we got a job to do."

"What news?"

"He's got her." Tobias's whisper hissed into the darkness. "Windlass has Bettina."

Shock pierced her like cold steel. It was over, then.

"Charlie?"

She swallowed away dryness so she could speak. "How do you know?"

"Pigeon post."

"What?"

"Carrier pigeons. Peter sent spies to Durchland, and they've been sending back information by pigeon. Numbering the messages so we know how many get through. I've been helping look after the birds. We've only lost two so far. They have these little metal containers attached to their legs and—"

"Will you shut up about the blinking pigeons!"

"Shhhh! Watch is—"

"To heck with Watch! How do you know Windlass has Bettina?"

"Peter's spies found out that someone called Bettina Hoffman was an old school friend of your mum's. When she was fifteen, your mum was sent to school in Durchland for two years, a sort of finishing school for posh girls. She met Bettina there and they got to be mates. Then your mum came back to Quale, and they never met up again until she ran away. I guess she chose her old school friend because nobody here was likely to know about her. Peter's spies tracked Hoffman down in Durchland," Tobias continued. "She'd been a teacher, and now she's headmistress of her own school. Or she was, till she was kidnapped."

"Windlass kidnapped her?"

"All Peter knows is that the woman's gone. She lives near the school. Peter's men found her house ransacked. And Bettina Hoffman has disappeared. So it's a fair bet Windlass has her and is bringing her back here."

"And if my mother was with her?"

"That ain't likely. Folks remembered a pretty blonde lady living with Bettina a few years ago. That must have been your mum."

"But if Bettina knows where she is..." Charlie groaned. "Windlass has won!"

"Not yet, he ain't."

"But if he's got Bettina—"

"Having ain't keeping."

"What do you mean?"

"There's only been one ship flying the Qualian flag leave Hanver in the past week. It sailed two days ago and should come in tomorrow. Bettina'll be offloaded and brought to the City under armed guard. Windlass will probably meet the ship. He'll want to question Bettina himself as soon as possible."

"But if there's an armed guard—"

"I know. We can't tackle them at the docks. And once he gets her back here it's all over. We won't be able to get at her, and he'll have all the time in the world to torture everything she knows out of her."

"He wouldn't—"

"Don't fool yourself, Charlie. That man would do anything to get what he wants."

"Then it's hopeless!"

"There's one chance. He's got to move her from the docks to the City. He could use a carriage and outriders, but that's slow and dangerous. Too many places for an ambush. No, he'll have a special train ordered. He'll use the atmospheric railway. We need to know when the special is running. If we know that, we can block the line and stop the train. Then it'll come down to a fight. We got a chance, at least."

Charlie sat, staring into darkness. A fight. People would get killed. And it would be her fault—all because she had given Windlass the letter. A strange, scratching sort of pain sharpened in her head, and she hunched her shoulders and glared into nothingness. If there was to be fighting, she would fight too. It was the only thing she could do to make things even a little bit right. Somehow it felt like, by risking her life, she might somehow save someone else's. *Stupid nonsense,* her brain told her. *I don't care,* she answered back.

"I told you we've got a job," Tobias said. "We gotta tell Peter the moment Windlass leaves to go to the docks."

"How are we going to do that?"

"Easy!" She could almost hear him grinning in the darkness. "Pigeon post!"

When she woke the next morning, the sun was a reverse shadow just visible in the grey sky, and the winter birds were shrilling and screaming in an attempt to thaw out after a bitter night. Charlie stuck her nose outside her eiderdown and wished she'd thought to put her clothes under the covers to keep them warm. She jumped out of bed and began to dress, shivering as she pulled on the first chilly layers. She would give washing a miss this morning. There was a layer of ice floating on top of the basin.

As she clattered down the freezing stairwell on her way to the lesser dining room and a bowl of hot porridge, it felt like she had imagined Tobias's visit in the night. He'd waited in her room for another hour, then left as silently as he'd come. Remembering Watch, Charlie had locked her door behind him.

They had arranged to meet beneath the old yew tree

after Charlie's Statecraft lesson with Windlass. "I can keep an eye on the drive till then," Tobias had said. "See if he takes out a carriage. He might even ride out on horseback; depends how quick he wants to get to the docks."

But when she had asked him how he'd got into the Castle grounds, he'd refused to tell her. "That's my secret, Charlie, and I'll keep it."

"Where are you going now?"

"I got a place I camp out sometimes. The old pineapple pit. I already filled the trenches with fresh muck. I'll be warm as toast."

"And a great deal smellier," Charlie said. "Just don't get caught. Windlass meant it when he said he'd ship you off to the colonies!" But Tobias had gone.

Time played tricks on her all through lessons. It leapt ahead, racing so that she couldn't remember what Professor Meadowsweet had said to her a minute before. Then it would balk, rear back on its haunches and refuse to move, so that each second was agony.

Fifteen minutes before the end of lessons, the pneumatic messenger whistled and a capsule plonked into the catch basket. The Professor managed to retrieve and open it, looking very pleased with himself. "Ah," he said with a smile. "You're to have a half-holiday today, Your Highness. The Prime Minister sends his apologies. He is unable to give you a Statecraft lesson. So you have the afternoon to yourself. If I may suggest, you might enjoy spending the time revising Esceanian grammatical tenses, especially the pluperfect."

"Thank you, Professor," said Charlie. "That does sound fun."

This was it! Windlass was going after Bettina this afternoon!

She was out the door a second after Meadowsweet dismissed her, racing down flight after flight of stairs. No one was expecting her. No lunch would be prepared and waiting in the lesser dining room. O'Dair and the other servants would be eating in the servants' hall. Even Fossy would be tucking into his lunch in the greenhouse, then snoozing half the afternoon away.

She ran all the way to the library, opened one of the casements, and slid outside. Then she was off, loping across frozen grass, dodging corpse-like bushes, making for the ancient yew. It was still bitterly cold, but the wind had dropped. Heavy, yellowish-grey clouds hung low in the sky and the air felt damp and sullen. *It will snow tonight,* she thought, as she pushed beneath the yew's branches, through the hanging fringe of green-black needles, and stood in semi-darkness, waiting for her eyes to adjust.

"Had any lunch?" Tobias was sitting on a bed of russet brown needles, leaning against the massive tree trunk. A canvas knapsack lay on the ground beside him. He reached inside and pulled out a packet wrapped in greaseproof paper. He tossed it to her.

"Thanks." Charlie squatted beside him and explored the packet. A slice of ham layered between buttered brown bread. Her stomach growled appreciatively. She'd been too excited to think about food, but she was starving. She took a big bite, leant back and closed her eyes as she chewed, relishing the taste of ham, bread and butter; relishing even more the odd sensation that had been buoying her up all morning.

Excitement, but more than that. Anticipation. And relief, if she was honest. Windlass might have Bettina, but they would rescue her. And at least now she didn't have to decide whether Windlass lived or died. With any luck, Mr. Moleglass and Tobias need never know what she had done. As for the coming fight—perhaps no one would be hurt. It all seemed so unlikely: a proper battle with guns. She couldn't quite believe in it now, in daylight.

Bettina. The name had taken on a magical quality. Soon she might meet her. Soon she might know where her mother was. Charlie shivered.

"Cold, ain't it?"

She'd almost forgotten Tobias. She sniffed. Yes, there was a definite odour of manure in the air. But, considering recent events, she decided not to say anything. "Windlass cancelled my Statecraft lesson," she mumbled through chunks of bread and ham. "That's why I'm early. He must be going this afternoon. Shouldn't one of us be on watch?"

"He's been in his office all morning. If he orders a horse or carriage from the stables, we'll know. You'd hear either one clumping up the drive. We'll know he's about to leave before he even puts on his coat and hat to go out."

"So have you just been sitting here all morning?" Charlie, forgetting her friendly resolution of a moment before, turned and glared at him. "How do you know he's even in his office?"

"Course I ain't been under here all morning, you gurnless idiot." Tobias grinned at her and fished an apple out of his bag. He polished it on his jacket sleeve. "I been out since dawn. I got a good hidey place where I can see the main drive from the gates. I seen Windlass's carriage arrive at seven-thirty this morning. I seen him get out and go in the ministerial wing. I seen his office light come on. I seen his carriage and horse wheeled off to the stables. That's when I come under here, to stay out of Fossy's way. Happy now? There's another apple in there if you fancy it."

Charlie pulled the apple out of the bag. It was a bit old and withered, but it still tasted of something resembling apple. She enjoyed each mouthful. "Sorry, Tobias. Thanks for the food. And . . ." She frowned in embarrassment, but the words had to be said. "I won't forget what you did for me in the laboratory."

"It weren't for you," he snapped. "I'm just . . ." He broke off and glanced at her. Looked away. "I ain't no hero, Charlie. I got my own reasons for what I'm doing."

"And you won't tell me what they are."

"Nope." He grinned at her. She smiled back and relaxed against the tree, blotting all the worries from her mind, concentrating on enjoying this moment as much as possible. She was happy. It didn't happen often.

Two hours later it began to snow. A sharp, spiteful sleet battered the yew's canopy, but soon the mood of the storm changed, and enormous snowflakes drifted down out of the thickening sky. An hour later daylight was fading, and three inches of snow encircled the tree where Charlie and Tobias paced round and round, beating their arms to keep warm. "Why hasn't he gone?" Charlie asked for the twentieth time.

"I don't know! Go ask him, why don't you?" Tobias replied for the twentieth time.

And then they heard it: the clop of horses' hooves; the clink and chink of harness, the rumble of iron-rimmed wheels on gravel. "He's ordered the carriage!" Tobias said. "Right! Time to send that message!"

They slid through the snow in a strange, greyish half-light. The sun had set. "What about the hounds?" Charlie hissed, suddenly remembering.

"It's only just gone four. Fossy don't let out the hounds till last thing. He'll be tidying up for an hour yet. They know me, anyway. It's you they'd tear to pieces."

"Well, that's reassuring!"

They ran side by side. Tobias grabbed her hand, and they ran even faster. Snow continued to fall. It had transformed the gardens into an unrecognisable place, smoothing away familiar landmarks. A wedding cake of glass and icing reared out of the gloom: the summer-house. Tobias slid to a stop and pushed in through the door. Charlie looked over his shoulder as he knelt before a small wooden crate.

"Bird's in here," he said. He had pulled the knapsack off his back, was scrabbling about inside it. "Got it!" He pulled out a scrap of paper wrapped around a pencil, held the paper on his knee and scribbled something. "Telling them he's going by carriage. That'll give them an idea of time. Mind you, the snow'll slow him down. If it keeps up, the train may not be able to run. Here."

He had slipped the paper into a narrow metal tube. He handed it to her and bent to unfasten the crate. There was a flutter of wings, and Tobias turned to her, his grin just visible. "She's a beauty! Want to touch her?"

Charlie reached out, smoothed the breast feathers. They were soft and warm. She felt the pigeon's heart fluttering beneath her fingers.

"Best get her off, then." He cradled the bird in the crook of his arm and slipped the message tube into a holder fastened around the pigeon's leg. "Done."

They stepped out of the summerhouse into deepening twilight. "Wish her luck, Charlie." The snow muffled Tobias's voice. He threw up his hands. She heard a whirr of wings, saw a blur fly upwards to meet the falling snow, and the pigeon was gone.

They hid in overgrown hedges bordering the drive and watched Windlass's carriage glow out of the darkness towards them, snow sifting through the twin beams of light cast by its carriage lamps. Like some crunching, lurching, orange-eyed monster, it wheeled past them. The last Charlie saw of it was the red tail-light winking as it rounded a bend.

She crawled backwards out of the hedge, stiff with crouching and cold. As she stamped the blood back into her feet and brushed the snow from her skirts, the moon broke through the cloud, pouring a stream of silver onto the snow. "Look," Charlie whispered, tugging on Tobias's sleeve and pointing to the sky. "The snow has stopped. The train will run."

# Twenty-Two

"Right, I'm off." Tobias shouldered his knapsack. "Get back to the Castle. Fossy'll let the hounds out soon. We'll get word to you." He turned and strode off into the garden.

Charlie waited until he was nearly out of sight, then ran after him, her feet punching through the snow. He was heading deep into the wilderness of untamed garden, away from the gate. He must have a way to get over the wall.

The moon was waxing full, and the snow reflected its light so that it seemed nearly bright as day. The Castle grounds flickered with strange blue shadows. Tobias's footprints made him easy to follow, which was good because he kept disappearing behind trees and bushes. She was terrified in case he looked back and saw her. She strained to hear any sound above her panting breaths and the soft crunch of her boots in the snow; strained to hear the first howl that meant the hounds were on her trail. Would the snow hide her scent?

He had disappeared again. She broke into a stumbling run, following his footprint trail until she reached an overhanging canopy of trees shrouded in bramble, and the snow faded and took his footprints with it.

She stood in the darkness beneath the trees. He was lost. She was alone. The hounds would be out. The hounds . . . Something rustled, shifted, scrabbled a few feet to her right. "Tobias?" Charlie asked in a shaking voice. "Tobias, I hope that's you!"

The rustling stopped. A rich, fruity stream of swear words emerged from the shadows. It was the most beautiful sound she had ever heard. More rustling, and Tobias broke free of the bushes and moved towards her. Charlie took one look at his face and stepped back.

"I'm coming with you," she said. She noticed she didn't sound all that certain about it.

"Of all the puddingheaded . . . selfish . . . thought-less . . . dimwitted,"—he paused for inspiration—"addlepated . . . pigheaded *brats!* Right! I'll take you back to the Castle and shove you in at the window myself, and it'll be your own blame fault if the hounds have you for supper!"

He grabbed for her. Charlie dodged. A long, mourn-ful howl sounded somewhere behind them. Tobias hissed in fury. "In here, and be quick!" He reached out his hand, and Charlie took it. He pulled her after him into a thicket of weeds. She stumbled and nearly fell. He was wrenching her arm from its socket. He dived beneath an overhanging curtain of ivy. It creaked in pro-test as they pushed beneath it. Dirt, leaves, snow, and a multitude of unguessable dead things showered down on them, some filtering down the back of Charlie's neck. Tobias waded forward. It was completely dark beneath the ivy. When he suddenly stopped, she ploughed into him and only the pressure of the hanging plant kept them upright.

"Get off!" he growled and shrugged away. Stood still. Nothing happened. Another howling bay pen-etrated the darkness. Much nearer.

"What are you doing?"

"Shut up!" And still he simply stood. And then, suddenly, a rectangle of light appeared in front of them. Tobias disappeared into it, reached back, and pulled her through.

The stitch in her side had begun as a niggling sharpness. Now it was a huge tearing pain that made her gasp with every breath. She had never run so far, so fast. Tobias was giving no quarter, and she wasn't going to ask. The train would be on its way soon, carrying Bettina and her mother's fate. If the Resistance managed to ambush it, she intended to be there.

Tobias hadn't wasted time venting his fury after he pulled her through the door in the Castle wall and re-locked it. He had simply stared at her for a long second, then said: "This ain't a lark, Charlie. And I'm no babysitter. I'd take you to me mum and lock you in the cupboard under the stairs if I had the time. If you can keep up, you can come. But I promise, when Nell and Peter catch sight of you there'll be hell to pay!" And he turned and ran.

Forty-five minutes later, he was still running. He was a hundred feet ahead of her, and the gap was slowly widening. Charlie redoubled her effort; gasping more breath into her lungs, ignoring the pain stabbing her side. If she lost him, she was truly lost. At first they had slithered over snow-covered cobbles. When the streets changed to macadam, the crushed gravel underfoot gave a better purchase, and they made good speed. Now the lanes were dirt, the houses smaller and less frequent. They were nearing the edge of the City.

Tobias veered off the lane onto open ground and slowed to a walk, tramping through the four or five inches of snow cover. She could see it now: a raised hump like a dike, rearing out of the flat field. Even the snow drifting over it couldn't disguise its relentless straightness, like a line drawn by a giant across the surface of the earth. They had found the railway.

They followed the railway line away from the City. Tobias had stopped running, settling for a brisk walk. Charlie managed to catch up with him. They walked in silence for some time. "Will the train run in this?" she asked at last.

"Yes." And that was all.

Fifteen minutes later, Tobias began to trot again, ploughing doggedly through the snow. Charlie groaned, but kept up. They were approaching a small hill with a circular grove of trees on its top. Charlie was gasping and panting as they climbed the last few feet towards the edge of the grove. The railway cut through it, carving through the hillock and splitting the circle of trees down the middle. Even in the snow and moonlight, the cutting looked raw and brutal.

Tobias slowed to a walk. Charlie stopped altogether, bending over with her hands on her knees, struggling to get breath back in her lungs. Her legs were shaking with exhaustion. So she didn't see the people advance out of the darkness beneath the trees until they were nearly upon her. She looked up, and the first thing she saw was Nell's furious face as she rounded on Tobias and clipped him so hard on the ear that he staggered and fell into the snow.

"What do you mean by it, Toby Petch?" Nell panted as Tobias scrambled to his feet and backed away. "I'll have your hide for this! I promised Rose! You're to have no part in any fighting. And to make it worse, you bring *her*? Are you mad?" Nell dodged forward and took another swipe, but a man Charlie recognised as Joseph pulled her back.

"I've got as good a reason as any of you to be here!" Tobias growled. He was rubbing his ear, shaking his head. He looked angry and sullen and stubborn. "And I'm a fair shot with a rifle. Better'n most of you, I reckon."

So Tobias wasn't supposed to be here either. Charlie grinned. Served him right for his high-handedness. But then she saw Peter step forward, and her grin faded. "You can shoot, can you, boy?" His voice was cold.

"Yes." Tobias straightened and stared back at him. "I been shooting rabbits, crows, and other garden vermin since I was seven. It's my job."

"You want to fight?"

"That's why I'm here."

"Give the boy a rifle."

"Peter! No! He's only twelve!" Nell cried.

"He's old enough to disobey orders. A good shot is a good shot. Twelve is old enough to kill and be killed. You'll find that soon enough when the Esceanians invade. Give him a rifle." He turned to Charlie. His eyes were as cold as his voice. Her mouth dried to cotton wool. "And are you a good shot, too, Your Highness?"

Her mouth fell open. "I-I can try. I've never—"

"*Then why are you here?* The boy at least is some use. You are a liability! I can't spare a fighter to look after you. And if you get yourself killed Quale is the loser.

Did you think of that?" He whirled on Tobias. "Why did you bring her? I wouldn't have cast you as the fool till now."

"He didn't!" Charlie cried. "I followed him. He didn't know until it was too late. I need to be here. More than any of you! It's my mother Windlass is after. And none of this would be happening if I hadn't shown him that letter. It's my fault! If anyone dies . . . I'm responsible!" There, she had said it.

Peter looked at her. Some of the coldness faded from his eyes. He nodded. "Very well, ma'am. But no fighting for you. Can you climb?"

"What?"

"Can you climb a tree?"

"Of course!"

He smiled for the first time. "Good. You can be lookout. Go and pick the best climbing tree in the grove. Get as high as you can and watch seawards. The train'll run with lights. As soon as you see it, holler, and we'll block the line. Then, Your Highness . . ." He reached forward, grabbed her by the shoulders, and stared down into her eyes. "You stay in that tree! You stay till it's all done, one way or the other. When it's safe, someone'll fetch you down. If you stir a limb out of that tree before the fighting's done, I'll give you the whipping of your life! Do you understand?"

"Yes," Charlie said. He gave her a gentle shake, another smile, and turned away.

Nell swooped, grabbed her hand and pulled her up the slope into the shelter of the trees. "He had a daughter who would have been your age," she whispered. "She died two years ago. He couldn't afford the doctor." Charlie stared up at Nell, then her eyes sought out Peter. He strode ahead of them into the shadows beneath the trees and disappeared.

At first, Charlie thought it was a star, dimly visible just above the horizon, where the sea and the sky met. A few minutes later, she saw the light again, and saw that it was not above, but below the horizon. And it was moving. She clutched the branches more tightly, hoisted herself higher and squinted. She had to be certain. It was definitely moving, coming towards them, growing brighter.

"I can see it," she shouted. "I can see the train! It's coming!"

"How far away is it?" Peter's voice drifted up through the branches.

"It cleared the horizon about a minute ago. I'd say it was about a third of the way here."

"Thank you, Your Highness. Fifteen minutes, people! We have fifteen minutes. Let's get this line blockaded!"

Charlie heard Peter's voice calling out orders, the milling hum of people shifting into action. She peered down out of the tree, trying to see what was going on. There seemed to be two groups of people, one on either side of the cutting. Peter was shouting across to the opposite group. The Resistance members ran to and fro in the snow, small dark figures.

There were two mini mountains of stone and rubble heaped either side of the cutting itself. They were piled at the very edge, kept from falling by crude wooden walls supported by wooden props. On Peter's order, the props would be pulled away, and an avalanche of stone would block the rails.

She stared out towards the sea again. Yes! The light was brighter, clearer. She knew that carriages on an atmospheric railway could travel at up to forty miles an hour. This train wouldn't travel so quickly in the snow, but it was coming fast.

A clattering roar startled her half out of the tree. She grabbed the nearest branch and watched as the

Resistance members on both sides of the cutting flung their arms in the air and cheered. They had done it! The railway line was blocked.

The approaching light grew brighter. Now Charlie could see the train itself. "Two carriages, Peter!" she shouted. "I see two carriages." One, she knew, would contain Alistair Windlass and his prisoner. The other would be full of soldiers. Her heart began to thud in her ears. She wanted to be out of this tree, down with the others, doing something! But she had promised.

Now Peter knew how many they would be facing. No more than ten to twenty soldiers. She had counted at least forty Resistance fighters. But the soldiers would be sheltered inside the carriage and armed with the latest rifles. No barrel-loading muskets or pistols, like some of the Resistance fighters carried. She looked for Tobias, but couldn't spot him among the dark figures darting to and fro. For a moment, she thought she saw Nell, running with Joseph towards the cutting, a rifle in her hands. And then, quite suddenly, silence fell over the grove. All the scurrying figures had disappeared. It was as though Charlie was totally alone, perched high in a tree above the snow-clad Qualian plain. The Resistance was lying in wait. The ambush had begun.

# Twenty-Three

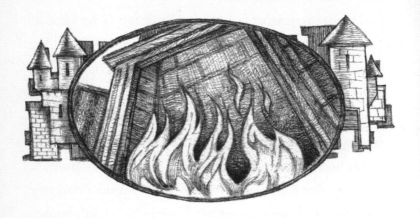

Charlie heard the whine of the approaching train. She shivered with excitement as she watched it speed towards her. She had read about atmospheric trains, but she had never seen one before. She caught her breath at the sight. The two carriages flew towards the cutting, driven as though by magic, without engine or horse. She couldn't see the pneumatic vacuum tube which powered them, only the snow catcher on the front carriage, peeling the snow from the track like skin off an apple. A driver stood on the observation platform, his hands on the braking wheel.

But Peter had chosen his place well. The rock fall was hidden in the shadow of the cutting itself. The driver wouldn't see it until it was too late. She watched the figure on the platform, wondering if he would survive. It wasn't possible to derail an atmospheric train, because each carriage was connected by an iron bar to the pneumatic tube between the rails. But the crash would be violent: the train was thundering down the track at nearly thirty miles an hour.

Nearer! Nearer! She could see lights in the windows. She had a glimpse of figures sitting inside the first carriage as it sped into the cutting. Charlie held her breath. She saw the driver leap from the platform a second before the train slammed into the rubble. The carriages bucked and stopped with a *CRASH!* that echoed across the plain and jarred snow from the branches over her head.

She wiped snow from her eyes. Dark figures spewed out of the trees on either side of the wounded train, tumbling down the cutting like a human avalanche, shooting, screaming, yelling. The sound of gunfire was unreal, like the noise of so many fireworks. The smell of cordite drifted through the air towards her. The lights in the carriages had gone out. Flashes and puffs of smoke, showing dark against the snow, meant that the passengers were returning fire.

Charlie clenched her fists, searching among the running figures for Tobias. A few of the people sprinting towards the train were stumbling, falling over to lie in the snow. A horror colder than any winter storm swept over her. And then she saw him. She knew him at once. He had paused, the one still figure in a maelstrom of movement. Tobias was bent over his rifle, reloading it. He darted forward. And fell.

In a moment, she was down the tree and running. Not Tobias! Please, not Tobias! The fear was unlike anything she had known. And then it was burned away by a fury unlike anything she had felt. If they had hurt him she would kill them all!

Charlie was at the edge of the cutting in a flash. She flung herself down the slope, bounding from rock to rock. Something spat a hole into the snow near her foot, and part of her mind realised it was a bullet, but she kept running. She raced towards the lead carriage.

The door onto the platform was open. In the moonlight, she saw Alistair Windlass, bareheaded, coatless, a pistol in his hand and a look of intense concentration on his face. She slid to a stop, watching in horror as Windlass raised his arm to aim at a man running towards his platform. Peter! He had taken his jacket off. He held his rifle in one hand and ran like a boy half his age, his hair streaming behind.

Windlass's pistol clicked. Nothing happened. Charlie saw his frown of annoyance. He threw the pistol at Peter, who batted it away with his rifle and kept coming. Windlass reached down, and she saw a flash of steel in the moonlight. He had his swordstick!

Five feet from the platform, Peter stopped running and took aim. Charlie saw his rifle jerk and heard the shot, but in the same instant Windlass ducked through the iron railing, dropping to the ground. In one fluid movement his arm extended, his sword point flying towards its target, and he lunged until he was almost kneeling in the snow. As quickly, he stood again, drawing his sword back. The two men faced each other, motionless. The tip of Windlass's blade no longer shone where the light struck it. He was watching the Resistance leader intently, as though waiting for his adversary to speak. The rifle slid from Peter's hands. He stepped forward, staggered, and fell face down in the snow.

There was a roar from the Resistance, a volley of gunfire. Bullets spattered the snow around Windlass. He stooped, snatched Peter's rifle from where it had fallen and ran for the second carriage. The door opened, and he vanished inside.

Charlie's knees gave way. First Tobias. Now Peter. She knelt in the snow, staring at his body lying less than twenty yards from her, a dark stain spreading from beneath him, blotting the snow like ink. She barely noticed the group of Resistance fighters swarm into the lead carriage, pull out a short, plump woman and drag her away up into the grove, towards the waiting horses and escape. A small circle of people gathered around Peter. She recognised Nell and Joseph, and then three things happened at once:

Tobias ran to the group standing over Peter, pushed in beside Nell.

Charlie leapt to her feet.

The door of the second carriage burst open, and Windlass jumped out, followed by his soldiers.

"Run!" shouted Joseph. He sprinted towards the side of the cutting. Tobias followed, pulling Nell. Charlie began to back away. No one had spotted her yet. Half a dozen soldiers lined up neatly, as if on parade. As one man, they raised their rifles, aiming at the fleeing Resistance members, at Tobias and Nell. Charlie opened her mouth to scream.

"Don't fire!" shouted the Prime Minister. "Lower your rifles."

"But they're clear in our sights, sir!"

"That was an order, Sergeant! Let them go. I've killed the one that matters."

"But they got the woman."

"And I shall get her back. But not tonight. Find any Resistance that are still alive. Keep them that way and get them on board. I'll want to question them. Send your fastest runner to the City. Get dray horses and a work detail out here to unblock the line. And a saddle horse. Be quick, man!"

All the time Windlass had been speaking, Charlie had been backing away. Now she turned and ran. "There's one!" shouted a soldier. "It's just a kid," another replied. "You heard the man. Leave 'em to rot."

She bolted up the slope and scrabbled into the trees. Someone swooped out of their shelter and grabbed her by the wrist. It was Tobias. His face was white and grim. "You never can follow orders, can you?"

"Same as you, I guess," she said. And then she reached

out and hugged him fiercely. "I thought you were dead," she whispered, hiding her face in his shoulder. "Like Peter."

"You saw?"

She stepped back, wiping her eyes. She nodded. But she didn't tell him the other things she'd seen. That she'd seen him let go of Nell and turn, halfway up the slope of the cutting, to look back down at the soldiers. That she'd seen the shock of recognition on Windlass's face the moment before he ordered them to hold their fire.

"I can't believe he's dead." The elderly lady in black sat in a narrow, high-backed chair beside the fireplace, her hands clasped in her lap. She stared into the flames. "He had more life than all the rest of us combined."

Charlie was sitting on the floor. She looked up at the old woman as she spoke, but saw instead the image of Peter's body lying in the snow. It had haunted her during the panic-stricken retreat from the copse. It had trailed after her as they waded through the snowbound streets of the City, darkening her terror of being caught in those last moments before reaching sanctuary.

Charlie shivered and hunched nearer to the fire. She

couldn't seem to get warm. Then her eyes sought out Bettina Hoffman once more. Her mother's old school friend sat in the only other chair, her round face white with exhaustion. Charlie swallowed a surge of frustration. How much longer would she have to wait before they could speak alone?

"There's seven others missing. Dead or wounded. Don't forget them." Joseph prowled about the room, his powerful shoulders hunched beneath his jacket.

"I forget no one, Joseph," the old woman replied, not removing her gaze from the fire. "But Peter was our leader. We will not survive without him."

"Rubbish!" Joseph whirled around. "I'll have no such defeatist talk here, Winifred!"

This, at last, roused the old woman from her grief. "And who are you, to order me about in my own house?" she snapped. "Be still, boy. You are not leader yet. Nor will be, if I have my way."

"Alistair Windlass would be pleased as punch to hear the two of you, yammering away at each other," Nell said. She moved forward into the firelight. Her eyes were swollen with crying, but she was calm. "Peter's dead, but he didn't die for nothing. We won! We beat Windlass, and we're going to do it again. We took something he wanted, and now we need to make use of that! We ain't got time for mourning now. Nor for bickering!"

Bettina Hoffman nodded. "You are quite correct, young lady." She spoke grammatically perfect Qualian with a slight Durch accent. "No, do not tell me your name. Names are best kept secret in the present circumstances."

"Please!" Charlie climbed to her feet. She couldn't wait any longer. "I need to talk to you! Now!"

Bettina looked over at her and smiled. "Yes," she said. "Years you have waited, I think. It is long enough. You are the only person here whose name I wish to know."

"Charlotte Augusta Joan—"

"So I thought. You are right. We must speak now. In private. If there is another chamber to this dwelling, where the child and I might be alone for a few moments?" She directed her question to Winifred.

"Of course," said the old woman, getting to her feet. "Let me show you upstairs."

"Hang on!" interrupted Joseph. "I think we ought to hear anything the two of you have to say to each other. It's us who's risked our lives. Some have died. And we didn't do it for the sake of the monarchy!"

"It is nothing to do with you, young man!" snapped Bettina. "I wish to speak with the child in private, and then I wish to retire. I am exhausted." She pushed herself out of her chair, motioned to Charlie, and marched from the room and up the stairs.

Charlie leapt to her feet and followed. She cast a last look back. Joseph was pacing, Nell was staring into the fire, and Tobias was slumped in a corner, asleep. When she saw him again, she would have the answer to the most important question of her life.

"Do you know where my mother is?"

The words burst out of her. Bettina finished closing the door and turned to her with a weary smile. "Patience, my child. I will answer all your questions, but in my own time. There is a story to tell, and I wish to tell it properly. Now, let me sit down. I am a bad traveller and was dreadfully seasick on the ship. And then that extraordinary man arrived, and I was in no condition to engage in a battle of wits, I can tell you. Quite terrifying, your Mr. Windlass."

"He isn't 'my Mr. Windlass'! I hate him!"

"Yes." The Durch woman looked at her, the smile draining from her eyes. "I would think you do."

They stood in a tiny bedroom. The room was freezing; the fire unlit, and the only light a single candle that Winifred had provided. There was a narrow iron bedstead, and a simple wooden chair. Bettina settled herself on the chair and motioned for Charlie to sit on the bed. Shivering with impatience, she did so.

"Your mother, Charlie—may I call you Charlie? Thank you. Your mother is one of my dearest friends. We were girls together at school. She was beautiful and clever. I was moderately intelligent, but by no means beautiful, as you see. And yet, from the very start, we were inseparable. She taught me to speak Qualian. I taught her Durch. She tried, and failed, to teach me physics. Even then, the boys were mad on her. Whenever we walked in the town, a string of them would form, waddling after her like a row of daft ducklings. Poor Caroline."

"Why poor?"

"Because she never enjoyed it. She was as unconscious of her appearance as it is possible to be. And she was far too intelligent to want any man who loved her for her looks alone. Which is why, I think, she married your father. Apparently, she overheard him talking about her at a party soon after they first met. Another young man was praising her beauty, and she heard your father say: 'What? The tall, gangly girl with all that yellow hair? She does well enough, I suppose, but I don't rate her particularly.' I think she fell in love with him on the spot!" Bettina sighed. For a moment, she looked sad. Then she smiled at Charlie again. "Yes, your mother ran away to me. I had the pleasure of her company for just over three years. They were very sad years for her. She missed you terribly, Charlie."

*She missed you terribly . . .* Strange how four simple words could cause such a jumble of pain and joy. She couldn't bear it; the question burst out again: "Where is she? Is she still in Durchland? Please, tell me!"

Bettina shook her head. Her round blue eyes were grave. "Your mother returned to Quale nearly two years ago. She is here in the City somewhere."

"What?" Charlie stared at her, shocked.

"Yes. But I do not know where. She disguised herself and returned to Quale. Her intentions were to seek enough casual work to live while attempting to find out whether or not Mr. Windlass had succeeded in duplicating her research. And also to try to find out more about you and your father. She had become increasingly worried for you, Charlie. The rumours coming out of Quale have been dreadful these last years. It is said . . . it is rumoured that your father is mad, and that Mr. Windlass is ruler in all but name."

Charlie nodded. "That's true. But he says . . . he told me . . ."

"Who?"

"The Prime Minister. He says my mother didn't leave because of him. He says they were working together. That she was doing the research at his request. He claims that he is double-crossing the Esceanians, promising them her research in order to delay their invasion until he can create this weapon for our country to use against them. He says he is trying to save Quale!"

"And do you believe him?"

"When he's talking to me? Yes. Almost always. Later . . . I don't know. I don't know what to believe."

"Believe this, Charlie. Your mother is terrified of Alistair Windlass. She is a brave woman. It takes a great deal to scare her. I have not mentioned her nightmares . . . well." She shook her head. "That man haunts her every waking and sleeping moment. Now that I have met him I understand why." She paused; her blue eyes blinked twice. *She's afraid of him too,* Charlie thought.

"I do not know Mr. Windlass's ultimate motives,"

Bettina continued, "but I do know that he is the reason your mother ran away. She wanted to keep her research out of his hands. In order to do so, she destroyed over two years of work! She burnt her papers! Do you know what that means to a scientist—to destroy knowledge? Her research still exists, of course. It is in her head.

"That is the reason I needed to speak with you in private, Charlie. I do not know where your mother is, but I know how you can find her. I have a name and an address. I will tell them to you and you must memorise them. You must go to that address yourself! You and you alone will be told your mother's whereabouts—no one else. Do you understand?"

Charlie nodded.

Bettina reached out and clasped Charlie's hands in hers, holding them tight. "Caroline knows that you have suffered because of her. Her guilt is the burden she must bear. But if she were sitting here now, she would see that her actions have not destroyed you.

"It took great strength for you to survive those dark years. Now you face a clever and ruthless adversary. You have shown courage and resourcefulness to get this far, Charlie. You must be strong a while longer. Bless you, child, and believe this: you will find her. I know you will."

# Twenty-Four

There was no beginning to her journey and no end. The snow stretched as far as she could see. It scorched her bare feet. Mile after mile, she trudged. She was alone. All the others were dead. Their bodies were mileposts, staining the snow black. The moon shone on their faces. She wanted to stop, press closed their staring eyes. But she had to continue. It was her journey. She walked past the dead, counting them as she went.

———

"Father? Father, I need to talk to you."

The King floated above her. He soared over his greatest creation. He had completed forty-nine towers, each taller than the last. He was hard at work on the fiftieth. The dust of five years mounded at the edges of the room, tracked like sand through the castle, drifted over its crenellations.

He had not heard her. Charlie sighed and settled into the dust to wait. She had slept badly. Tobias and Nell had helped her return to the Castle through the pneumatic freight tunnel. When she had at last crawled into bed it was nearly four a.m. She had collapsed almost at once into sleep, but strange dreams and images had woken her time after time.

The memory of Peter, lying dead in the snow, would not leave her. She had made one mistake. She had trusted the wrong person. And now Peter was dead. She remembered what Nell had told her about his daughter. As soon as it was light, she dressed and ran to find her own father. Now she watched him float above her, playing with his cards, and she trembled with an almost savage fear.

When at last he spotted her, her father gave a cheery

wiggle of the fingers. Twenty minutes later, he began his descent. "Hello, my child," he said, as he joined her in front of the castle. "Come to see how it's going, have you? Ah, Charlotte, there has never been a castle like it. This will be my crowning achievement. I feel it. Nothing can go wrong."

There was such joy in his face that she smiled in spite of herself. For the first time, she noticed a few grey hairs twined among the auburn. For some reason, they made her want to cry. "Father, I need you to do something for me. Something very important. Will you promise?"

"Ah, child. Promises, now. Dangerous things, promises. I'll try, of course. If I can. If it doesn't interfere with the castle, you know."

"It won't interfere, Father." Charlie reached out and caught hold of his hand. She grabbed it and held on tight. He stared at her in astonishment. "Don't take your medicine, Father," she said slowly and carefully. "It isn't good for you. It will stop you making any more castles. Listen to me. Trick Mrs. O'Dair. Pretend to take it but don't . . . for Mother's sake!"

Her father stared at her blankly. He closed his eyes in a frown of pain. "Go away now, Charlotte," he said, pulling his hand from hers. "Go now. I have work to do." He turned and began to climb the scaffolding. He climbed slowly, as though he were tired.

Charlie sank onto the floor, tears trickling down her cheeks. She turned her head and a cold fist squeezed her heart. Alistair Windlass stood in the door, haloed in sunlight, watching her with eyes like chips of ice. His hair gleamed as the light struck it, faded gold against his dark clothes. "Your Highness," he said. "I have something to discuss with your father. If you will excuse us?"

As she passed him in the door he took hold of her arm. Charlie gasped and tried to pull away, but Windlass gripped her shoulders and turned her to face him. His hands were gentle, but she could not break free. "Mrs. O'Dair reports that you did not present yourself for dinner last night. You were not in your quarters when the maid was sent to find you. Where were you?"

She stared up at him, hating him, fearing him. He thought she was powerless, but she had succeeded where he had failed. She knew how to find her mother! "I wasn't hungry." She wouldn't let him stop her now. She made her voice sound soft, defeated. "So I visited Mr. Moleglass."

"Ah." Windlass's eyes never left her face. "I think Mr. Moleglass may need to find another situation quite soon. Perhaps you could pass that message on. And I think it would be best if you did not visit your father for a while." His voice was as gentle as his hands, but his eyes were pitiless. "For your own sake and his. He should not be upset. You need to dedicate any spare time to attending your studies. The day is nearly here when you will be invaluable to me and your country."

He let her go, and she stumbled past him into the antechamber. She didn't begin to run until she was in the corridor.

Charlie picked up the white queen and moved it diagonally across the board, taking Mr. Moleglass's last knight.

"Excellent move!" He bent over the board, a frown of concentration centred precisely in the middle of his brow. "You make it difficult for me, Charlie. You are playing with élan!" He smoothed the fingers of his dove-grey gloves, then shifted his rook three places to the left. Charlie had anticipated the move. Instead of sending her queen to safety, she pushed a pawn forward. It now stood one square from Moleglass's end of the board. He glanced up at her and smiled. "So," he said. "If I take your queen, the pawn becomes another, and my king is in check with no hope of escape. Well done." He reached out and toppled his king onto its side. "You have won, my child."

Charlie nodded. Normally, she would be delighted to have beaten Mr. Moleglass at chess. He paid her the compliment of never letting her win. But today, the game was merely a way of putting off an unpleasant task. She had to tell him, and she didn't want to. It was almost time for lessons.

Charlie glanced at Tobias, sitting slumped in Mr. Moleglass's armchair, staring at the floor. He had stayed the night here, too tired and too worried about being caught to risk another trip through the grounds or the freight tunnel. He looked as though he had not slept well either. She remembered seeing him pause to reload his rifle during the fight. Had he shot someone? Was that what he was thinking about?

She took a deep breath. "I'm leaving the Castle tonight, Mr. Moleglass. That's what I've come to tell you. I need your help so I can use the freight tunnel. Last night Bettina gave me an address and the name of a contact. I'm going to find my mother."

Mr. Moleglass looked up from the chess table, where he had been arranging the pieces on their squares. He rose to his feet, sat, then stood again and began to pace.

"You have only just escaped death," he said at last, "and now you want to run into its jaws again?" He shook his head. "There's too much we don't know. This information is over two years old. There is no guarantee that this contact will still be there or that they will still be in touch with your mother." He paced from sink to hob, from hob to door, from door to sink. Then he started all over again. His dove-coloured gloves corrugated into wrinkles as he wrung his hands.

The last thing Charlie needed was an argument with Mr. Moleglass. She looked at Tobias. He raised his eyebrows and shrugged.

"I have to go," she said. "I have to find my mother. Windlass could recapture Bettina at any moment. The Resistance are hiding her, but some of the people we lost last night might be alive. They could be being tortured right now. They'll tell names, addresses!"

Mr. Moleglass stopped halfway to the sink. "Wait a little, Charlie. Give me a few days to make enquiries. Then we'll decide what to do."

"I haven't got a few days! Didn't you hear me? Windlass knows I don't trust him. He heard me tell my father not to take his medicine. And he knows I wasn't in my room last night. I told him I was visiting you, but I'm not sure he believed me." She wasn't going to pass on Windlass's threat. It had been meant for her: a punishment. She would just have to make sure that the Prime Minister never got a chance to carry it out.

"If that were the case, he would have questioned you. I think you must be mistaken."

"I'm not mistaken! For the moment, he thinks I'm trapped inside the Castle. I have to act now. I'm going tonight."

"Tobias! You of all people should know how dangerous this is for Charlie. Persuade her. Help me."

Tobias shook his head. "I'm sorry. It's no more dangerous than what she's done already. And nobody's safe any more, Mr. M. Especially not Charlie. Not with Windlass this close to finding her mum. He'll not stop now! Not till he's tracked Bettina down and then the Queen. But don't worry. She won't be alone. I'm going with her."

"What?" She stared at Tobias.

"You don't know your way around the City. And you got no more idea of what happens on the streets than a newborn babe. It's not just Windlass. There's people out there who aren't nice. I know how to avoid them— you don't. I'm coming."

She opened her mouth and then shut it. He was right, and if she was honest, she wasn't sure she could have managed the journey through the freight tunnel by herself.

Mr. Moleglass approached the chess table and lowered himself into his chair. He sighed and looked across it at her. His eyes brimmed with pain, and the sight squeezed her heart. She was hurting him, and there was nothing she could do about it.

"Perhaps you are right," he said. "For years I deluded myself with the hope that by staying here I could somehow keep you safe. I am an old fool: I never had any power to protect you. Still, old habits die hard." He picked up the white queen from the chess table. "Hold out your hand."

It dropped into her palm, cool and heavy.

"A talisman," Mr. Moleglass said. "To bring you back to me."

She was mildly surprised when Tobias accompanied her out the door; more surprised when he grabbed her arm as she started for the dumbwaiter. "Hang on, Charlie." Even in the half-light his face looked strained, and she realised how much she missed the smiling, joking Tobias of a few weeks ago. "You sure you don't want to wait a day or two, and let me or Nell check this place out?" His eyes searched her face. "Be sure. There's no coming back this time. You won't have gone missing for a few hours: it'll be a day or more. They'll know you're getting out of the Castle. And then if he catches you, Windlass'll lock you up tighter than a tick on a dog's ear. If we go, we gotta finish it. If we don't find your mum—"

"I have to go. Not you. Not Nell. It has to be me. And I want to go tonight."

He nodded. "This is for you, then." He picked a bundle up from beside the door and handed it to her. "I meant to give it to you days ago; it's been in the pineapple pit but it don't niff too bad. Me mum made this lot up for you. We reckoned you might have to scarper one day. I'll come to your room at midnight." Despite the faint odour of manure, she clutched the bundle to her tightly as she watched him turn and disappear through Mr. Moleglass's door.

When the pneumatic messenger whistled and a message capsule dropped into the catch basket, Professor Meadowsweet rose from his chair to tackle the modern technology with all the aplomb of an old hand. "Ah, your recent half-holiday is to be paid back this afternoon, I fear, Your Highness." He smiled at her. "You are to report to the Prime Minister as soon as we have finished our lessons."

Charlie stared at him and felt a sickness of dread settle in her stomach. Had Windlass found out that she was planning to run away? Had he caught Bettina?

The Prime Minister did not stand as she entered. He did not look up from his desk. Charlie paused in the middle of the room, waiting to be invited to sit down. Her stomach squirmed.

For several minutes she stood and watched Windlass's pen travel across a sheet of snowy white paper, filling it with elegant loops of copperplate. He wrote quickly, his face as perfectly composed as his handwriting.

He lifted his pen and, taking a pen wipe, began to

clean the nib. She was reminded of his sword, the tip dark with Peter's blood, and shuddered. As though he were standing in front of her, she saw again Peter's funny wide mouth, his eyes sparkling with humour and intelligence. He was dead. Because of her. Because of this man. She stared at Windlass. Why should this man be alive, when Peter was dead?

Only when he had replaced the pen on its stand and the lid on the inkwell did Alistair Windlass raise his eyes to hers. He did not smile. "Your Highness."

"Prime Minister," she replied. "I've come for my lesson."

His eyebrows rose. "Have you resolved to attend to your studies after all? I was beginning to think you had decided the effort to help your father was too strenuous."

The worm of unease in her stomach grew into a writhing snake. How much did he suspect? How much did he know? "I don't understand," she said.

"I've just had a report from Professor Meadowsweet. Your lack of application in Geography and Latin is abundantly evident. It makes me wonder how you have been spending the time when you should be revising." His pale eyes watched her coolly as she struggled to keep her face blank. "And now it seems that you have taken to wandering about the Castle in the middle of the night."

"I'm sorry. It won't happen again."

"I think we must make sure it doesn't. I confess to being disappointed in you, Your Highness. I had assumed that you were devoted to your father. It seems that I was mistaken."

Her breath caught in her throat. She stood, choking the hatred down, swallowing the words she wanted to scream at him. Her fists clenched. She made them relax. She would not give him the satisfaction of seeing how much his words hurt.

"Do you think it helpful to interfere in your father's care and advise him not to take his medication? Someone listening to you might think you believed Mrs. O'Dair to be involved in a plot against the King's wellbeing. Is that what you believe?"

"No!" She managed to spit the lie out.

"I'm relieved to hear it. Otherwise, I would have to wonder if you doubted my intentions as well. I thought I had explained the danger facing this country. I thought I had gained your trust and cooperation. And it is vital that we trust one another if we are to work together to save the Kingdom for your father. Do you agree?" He was watching her every expression. His eyes never left her face. Agree? He knew she had no power to do anything else. And he was making sure she knew it too.

He was playing with her. Cat and mouse. She had never felt hatred like it. It burned in her throat. She swallowed and found her voice at last. "I would do anything to help my father."

He studied her without speaking, then nodded. "We understand each other, then. No lesson today, Charlie. I'm too busy." He picked up his pen, turned over a fresh piece of paper. He had dismissed her. Her punishment was over. She was invisible again.

"I will leave, Prime Minister." She was amazed at how calm she sounded. "But don't ever call me Charlie again. That was my mother's name for me. Only my friends may use it. I am Her Royal Highness, the Princess Charlotte Augusta Joanna Hortense of Quale." His pen stuttered, and a blot began to curl onto the paper.

# Twenty-Five

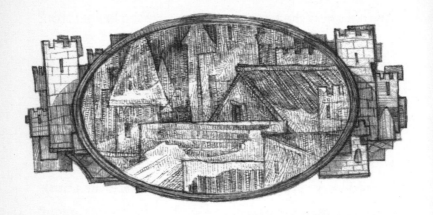

Charlie could scarcely eat her dinner for excitement. She slurped her soup, gnawed her mutton and picked at her mashed swede, thinking constantly of the bundle hidden in the bottom of her wardrobe. And what it meant. She didn't even mind when the footman splashed soup on her hand and dropped hot swede in her lap. "Don't bother about it, Alfred," she replied to his aspidistra-like apologies. "You can't help being clumsy, can you?"

She ran all the way to her bedroom after dinner, pulled open the wardrobe, yanked out the bundle and unwrapped it again, tearing away the layers of brown paper. It was all here, just as she had remembered—a set of Tobias's old clothes: trousers of sturdy brown canvas, collarless shirt, waistcoat, boy's flat cap, and a thick wool jacket.

She unfastened her boots, took off her dress and unpeeled the layers of petticoats, shifts and chemises. She re-dressed herself in the new clothes as quickly as she could and began leaping around the room, intoxicated by the freedom from heavy, hampering skirts. *When I am Queen,* she promised herself, *I shall never wear anything except trousers ever again!*

When she had worn out her first frenzy of excitement, and looked long and often enough at the unrecognisable person in the swivel mirror, she curled up in her armchair with a book and her eiderdown and began the wait for midnight.

A few minutes before Tobias was due, Charlie pulled on her boots and buttoned them with the buttonhook. Her shiny black boots looked odd with boy's clothes, but it couldn't be helped.

A faint tapping noise came from the door, and she shoved the buttonhook into her pocket and ran to open it. Tobias placed his unlit lantern on the table and turned to her. "Are you rea—" His eyebrows flew skywards. He grinned.

"Don't you dare tease me, Tobias Petch. It was your idea, after all!"

"I weren't gonna tease you." His smile stretched. "Just thinking what a grand chap you make. Only trouble is your hair. You look like a boy right enough from the neck down, but what are we gonna do with those red curls?"

"My hair isn't red," she snapped. "It's auburn. Like my father's."

"If you say so. But it don't look like a boy's hair. It's grown a deal since you started being civilised. Almost looks pretty. Can you shove it under that cap?"

"I'll do better than that," said Charlie, and she ran to her table. "Here they are!" She brandished a pair of scissors. "You cut it off for me!"

He backed up, alarm replacing the grin. "I will not! That ain't right—cutting off a girl's hair."

"Then I'll do it myself. Hold the candle at least!" She stood in front of the mirror, held her hair up in bunches and hacked it off.

"Blisters!" Tobias said in dismay, watching the feathers of hair swirl to the floor. "I guess it'll grow back."

Charlie grinned at her reflection. Cut short, her hair framed her eyebrows and ears with a tangle of soft curls. She pulled on the cap and turned to him.

"Well?"

"That's done the trick. No one would know you wasn't some snarky little lad."

She gathered the cut hair and threw it onto the fire, where it frizzled up at once and gave off an appalling stink. "There," she said. "No clues! Even Windlass won't think to look for a boy! Come on, then!" She was nearly bouncing with excitement. In a few hours she would see her mother's face again!

He caught her arm. "Calm down, Charlie. We've got to go careful getting out of here."

She shrugged. "I know that! Mr. Moleglass will be waiting in the freight room. We only have to get there, and we've dodged Watch before. You didn't have any trouble getting up here from the cellars, did you?"

"That's just it." He frowned and shook his head. "There weren't no sign of Watch about the place. I don't like it."

"He's probably snoring away in the library. No one knows you're here. Not Windlass or O'Dair. And they don't know we're going tonight. They can't!"

"I don't see how they could, no. But we still need to go careful, and you're larking about like this is some sorta game. It ain't, Charlie. I don't care to end up dead tonight, with Watch's bullet in me back."

The spark of excitement dimmed. He was right. Windlass might be waiting to catch them. Watch might be waiting to kill them. If she was careless, or unlucky, she might never see either of her parents again. And then there was Tobias. She felt something catch at her heart. He was risking death for her. He might have his own reasons, but that wouldn't make her feel any better if anything happened to him.

"Maybe . . ." she said. And stopped.

"What now?"

"Maybe you shouldn't go with me."

*"What?"* His mouth dropped open. "Are you crazy?"

"It's too risky. I'll go on my own."

He shook his head. "I don't know what's got into you, Charlie. Forget it. I know the City. You don't. We go together or not at all. Your choice." His mouth went thin and stubborn, and she knew there was no arguing with him.

She thought of her father, asleep in his cheerless bedroom, a new bottle of medicine on the bedside table. Was she doing the right thing, leaving him? She was all he had. The only one who could help him. If things went wrong... She shuddered and shook her head. There was no turning back. "All right," she said. "Let's go."

Charlie led the way. She chose devious routes, circling back, waiting, listening. They crept down the staircase that led to the third floor. It was a sullen night. The wind chased ragged clouds across the sky, and moonlight shone fitfully through the windows. Tobias had brought his dark lantern. They kept its eye half shut and travelled in the light of the feeble beam it cast. Her heart thudded uncomfortably. She wondered if this was the last time she would do this: creep fearfully through the Castle at night, listening for Watch.

On the third floor she left the servants' stairs behind and headed for the main staircase. They would travel to the cellars in the dumbwaiter; it was safer than using the servants' lift.

She heard it before she saw it. *Wheeze...creak.* A massive black shadow detached itself from the wall in front of them. Moved forward. "Right on schedule," said Mrs. O'Dair.

Lantern light flickered as Watch slouched around the corner. He stood, holding up his lantern and smirking at them, his other hand resting on the revolving pistol in its holster. Charlie stared at Mrs. O'Dair. The housekeeper was smiling too. She looked happier than Charlie had ever seen her.

"I have to thank both of you for making it so easy for me," O'Dair said. "Did you really think, Petch, that I wouldn't notice that someone had been using the freight railway? You should have replaced the coal! You're a thief and an outlaw. The Prime Minister will doubtless give Watch an award for shooting you. And you . . ." The look she threw Charlie gleamed with anticipation, ". . . so clever of you to dress yourself up as a boy. Now there will be no awkward questions when you're found dead as well! Watch can hardly be blamed for not recognising you. Who would expect a princess of Quale to be running around the Castle at night dressed like a chimney sweep?" O'Dair laughed: a rich treacly gurgle that turned Charlie's skin to gooseflesh.

"Watch!" Tobias took a hesitant step towards the night watchman. "Watch, we're mates. Don't listen to her! You wouldn't shoot a mate—not you! A-and Maria'll never look at you again if you kill me!"

Watch shrugged. His hand never left the pistol. His watery eyes shifted in the lantern light. "Sorry, kid. Ain't nothing personal. Times is hard. Hard as Maria's heart. Just stand still, and it'll be over quick."

All the time he'd been talking, Tobias had been inching towards the housekeeper. Charlie saw his body tense, and she knew what was about to happen. He threw his lantern at Mrs. O'Dair, straight at her face. Charlie didn't wait to see if it hit her. She ran. Ran alongside Tobias, faster than she had ever run before.

A bellowing scream, then: "Get them!" shrieked Mrs. O'Dair. "Shoot them, you fool!"

Charlie heard the sound of a banger exploding; at the same time, a giant mosquito whined past her head. She found she could run even faster. But as she ran, she realised there was no place to run to. Mrs. O'Dair would not let her hide safely in her bedroom. Charlie was a witness to her own attempted murder. The O'Dair would not stop now until they were both dead. No place in the Castle was safe.

"Follow me!" she screamed to Tobias.

They ran, hearts hammering, lungs screaming, breath burning their throats. Watch pounded after them. Never much closer; never much further behind.

"We've got to lose him," gasped Tobias. "You know this rats' run. Come on, Charlie!"

She didn't bother to answer. She was saving all her breath for running. There was no way down from here; they would have to go up.

She bolted up the first staircase. Then out on the fourth floor. Sprinting. Up another staircase to the fifth floor. She ran out into the corridor and along it, around a corner. A short flight of stairs. Another corridor. Another corner. She passed the door she wanted and was thirty feet further on before she realised. "Wait!" Her brain switched back on. "This way!" And she turned back the way they had come. She looked over her shoulder. Tobias was just standing there, his mouth open. "Come on!" she insisted. "It's the only way!"

With a groan, Tobias sprinted after her. Neck and neck they rounded the corner. Charlie saw the glimmer of a lantern hovering at the other end of the corridor. She felt Tobias hesitate. She grabbed his arm and yanked him the last few steps and through a door into total darkness.

"Careful!" she whispered. "This stairwell is half rotten. No one uses it now. Find the handrail and follow me down. Don't fall, or you'll break both our necks!"

It was an ancient servants' stair: windowless, narrow, winding. Charlie's heart pounded in her ears. Would Watch be fooled? If not, the door behind them would swing open any second now, and they would be pinned in the light from Watch's lantern. Would he shoot them in the back?

"Hurry!" Tobias's voice bubbled with fear.

She groped; her fingers clutched the handrail. They began to climb down, feeling with their feet for each new step. It was pitch-black; the air stale. Each step seemed to take an age. Her old terror of the dark, of being shut in, skittered out of the corners of her brain. "Not now!" she pleaded, but her heart skipped a beat, lurched, began to race.

The stairs were old, wooden, worn smooth by thousands of footsteps. They had warped into odd heights and angles. Some treads were completely missing. The stair beneath her foot creaked. So did the next. And now Tobias would step on it after her, and its wooden mouth would scream again. She felt sick with fear: fear like death. Almost, she wished Watch would hurry and find them. Anything would be better than this.

Without noticing, she had stopped moving. Tobias stumbled against her. She felt herself falling and clutched the railing with both hands and lay against it, shaking. Tobias was half-sitting on her. He pulled himself off and grabbed her shoulder. His hand hurt: it felt angry.

"Why did you stop?" his voice hissed in her ear. "You damn near killed us!"

Light boiled down the stairwell. They froze, not moving—not daring to move in case the stairs screamed again. Tobias's face floated above her, white and grim. The winding stair hid them from Watch, but they could hear his raspy breathing. Tobias's eyes were locked on hers. They waited, wound tight as springs, ready to race for their lives.

Then the miracle happened. Somewhere above them Watch grunted. He shut the door and the sound of his feet running on down the corridor faded with the light. Charlie found she could move again. She pushed past

Tobias, up and out. Time was short. Watch might return at any moment.

They climbed the rickety stairs, opened the door onto the corridor and turned back the way they had come. A piece of wall near Charlie's head exploded. Watch lunged out from behind the corner. He had been lying in wait! Tobias cursed as they ran. Charlie thought: *two bullets. Four left. Unless he has more on his holster.*

There was only one way now. And it was almost as deadly as Watch. She grabbed Tobias's hand and tore up the twisting stairs to her attic. They had gained a fraction of time: Watch was slower on stairs.

Charlie ran to her bedroom, flung open the door and tore across it. Bashed open the window. "Out!" she screamed at Tobias.

He stood frozen. His face white. "I can't—"

"Out!" she shrieked. She pulled him to the window, pushed him through and scrambled after him. They stood on the parapet. The wind howled and shoved, making them stagger. Charlie grabbed Tobias's hand and began to climb.

She had spent five years playing on these rooftops.

She knew every inch of them. Every slope and slide, gully and drain. But she never went on the roofs in winter. In the dark. Over the ice.

The first part was easy. A low-pitched roof to scramble over, then a lead gutter. Tobias slipped and fell to one knee. "No!" he shouted. "You're gonna kill us."

Golden light spun out of the sky and pinned them against the roof. Another metal mosquito whined past, exploded into the slates behind them, shattering one, sending chips of slate flying. "Ow!" Tobias clapped a hand to his cheek. Blood oozed between his fingers.

"That's what'll kill us," Charlie screamed. "Now come on!" She grabbed his hand and pulled. He followed.

Her mind was full of pictures. Pictures clear and sharp as crystal. She found a fragment of a second to be surprised by this and then concentrated on the image she needed. She knew the way they had to go. It was possible. Even with ice. There was only one place . . . *Think about it when we get there. Concentrate.*

They slithered and slid out of the gutter, free falling down a slide of roof to a lower level. *Now climb,* thought Charlie. Watch surely couldn't still be following them. But he was. She turned her head and saw the lantern dancing behind them, will o' the wisp light, death in its eye.

Tobias followed. She had let go of him now. He seemed to be over his first terror, if the solid stream of curses was anything to go by. "Slow down here," she called. "Take your time. Feel for it." They were drawing away, little by little, from the deadly gleam of the lantern. Just one last bit. The bad bit. She stopped. Put out her arm to steady him. They crouched at the top of a slope, and she saw that the cut on his cheek was still bleeding. Tobias didn't seem to notice. He looked over her shoulder at what lay before them, and his face went rigid with shock. "Oh my God!"

It was the ridge. The one where the wind had nearly murdered her weeks before. Part of her mind wondered if she had always been meant to die here, and fate had just postponed it, as a sort of joke.

"We can't cross that!" Tobias reached out and grabbed her shoulder. "I can't do it, Charlie. I'm terrified of heights. Always have been. I can't do this!"

"Remember what you told me about the dark?" she shouted back to him over the roar of the wind. "The dark can't kill you."

"Yeah? Well, the dark *can't* kill you. This can!"

Light crawled up the slope behind them. "So can he!" Charlie cried. "I know which one I'd rather have kill me, and it isn't Watch! I've got to go first. Promise me you'll follow."

"I can't!"

"Don't let them win, Tobias. Please!"

He groaned. "I'll try," he said.

She got to her feet. A bullet whizzed by her head. She flinched and nearly fell. Tobias grabbed her leg. "Let go!" She balanced against the push of the wind, stepped onto the ridge. Five more steps, and *jump!* She landed flat on her stomach, scrambled up and turned. "Come on, Tobias!" she screamed.

He staggered to his feet. The wind shoved him. He crouched down. A bullet shattered the air where his head had been a second before. Charlie looked past him and saw Watch. He had nearly reached the ridge. The gun was tucked back into its holster, and he was crawling up the slope, pushing the lantern in front of him.

"Go now, Tobias! He's coming!"

Tobias stood. He looked across ten feet of nothingness at her, and she saw the terror in his eyes. He was shaking.

"Please, Tobias!" she moaned. "Now!"

He stretched out his arms for balance and stepped onto the ridge. Took another step. Two more. Wobbled. Looked down. And froze.

*"Tobias!"*

Watch stopped crawling. Pulled his pistol from its holster. Took aim.

The sound of her scream was lost in the roar of the pistol. Tobias thudded onto the roof beside her. He lay face down, unmoving, his legs dangling in empty air. Charlie grabbed him under the arms and tugged, trying to pull him away from the edge. He was too heavy. She couldn't shift him. "Tobias!" She shouted his name in despair, then turned to face their pursuer.

Watch had reached the ridge. He set down his lantern, calmly reloaded his pistol. *Damn!* thought Charlie. He put one foot on the ridge, looked up, saw her, aimed the pistol at her head. The wind screamed with her. It picked Watch up and threw him off the roof.

# Twenty-Six

"Are you shot?" Charlie shouted, shaking Tobias. "Did he kill you?" Her hands were sticky with blood.

She grabbed his jacket collar, tried to turn him over. She heard a moan. Tobias lifted his head. "The only person likely to kill me is you," he wheezed. "Stop throttling me!" Groaning, he drew his legs beneath him and crawled away from the edge. He struggled to sit up. His face was smeared with blood. "I knock the wind out of myself, and you help things along by half-strangling me." He looked around. "What happened? Where's Watch?"

Charlie shivered. "He fell. The wind got him."

Tobias's eyes went cold. "Good," he said. He dug a handkerchief out of his pocket and clamped it to his cheek. "Let's get out of here. Before someone stumbles over him and raises the alarm."

"O'Dair."

"She won't." His lip curled. "She don't want us found alive. If she knows what's happened the best she can do is hope the roofs kill us as well."

"She'll be disappointed," said Charlie. "It's easy from now on."

"Oh yeah?" Tobias managed a weak grin. "I'll believe that when me feet are back on the ground."

In fifteen minutes he got his wish. They climbed from the lowest roof into an ancient wisteria with branches thick as Charlie's waist. In seconds, they were on the ground. Dim moonlight washed out of the sky, hinting at the shape of trees and hedges. Tobias did not even pause to get his bearings. He grabbed Charlie by the hand and pulled her after him.

On the roofs, Charlie had been too frightened to notice she was cold. She knew it now. The wind sliced through her jacket. Breathing felt like swallowing lumps of frost. Only Tobias's hand was warm. It dragged her through a maze of looming dark shapes. Her feet were blind, not knowing where the ground would meet them. His hand kept her upright as they scrambled over weeds and roughly dug ground. She winced at the sound of their feet crunching iced grass, frost-crusted earth, breaking the frozen carcasses of weeds with sharp cracks that reminded her of Watch's pistol.

*"Arrrooough!"* The sound exploded out of the darkness. Tobias froze. *"Rooouugh, grrrouugh!"* Charlie heard the hounds crashing through the undergrowth, rushing towards them. She turned to run, but Tobias grabbed her jacket.

"Stand still, or they'll tear your throat out!" He pulled her to him, holding her so close she could barely breathe. Two enormous shapes bounded into the starlight. Stopped. Sniffed. Whined. "Get on out of it, Belle!" Tobias ordered. "Go back to the kennels! Go on!" The leading hound whined again, stepped forward, wagging her tail. "Get!" shouted Tobias. Both animals turned and loped off into the darkness.

"Well, you were wrong," Charlie said, a moment later, when she could talk without the scream she had swallowed churning back. "They didn't tear me to pieces."

"You're in my clothes. You smell of me. I helped raise

'em. We were lucky, is all." He let go of her, turned his head as though listening. "Where's the guards? The place ought to be crawling with them. 'Specially after all that shooting on the roof. They must've heard it. I don't like it. Something ain't right."

"We can't go back now!"

She saw the dark outline of his shoulders hunch as he shrugged. Then he grabbed her hand, and they were running again. The ground underfoot grew rougher. Brambles caught at Charlie's trousers, snagged her feet. Tobias stopped. "We're here. This is where we go out. Grab onto the back of my coat." He pushed under the hanging ivy curtain.

Charlie followed, her hands clutching the back of his jacket. She heard the now familiar sounds of lock picking, the faint rumble of oiled hinges rolling open. Tobias pulled her through a low doorway, and she felt cobbles beneath her feet. They were out.

She had to crane her head up to see the stars. They seemed further away. The air felt oilier, damper. It smelt of sewers. The Castle wall was behind them; another wall loomed in front.

"Come on. Let's get out of here." Tobias walked quickly and silently, his head constantly turning as if he were listening. He kept a painful grip on her hand, as though afraid she might suddenly disappear. She found she was glad of it.

Her arms and legs had been powered by sheer terror since O'Dair had pounced on them in the Castle. Now terror had given way to a different sort of fear. Was Tobias's instinct right? Was Alistair Windlass lying in wait around the next corner? She didn't even know if they were risking everything on a fool's errand. The name and address Bettina had given her were two years old. Anything could have happened in that time. She hadn't allowed herself to doubt until now. Perhaps it was the cold darkness of the night . . . the horror of what had happened on the roofs . . . she shuddered. If only she could warm up.

They had left the alley. Buildings crowded both sides of their path, hanging their top floors over a road that seemed too narrow for all but the smallest cart. Tobias threaded their way through a labyrinth of similar streets, pausing from time to time to listen. Their footsteps echoed in the cold air, bouncing off the walls of the houses. He held her hand and led her deeper into the heart of Quale City.

As though in pursuit, the Cathedral bells rang out behind them, and then a single ponderous bass note tolled across the City. One a.m. The houses and shops they had passed so far had all been dark and shuttered, the streets deserted. But now Tobias led her into alleys so narrow they shut out the stars. And here, despite the late hour and the cold, there *were* people. Charlie's breath came faster at the sight of them.

The buildings were ramshackle and shabby: tilting, leaning, lit by the yellow glow of the lanterns hanging over the doors of public houses. People lounged beneath these lanterns, faces jaundiced by the light. Men, women, children, nipped and starved-looking, some clearly drunk. Ramshackle and shabby as the buildings. Eyes watched as they passed.

"Tobias!" Charlie hissed. Why had he brought her here?

He tightened his grip on her hand. "Don't look no one in the eyes. Don't stop walking and don't look scared." He was whispering. She could barely hear him over the clattering of their boots on the cobbles. "This is Flearside. It ain't pretty, but it's the quickest way. We don't know how much time we got before Windlass finds out we're gone. We need to get to where we're going before morning, or he'll have the Guard and the Army searching."

He didn't speak again for over an hour. Flearside slid behind them, and Tobias let go of her hand at last. Alleys became lanes, widened further, straightened into streets. The smell of age, of ancient sewers, damp stone, rotting timber, faded. Charlie looked up, and saw that the stars had returned.

Some time later, the sky in front of them melted from black to purple. It turned a deep rich blue, like velvet. Charlie forgot the ache in her legs. She watched in fascination as the sky glowed, lightened through every shade of blue to palest silver. Fire melted the silver, and the sun rose, red as an orange. Her heart soared with it. They had made it this far. It seemed impossible that they should fail now. Each step must surely bring her closer to that moment when she would see her mother again!

She turned to look at Tobias. He was staring up at the sky. The cut on his cheek had finally stopped bleeding, but his face was the colour of whitewash under the streaks of dried blood, and he had dark circles beneath his eyes. She wondered if she looked as ill and tired.

Her head was buzzing with thoughts of her mother, but it was growing more and more difficult to lift her feet from the pavement. It was as though her boots were becoming heavier with each step. She yawned and tried to ignore the blisters rubbing her heels raw.

They were in a terraced street of new-looking houses, built primly of dull red brick. They passed shops, still shuttered and barred against the night. Smoke uncurled from a dozen chimneys, poking dirty grey fingers at the sky. The acrid smell of coal drifted through the air. They passed a flower-seller setting up her stall on a street corner. A milk cart trit-trotted down the gravelled road behind them.

Charlie watched the old man on his cart, the shiny milk churn lashed on the back. She swallowed and realised her own hunger and thirst had been waiting a long time for her to notice them. Why hadn't she thought to bring some food? Water, even. As for money, she had never had any—other than the silver thruppence she had found years ago in the crease of one of the library chairs. And Mrs. O'Dair had stolen that.

The morning sun had no warmth in it, but the wind had dropped. Hunger burnt like fire in her stomach. She wasn't used to hunger now. She had forgotten how it gnawed at your insides till you could think of nothing else.

The street narrowed and became a lane. It twisted round a green bit of ground, with an old timber-framed inn on one side of it and a row of tiny cottages on the other. A small wooden bench sat on the edge of the green. Tobias limped to the bench and collapsed onto it. Charlie sat beside him. She leant back and closed her eyes. She groaned aloud with the bliss of not moving. Her legs twitched as they relaxed. She was nearly asleep when Tobias dug his elbow in her ribs. "Don't go nodding off. We need to have our wits about us when we go in."

She stared at him. "Do you mean . . . ?"

"That's right. We're here. I thought you could read." He pointed to the sign hanging over the inn door. It showed the picture of a giant pie with the heads and beaks of birds poking through the top crust. Above, in flowing gold and green script, were the words *The Four and Twenty Blackbirds.*

# Twenty-Seven

The lemonade was sweet and sticky. Charlie drained three bottles. She longed for cold, fresh water, but the best to be had in the Four and Twenty Blackbirds was lemonade or ginger beer. She tilted an empty bottle, making the marble stopper clink round and round in the neck, and waited for the fat man to bring their food.

When it came, it was not worth the wait, or Tobias's two silver sixpences. The bread was oily and hard, the bacon stringy, the fried potatoes slippery and yellowish-green. Charlie wolfed every crumb and wished for more. The inside of the inn was low-ceilinged and dingy. It reeked of stale tobacco. The fat man reappeared and leant on the bar, smoking a cigar and staring at them. They were the only customers. The man removed the cigar, hawked and spat onto the floor. "Come far?" he said.

"No." Tobias nudged Charlie with his foot. She stared at her plate and felt sick. It had nothing—or not much—to do with the food. The place was wrong. The man was wrong. She looked up at his doughy face and felt the last of her hope drain away. This man could have nothing to do with her mother. It had been a fool's errand after all.

Tobias kicked her harder. "Ow!" She glared at him.

"Go on," he hissed, and she knew she would have to do it. After all they had gone through to get here, she couldn't quit now. She got to her feet and walked to the bar, gave the man a polite smile. He stared back at her. Blew smoke. Charlie coughed. Her smile grew grim.

"Excuse me," she said. "I wonder if you can help me. I'm looking for someone by the name of Emma. She left a message that I would always be able to contact her at this inn. Do you know who I mean?"

"Nope."

"Perhaps the owner—"

"That's me." He chewed on his cigar. "If you're done

with that lot I'll clear away." He blew more smoke.

"Wait," said Charlie. "This is really important."

"Can't help you," said the man. His doughy face was expressionless. He waded from behind the bar and began to stack the dishes. Charlie looked after him, stunned into silence. Her hope of finding her mother had just shattered into a million pieces.

The man balanced the dishes with surprising elegance and sauntered towards the depths of the inn. As he was about to pass into the back room he paused and turned round. "Mind you," he said, mumbling past the cigar. "I only had the place a year." He disappeared.

"Stop!" screamed Charlie. "Who had it before you?" Clattering and clanking wafted out. The man's head reappeared.

"Dead," he said, and withdrew like a turtle into its shell. Charlie gasped. Vaguely, she was aware of Tobias coming to stand beside her.

"What about next of kin?" roared Tobias. The man's head popped out again.

"Look here," he said. "I got work to do. Last question. Then you two clear off, or I'll get the law on you. You can ask your questions of them!"

"Next of kin?" asked Tobias again.

"Widow-woman. Three mile down Froghampton Lane. White cottage. On its own. Can't miss it. Get lost." He poked his head back in and slammed the door behind him.

The cottage stood back from the lane. It had been built at a time when the ground was lower, and now it stood in earth up to its knees. Wisteria and rose trees grew up its front, and the door was painted a soft, earthy green. The knot in Charlie's chest loosened for the first time since the Four and Twenty Blackbirds.

She took the polished brass knocker in her hand and let it fall onto the plate, twice. Nervous sweat prickled under her arms. Tobias was whistling through his teeth. She was about to scream at him to shut up when the door swung away from her hand. She found herself looking into eyes as blue and bright as flax flowers. They belonged to a white-haired old woman who seemed no taller than she was. Charlie looked down and saw that the woman was standing a foot lower in the ground.

The woman smiled at her surprise. "'Tisn't us who's sinking," she said. "It's you young things that keep growing higher. Come in now, and I'll give you a sup of milk."

"B-but you don't know who we are," Charlie stammered, her face growing warm at the kindness in the woman's eyes.

"Do I not?" said the woman. "I think I've been waiting for you nearly two years now, m'dear. Come in, do. My bones don't like the chill."

Her heart hammering in her chest, Charlie stepped down onto the flagstones. Tobias followed and closed the door behind them. Inside, the cottage was dark, but a cheerful fire glowed in the grate of the large fireplace. The room was simply furnished in an old-fashioned style, with a large wooden settle in front of the fire, and two wooden chairs either side. A child's stool stood to one side, with a well-loved china doll propped upon it. A hobbyhorse lay on the floor nearby.

"My granddaughter," said the old woman, seeing Charlie glance at the toys. "She lives with me, but she's resting upstairs just now. She'll not bother us with her chatter. Sit yourselves by the fire, m'dears, while I fetch some milk. Have you eaten this day?"

"If you can call it that," Tobias said with a grin. "At the Four and Twenty Blackbirds."

"Well, no doubt you'll survive. You're young." And she disappeared into the back room.

Charlie sank onto a settle which stood with its back to the door. Tobias collapsed into a chair beside the fire and stretched out his feet with a groan. Charlie was too bubbling over with dread and hope to speak. It was beautifully warm on the settle, and she could feel the stiffness and chill begin to seep out of her.

The woman came back into the room. She handed them each a steaming mug. Charlie breathed in the smell and took a sip. The milk was hot and creamy. She drank deeply. "Now," said the woman, looking at Charlie. "What's your name, child?"

"Charlie."

"Charlotte," corrected the woman. "And the rest?"

"Charlotte Augusta Joanna Hortense." She spoke in barely a whisper. The woman looked at her. She was smiling, but Charlie saw a tear glisten a snail's trail down the soft wrinkles of her face.

"Then come here and let me kiss you, Charlotte, for I have loved your mother from the moment of her birth." When Charlie just stared at her, open mouthed, the woman laughed. She sat beside Charlie and took her face in her hands. She placed a dry, soft kiss on her cheek. "I was her nanny, child. Emma Farleigh as was—till I married Mr. Goodenough. Emma Goodenough now, even though Mr. Goodenough went and died on me, bless him. Let me look at you now!" Mrs. Goodenough studied her. "You've the look of your father about you, Charlotte. But your mother is there in the shape of your head and your delicate bones. And you never got those curls from your father. Oh, the trouble I had with your mother's hair. She was all for cutting it off short, as you have done. But I wouldn't have that. You must grow yours back, as soon as ever you can. Promise me, now!"

"I told her not to cut it," Tobias said.

"I like it short," said Charlie.

"Stubborn, like her, I see." Mrs. Goodenough turned to Tobias. "And who might you be, young man?"

"Tobias Petch, at your service." He bobbed his head.

Charlie couldn't bear it any longer. "Where is she? Mrs. Goodenough—"

"Emma."

"Emma, then. Do you know where Mother is?"

Mrs. Goodenough's face grew serious. "I haven't heard from her for some time now. Not that that's unusual. Your mother's led a strange life these past years. I know little about it. But she sends me messages from time to time. Telling me where she is. I'll give you the last."

She got to her feet and walked to the fireplace.

She reached up into it and pulled something out. She brought it back to the settle, and Charlie saw that it was a small metal casket. Mrs. Goodenough took a key from a chain around her neck and opened the casket. A folded piece of paper lay inside. "Caroline hoped you might come looking for her," she said. "If ever you did, I was to give you her latest address. This is it."

She handed the paper to Charlie. The fire had warmed it, and it fluttered like a bird in her hands. Charlie unfolded it and read the number of a house and the name of a street. "I don't know where this is," she said.

"It's in the City, my love," said Emma Goodenough. "That's all I know."

"Let me look." Tobias took the paper.

"Do you know where it is?" Charlie asked.

"Aye," he said. "I know. Flearside."

Charlie stared at him in horror. Surely her mother wouldn't be living in that nightmare place?

Mrs. Goodenough wanted them to stay the night to rest, but Charlie would not. "In that case, Madam Stubborn, you will let me give you the money for a hansom cab. None of that! You'll still have to walk five miles to find one, child."

In the end, they walked six. It was nearly four in the afternoon as they climbed wearily into the cab, and the short winter day was dying. Charlie stared over the horse's ears, watching the sky fire crimson, then purple, then ultraviolet, then sink into a moonless black as the cab clattered and jolted slowly through the City. She fell asleep.

It seemed only minutes later Tobias was shaking her. "Come on, Charlie. Wake up. We're here."

"So quickly?" she muttered, the flood of excitement making her heart thump and waking her all at once.

"Quick? Slowest cab this side of four counties. It's gone eight o'clock!"

Charlie jumped down into the cold, black night and watched Tobias pay out a half-crown and a sixpence into the cabbie's hand. "Use that and get yourself a horse that's alive!"

"None of your cheek, lad! Where'm I to get good horseflesh? Them as ain't in the Army's needed on the land. The rest been et. Count yourself lucky to travel behind a horse at all!" He clambered back onto his box and clopped off into the night.

"Been quicker to walk. And a sight cheaper," grumbled Tobias.

"Don't worry. We're here now. Where's the house?"

They wandered along the street, reading the house numbers by the fitful light of the few street lamps that had been lit.

The houses were poor, thin things. Narrow-walled. Built cheaply in a poor, thin alley. "This one," hissed Tobias. Charlie ran to him. The windows were dark. Perhaps she had gone to bed. Perhaps she only lodged here. They would have to wake the house. "Go on, then," said Tobias.

There was no doorbell. No knocker. Charlie rapped on the door. Waited. Nothing happened. She knocked louder. She thudded on the door with her fist.

A window in the house next door crashed open. "Clear off!" shouted a man's voice. "They've flitted!" The window banged shut.

"Move over," whispered Tobias. He dug in his pocket. The lock clicked open almost at once. Charlie went in first. The only light was from the street outside. "I don't reckon they're on the gas here," he said.

"I'll find the kitchen and look for candles and matches," said Charlie.

The kitchen would be at the back. She felt her way down the narrow hall, blundered into a door and opened it. The curtainless window let in a faint light. Enough to see a bare table, a cold, unlit range, a shabby dresser, its shelves bare. Charlie went to the dresser and pulled open drawer after drawer. She found a few supplies: string, sealing wax, stamps, a broken toasting fork. In the last drawer, beneath a crumpled cloth, she found matches. A single candle stood on the mantel over the range. With shaking fingers, she lit it and went back to the hall.

Tobias shut the door. He shook his head. "The front room's empty. Bare as a beggar's bottom. Sorry, Charlie. Looks like she's gone."

"I'll check upstairs." She was amazed at how steady her voice sounded. Inside she was all in pieces. She walked up the stairs slowly, shielding the candle. There were two rooms at the top of the house. Mean, narrow rooms with mean, narrow fireplaces. They were both empty. It was over. It had all been for nothing. Charlie reached up a shaking hand to brush away a tear and heard Tobias come into the room.

He put a hand on her shoulder. "You all right?" She nodded but didn't turn around. "We'd best get you back to Mrs. Goodenough," he said. "We'll have to sleep here tonight and get an early start. Let's see if there's any coal in the lean-to. Come on, Charlie, best to keep busy. She'll be in touch again. You've got to wait is all."

He was right. But she had been so positive they would find her mother tonight. And now . . . She let Tobias lead her to the stairs. Tears blurred her eyes again, and she reached to wipe them away. She only knew something was wrong when his fingers dug into her arm.

Alistair Windlass stood at the foot of the stairs. He was too tall and elegant for the narrow hall. He had taken off his top hat and held it carelessly in a gloved hand. A brass lantern stood against the wall. He smiled up at them. "I hope you have enjoyed your little adventure," he said, "because it is at an end."

"You . . . *bastard!*" Tobias pushed past her, lunging down the steps. He immediately slid to a stop, grabbing the railing to keep himself from falling all the way to the bottom. Charlie leant to look past him and saw what had stopped him. Windlass had taken his other hand out of his overcoat pocket. It held a pistol.

# Twenty-Eight

"Technically, Tobias, it's you who are the bastard," said Windlass. "And name-calling is the last resort of the feeble-minded. I should hate to think that any son of mine was feeble-minded."

"Son?" gasped Charlie. She dropped the candle, and it guttered out instantly. "Tobias is your son?"

"Hasn't he told you that interesting fact? Sometimes I fear he's ashamed of me. Yes. My son. Although technically illegitima—Tobias! Do stand still. I may not know you very well, but I am your father. I should hate to be forced to shoot you. As you're halfway down the stairs, you might as well come the rest of the way. But be careful, Tobias." Windlass stepped back towards the door. He turned the pistol on Tobias and kept it pointed at his chest as the boy climbed slowly down the stairs.

Charlie's knees turned to soggy cardboard. She clamped her hands onto the banister. Her knuckles turned white as she watched Tobias edge past Windlass and back away from him down the hall.

"That's far enough, Tobias! Do not move from there. I share your disappointment, Your Highness." Windlass's eyes flicked up to Charlie before returning to Tobias. The pistol pointing at him never wavered. "I too hoped to find the Queen tonight. But never mind. As Tobias said, she will be in touch."

"How did you find us here?" Charlie tried to sound calm. "Have you been following us ever since last night?"

"I employ people to do that sort of thing," Windlass said shortly. "I've had a man watching Tobias's secret door in the Castle wall since the night of the ambush. Once the Resistance had Bettina, I knew it would not be long before you went in search of your mother. And

I trusted that Tobias would be gentlemanly enough to offer to accompany you."

Tobias caught her eye. His face was stricken.

"One of my men," continued the Prime Minister, "is outside this house. His job, Tobias, is to make sure that you don't attempt to follow the Princess and myself back to the Castle."

Charlie froze.

"What?" shouted Tobias. "You leave her alone!"

"You're not in any position to give orders, Tobias. Set one foot inside the Castle walls and I shall have you arrested and transported to a penal colony on the other side of the world. It would distress me, but I will do it. Your mother, I fear, would be severely traumatised by your loss. If you're tempted to embark on heroics I suggest you think of her. The Princess is in no danger. Particularly now that you've exposed Mrs. O'Dair's duplicity.

"You should really have come to me when you realised she was a threat," he said to Charlie. "Never mind. I shall deal with her in due course."

"I'm not going anywhere with you!" Charlie clutched the handrail even harder.

"Don't be childish. You have no choice. And you'll

343

be safer with me than you appear to have been for some time."

"And my father?"

"Ah." Windlass frowned. "I'm sorry. Sometimes sacrifices have to be made. The fact that I'm so close to locating your mother makes it urgent, I'm afraid. Which means I need you, Charlie. You have become essential."

Nell was right: he meant to kill her father. He had doubtless intended it from the moment she visited him in his office and presented him with a more convenient puppet. She stared at him in horror. But the only thing she could think to say was: *"Don't call me Charlie!"*

Windlass shrugged. "Come here, Your Highness. I have a carriage waiting outside. Now!"

There was nowhere to run. But he would have to drag her away, screaming and kicking! She shook her head. "No!"

"Leave her be!" roared Tobias, lurching forward.

Charlie heard a soft click as the Prime Minister cocked the pistol. It was pointed at Tobias's head. The boy froze. The blood drained from his face.

"Don't move, Tobias. Your life depends upon it. And if you, ma'am, do not come down those stairs at once,

I shall pull the trigger." The Prime Minister's voice was arctic.

"D-don't do it, Charlie!" stammered Tobias. "He's fooling." But Tobias's face was whiter than Windlass's silk handkerchief, and Charlie had already arrived at the bottom of the stairs.

Windlass reached out his free arm and swept her to his side. He pulled her backwards. The door opened. A man stepped to one side as they backed out. His face was a blur beneath a flat cap. Windlass carried her the few steps to the street and lifted her inside the waiting carriage. He pushed her onto one seat and sat opposite. The pistol had disappeared, but his right hand remained in his overcoat pocket.

"Drive on," he called. The carriage lurched forward. The sound of the horse's hooves echoed through the darkness as it trotted briskly over the cobbles. A young horse, no doubt, which would carry them to the Castle quickly. Charlie's hands clenched the leather seat either side of her. She couldn't take her eyes from Windlass's face. It was smooth, expressionless. A scream pushed up her throat. To stop it, she spoke one of the questions scouring her brain.

"If Tobias is your son, why is he working as a gardener's boy?" For a moment she thought he wasn't going to answer. Then Windlass shrugged.

"I married Tobias's mother when I was very young. Barely more than a boy. Oh yes," he said, noticing her frown, "we were legally married. But shortly before the birth of our son a singular opportunity came my way. I'm an ambitious man. You may have noticed." He grinned, and it was Tobias's grin. It shocked her.

"I was fond of Rose, but I was fonder of advancement. She wasn't the sort of wife who would have helped me to rise in the world. So I left her. Later, when I was in a position to do so, I destroyed all record of the marriage. Hence Tobias's illegitimate status." Windlass paused. Frowned. "In other circumstances I would have enjoyed his company. But that has not been possible. I did, in an effort to look after them both, find Rose employment as a seamstress, even encourage her to remarry. That was not successful. Mr. Petch met an early end in the canals. A quarrel over ill-gotten gains, I understand. He was not missed. He used to beat them both. I fear Tobias blames me."

"And do you think yourself blameless?" Charlie asked in amazement.

"I don't think in terms of blame at all, child. You should know that by now."

"And my mother? Tell me the truth! She ran away from you, didn't she?"

"Your mother is one of the great scientists of our age. I had set her to work on vital research when she stumbled across something unexpected. Something with the potential to change the course of history.

"Many scientific breakthroughs come about by accident, I believe. Of course, she told me about her discovery. She saw the implications at once. She was horrified by the sheer destructive potential. Your mother has a delicacy of conscience which is perhaps not suited to the application of science. I argued against her scruples, explained the political realities. She must have sensed my determination. She fled. Your father, I'm afraid, never really recovered. He is a charming man . . . but weak."

"You're drugging him!" Charlie shouted.

Windlass shook his head. She saw pity in his eyes, and it made her want to scream. "Only recently. He began showing an interest in things other than his castles. I asked Mrs. O'Dair to keep him pacified. A harmless drug. He hasn't suffered. He will have a quick end. I promise you that. As quick and painless as possible. And now, we have arrived."

The carriage lurched to a stop. The driver grunted as he jumped to the ground. The door opened. Windlass climbed out and motioned her to follow. She didn't move.

"If you do not climb down at once I shall instruct my man to carry you inside." His voice was bored. "Which is it to be?"

She climbed down. A white moth fluttered against her face and melted. Then another. Snow whirled out of the darkness. The dome of light at the entrance to the ministerial wing became a child's toy: a blizzard trapped in a glass globe. The guards' hut was empty. He had dismissed them. There was not to be even the slightest chance of help for her.

The Prime Minister hugged her to his side, shielding her from the snow, and strode into the Castle. He did not slow down or let go until he opened the door to his office and pushed her inside.

She heard the click of the key in the lock. She waited in the dark, her mind darting to and fro in a white blankness, as he lit one of the gas lamps. She looked for a weapon. Something to hit him with. There were only files and portfolios. She ran to a chair and tried to lift it, but it was too heavy.

Charlie looked up to see Windlass watching her. His mouth was twisted into half a smile. He looked tired, and his eyes were sad.

"Don't do this, please," she begged. "Why kill him? You have everything! You already rule Quale! Let him live. I'll take him away somewhere. You needn't see either of us ever again. Be king! I don't care! But please don't kill my father!"

"The Esceanian threat must be dealt with, Charlie. I will use whatever means are required. As things stand, it is only a matter of time before they invade. Months. A year at the most. Once their spies find out that our stockpiles of gunpowder are nearly depleted and that all my promises of a new weapon have been lies, the Emperor will invade. Do you really think that he would let your father live? Or you?"

Windlass sighed. He ran his hand across his eyes. A lock of hair fell onto his forehead, making him look younger, wistful. "I haven't time to explain. I doubt if you would be willing to listen. But Quale is only a part of this. There is much more at stake . . . so much more. I am sorry. I never wanted to hurt you. Or the King, if you can believe that. But this is more important than you can imagine. I have no choice."

"I'll tell!" Charlie cried. "If you kill my father I'll tell! I won't be your puppet!"

"I no longer need a puppet, Charlie. You have found your mother for me, for which I am extremely grateful. Now that I know she is in the country; that she is using Mrs. Goodenough for her contact, it will not take my men long to track her down.

"I had nearly given up hope. There were tantalising traces of her discovery in the papers she left behind, but not enough for my scientists to duplicate her work. Once I have you both safe, she will cooperate.

"I must go now and find some of your father's old notepaper in the library with which to forge his suicide note. He must be dead before the servants are up, which gives me only a few hours. Half the Kingdom believes he murdered the Queen; they will be easily convinced that he killed himself from a combination of remorse and an unbalanced mind."

He looked at her, and his eyes were blue ice. "Now, go into the cloakroom, please. I'm going to lock you in. You'll be safe here from Mrs. O'Dair."

She turned and ran, but in two steps he had caught

her, grabbing her by the shoulders. She twisted, kicked, tried to bite, desperate to stop him, to hurt him. He dragged her to the cloakroom and threw her inside. She crashed into the opposite wall and slid across the wooden seat of the thunderbox, stunned. The door slammed shut and darkness swallowed her. She heard the lock click. She heard him walk across the room. The second door closed.

Charlie screamed. She screamed and screamed until her voice shrivelled to a croak. The dark grabbed her by the throat and squeezed. She knew she was about to die, like her father. She staggered to her feet. Her heart hammered even harder, and she thought she might faint. She felt her way to the sink, fumbled the cold tap on and plunged her head beneath the freezing spray. Gradually her heart slowed. She stopped gasping for air. Her brain began to work.

She stumbled to the door and felt for the lock. Her hand found the buttonhook in her trouser pocket. Tobias had made it look easy. She found the keyhole with her finger, poked the hook into it, jiggled, twisted, levered from side to side. Nothing. Her fingers were wet with water and sweat. The handle slipped. She heard the ping as the hook hit the wooden floor and bounced. She used a word even Tobias had never heard, lowered her shaking hand and felt the floor with fingers soft as spiders' feet, fearful of knocking it out of reach. She gave a sob as she touched it. In a moment it was back inside the lock. She listened with her fingers, tried not to think of the time it was taking . . .

*CLICK.* Loud as a lightning bolt cracking the sky, she heard it. Turned the knob with disbelieving fingers and was blinded by gaslight.

The second door was easy. Her fingers had the hang of it now, and her eyes were able to help. She tore up the stairs, raced through the west wing and into the south, along the corridor towards her father's bedroom. She had never run so fast.

Moonlight poured in at the windows; it must have stopped snowing. The thick carpet swallowed the sound of her feet. She grabbed his door knob, flung his door open, ran to the bed and pulled back the heavy hangings. The bed was empty. Her father was gone.

The air shifted as the door to her father's dressing room breathed open. Charlie heard the creak of whalebone, the rustle of bombazine.

# Twenty-Nine

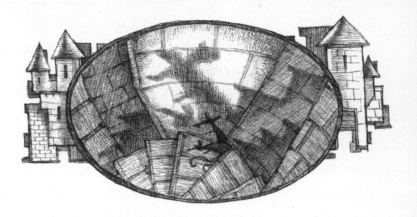

Mrs. O'Dair's face was a pale oval above the black pyramid of her body. The pistol in her hand winked in the moonlight. Charlie heard a hiss of delight.

"You!" the housekeeper breathed. "I expected Windlass, but this is even better! All of this is your fault, you ugly little brat! If it weren't for you, things would have continued as usual. Two more years and your mother would have been declared dead. Then your father could remarry."

Charlie felt sick. "My father would never marry you!"

"Your father does whatever I tell him! I look after

him! No one else does! No one cares for him but me.
I shall be Queen, instead of that insipid bluestocking
mother of yours. She never loved him!"

"Liar!"

O'Dair lunged forward and grabbed Charlie's arm.
Her face floated in front of Charlie, the eyes dark holes.
The smell of oil of cloves and mothballs pressed into
her nose. The pistol pressed against her chest. She tried
to pull away, but O'Dair's hand might have been made
of stone.

"You are going to pay for the trouble you have caused
me." O'Dair's breath scoured her face. "This is Watch's
pistol. It should have put an end to you weeks ago! I
shall enjoy killing you with it. But not yet. I need you
for a little while yet."

"Where's my father?"

"Safe. Out of Windlass's way."

"Where?"

"The dungeons, brat! Where I'll dump your body.
The rats can have you!"

The housekeeper tucked the gun in the reticule dangling from her waist and moved towards the door, pulling Charlie after her like a steamship towing a rowboat.
"Poor Ancel," O'Dair sighed. "I have kept him like a

blackbird in a cage for five years now. I knew I would have to kill him in the end, but I hoped it would not be for a while yet."

Shock stopped Charlie twisting and beating at the hand fastened around her wrist. O'Dair surged on—out the door, down the corridor, towards the servants' stair, dragging a stumbling Charlie behind her. "We'll go the back way," O'Dair said. "I don't want to meet the Prime Minister just yet. Not until I've dealt with you."

"You can't kill Mr. Moleglass!" Charlie cried. "He's your husband!"

"That's why, stupid girl! Otherwise the marriage to the King won't be legal."

"My father won't marry you! And even if you made him do it, my mother's still alive."

"Your mother doesn't worry me," panted O'Dair. "She'll not dare show her face here. I know things—"

"What? What do you know?" But the housekeeper had reached the door to the servants' stair. She dragged Charlie down into the dark. Charlie stumbled, slid two steps, grabbed the handrail with her free hand and got her feet under her again. She was pulled stumbling and slipping all the way down the twisting narrow stair.

O'Dair yanked her along the servants' corridor to

the lift and heaved her inside. Charlie crashed against a wall and slid to her knees. O'Dair had her back to her, closing the lift doors. She ignored Charlie. It was as though she was already dead. Charlie climbed to her feet and stood, shaking and sick, weak with fear, as—with a clanking of chains and grinding of gears—the lift plunged towards Mr. Moleglass's cellar.

The mouth of the pistol pressed against the back of her head.

"Knock on the door," hissed O'Dair. "Call out to him."

Charlie shivered. She thought of Mr. Moleglass lying peaceably asleep in his bed on the other side of the door, unaware that death waited in the cold dust of the corridor. She took a deep, slow breath. "Mr. Moleglass!" she shouted. "*Don't open the door!* O'Dair has a gun! She wants to k—" A massive hand clamped across her mouth and squashed her to O'Dair's bosom. Whalebone poked her shoulders, bombazine slithered on the back of her neck, oil of cloves suffocated her.

"Do you think that matters?" O'Dair chuckled. Her bosom heaved and her corsets groaned. "Ancel!" she called. "Ancel, open the door. I have your little friend here. There is a pistol at her head. If the door is not open in two minutes, I will pull the trigger."

Charlie twisted and kicked and writhed, but O'Dair took no notice. A light flickered beneath Moleglass's door, strengthened, rayed outwards. Charlie heard footsteps approaching and fought the stone hand in a frenzy of despair. The door opened inwards and the butler stood puddled in light. His hair stuck out from his head like black feathers; he wore a dark blue dressing gown tied across his egg-shaped stomach, and his seal's eyes were bitter with disappointment as he looked at Mrs. O'Dair.

"Let go of the child, Agatha," he said. "This is unnecessary and unbecoming. Come inside, and I will put the kettle on."

"You silly little man!" spat O'Dair. "You think a cup of tea can solve all the world's problems!"

"Better than a gun, at any rate. Let go of the child. She is powerless to stop you, whatever you intend."

Mrs. O'Dair's hand slid from Charlie's mouth, grasped her shoulder and shoved her forward. Charlie fell into Mr. Moleglass's arms and was gathered tight.

His hand smoothed her hair, and he kissed the top of her head. "Sit in my chair, Charlie. Try not to worry. I will deal with Mrs. O'Dair."

She looked up at him. His brown eyes met hers, and he smiled. His smile was sad. "Please, Charlie," it said. "Pretend to believe me."

She stumbled to the chair and crouched in it, shivering, her eyes fixed on O'Dair as the housekeeper advanced into the room, her pistol pointing at Mr. Moleglass's heart.

"I'm sorry, Ancel," she said. "You and the girl will come with me to the dungeons. No cups of tea."

"Leave Charlie here. She is no threat to you."

"Of course she is. Her father loves her, after his fashion. That is threat enough. Besides, I hate the brat."

"Then you will have to kill us here. I shall not make things easier for you."

Mrs. O'Dair's eyes narrowed. Her face flushed the colour of rusty iron. "You are too fond of your own way, Ancel! It has been your greatest fault as a husband." She raised the pistol. "Very well—"

"I am surprised at you, Agatha," Moleglass said. His voice shook, very slightly. "It is unlike you to throw away a fortune."

O'Dair's eyes flickered. The mouth of the pistol lowered a fraction of an inch. "A fortune? What are you talking about?"

Charlie wondered the same thing. She leant forward, staring at the butler, heart thumping.

"The Queen's papers. The Prime Minister would pay a handsome sum for them."

Charlie gasped. *Of course!* Clever Mr. Moleglass.

The housekeeper snorted derisively. "A fortune? For papers?"

"You don't know what Windlass is after, do you?" Charlie made herself speak. She tried to ignore the pistol as it swivelled to point at her head. "He's tricked you from the beginning. Letting you have the pickings from the Castle. Silver, china, wine, linens. How much have you made from those? Hundreds? A thousand? Alistair Windlass has robbed the entire Kingdom. He's stolen a fortune! And he would give half of it to you for my mother's scientific papers."

"Why?" scoffed O'Dair. "Why should he want that woman's scribblings?"

"Power," Charlie whispered. And watched the pupils of O'Dair's eyes widen with greed. "She invented something by accident. A new sort of weapon."

O'Dair hissed. Revelation lit her face, curved her lips in a moist smile. "*That's* why she ran away."

Charlie nodded. "Yes. She ran from him. She ran to protect her science."

The housekeeper's eyes glittered. "Where are these papers, then?"

"They're—"

"I will take you to them," Mr. Moleglass interrupted. "The Queen entrusted them to me before she left."

Charlie stared at him, appalled. He was trying to draw the housekeeper away. Using himself as bait in order to save her. Once he was alone with O'Dair, he would try to get the gun from her. And she would kill him.

"He's lying!" she shouted.

Moleglass's head whipped round, his eyes wide with alarm. "Charlie! Stay out of this!"

"What do you mean?" O'Dair advanced until she towered over her. The smell of mothballs and oil of cloves was tainted with the sharpness of sweat. The housekeeper's forehead was moist, her dark eyes glared at Charlie. She placed the pistol against Charlie's forehead.

"Leave her alone, Agatha! The child knows nothing!"

The housekeeper ignored him. The cold circle of steel pressed Charlie's head into the back of the chair. "Well?" hissed O'Dair. "Ancel is lying, is he? Then what is the truth, brat? *Where are those papers?*"

The gun pinned her to the chair. She couldn't move. "Unload your pistol and give me the bullets. Then I'll tell you."

O'Dair's full lips stretched in a slow smile. She took a step backwards, and a wave of giddiness swept over Charlie as the pistol released her. "You must think me a fool!" The housekeeper shook her head. "Tell me, or I shoot your beloved Mr. Moleglass. I will count to five."

"If you kill him, I'll never tell you!" Charlie shouted.

O'Dair's smile broadened. She aimed the pistol at Moleglass's heart. The butler flinched, took a single step back, then stood quite still, facing his wife. "One," she said. "Two . . . three . . . fou—"

"All right!" cried Charlie. "They're in my bedroom. My mother gave them to me the night she left. I've been hiding them for her ever since. They're stuck to the back of my wardrobe."

"No, Charlie!" Mr. Moleglass shouted. He jumped forward and yanked her out of the chair, shook her. "You betray your country! There was no need to tell her the truth! I could have got the gun from her, you stupid child!" He let go of Charlie and whirled to face the housekeeper. "Don't give those papers to the Prime Minister, Agatha. I beg you! If you do, you will cause the deaths of countless innocent people and put at risk the liberty and personal freedom of every citizen of Quale!"

Mrs. O'Dair laughed. "Always a flair for the dramatic! Really, you should have gone on the stage. What is a butler, after all, but someone acting a part for the whole of their lives? Do you think I care about any of that? You amuse me, Ancel. As a reward, I shall let you and the brat live. For a little longer." She backed from the room, pausing to take the key from the lock. The door shut her from view, and Charlie heard the click of the key in the lock, the creak and rustle of bone and bombazine, then silence.

Moleglass turned to her, panting, his eyes dark as coal in a chalky face. "Charlie! You should not have interfered! She nearly killed you!" He reached out, hugged her close, then pushed her away so he could look into her face. "Where is Tobias? What has happened? I waited in the freight room all night, and you did not come. I have been frantic!"

"Tobias is safe, I think. But we have to get out of here!"

"The door is locked, Charlie. I can try to break it down, but—"

She fished the buttonhook from her pocket and ran to the door.

"Charlie, what are you—"

"Not now!" She knelt and wriggled the hook into the keyhole. Five minutes later she was still jiggling and probing. Her fingers had lost the knack. "Sweet Betty!" she exploded and twisted the hook viciously. It found an edge of metal, pushed it to one side, and the lock clicked open.

"Psychology obviously comes into it," Moleglass observed drily. "Quickly now, child. We must get out of the Castle."

"No!" Charlie sprang to her feet. "Go and find Nell, Mr. Moleglass. Rose Petch will know where she is. Then go with her to fetch the Resistance. Windlass is in the library right now, forging my father's suicide note. We can't fight him alone. He's far more dangerous than Mrs. O'Dair, and the Guard will obey him, not me. We need help. And witnesses. And for goodness' sake, stay out of O'Dair's way. Oh . . ." She fished in her pocket and pulled out a folded piece of paper. "This is the address of the house where one of Windlass's men is holding Tobias. Have you got a lantern?"

Moleglass stared at her, then at the paper she had thrust in his hand. "Why do you need a lantern? What are you going to do?"

"I'm going to find my father."

The lift returned all too soon. Charlie stood in a circle of lantern light and heard the clanking approach. Mr. Moleglass had gone. Soon the lift would be carrying her deep beneath the Castle. She shivered.

The inner grille closed, and the outer doors groaned and creaked shut. The lift lurched and began to sink. Charlie leant against the side and tried not to think of the tons of earth and stone swallowing her. She felt her heart stutter, speed, start to gallop. Sweat beaded on her forehead. She gasped for air, grew giddy. The needle in the semicircle over the door jumped from B1 to B2. A lifetime later it lurched from B2 to B3. Her heart was winning the race. She would die before she reached the dungeons.

She stared at the golden glow of the lantern—the

frail circle of light keeping her safe. She felt the weight of the Castle over her head. Worse, she felt the infinite darkness of the dungeons lying in wait, ready to pounce the moment the flame failed or the oil ran out. What had Tobias said? "It's only dark," she murmured, hearing his voice again. "Dark can't kill you." Then why did she feel like she was about to die? "It's only fear," she told the lift. "Fear of the dark. Fear of being closed in. It can't kill me." She didn't believe it.

The lift juddered to a stop. She picked up the lantern, stumbled to the grille and tugged. She waited another lifetime, her heart rattling too fast to count the beats, until the lift doors groaned open. Air as cold and wet as an invisible river rinsed her face. The cold calmed her, gave her breath. She lifted the lantern and began to run.

"Father! *Father!* It's Charlie. Where are you?"

She ran inside her circle of light through the darkness, stumbling over paving stones, listening for her father's voice, hearing the rats skittering along the walls. Cell after empty cell. Then: "Charlotte? Is that you? Child! Why are you not safely in bed?"

Her father peered at her through rusty iron bars. His hair tumbled about his face and he was wearing striped pyjamas, a flannel dressing gown and slippers. Charlie grabbed his hand through the bar. It was ice cold.

"Mrs. O'Dair," said her father through chattering teeth, "has gone mad. Did you know that, Charlotte?"

"Yes, Father."

"She seems to think I want to marry her."

"I know."

"But I'm married to your mother. And even if I weren't . . ."

"Don't worry about it, Father. Now let go of my hand. I'm going to get you out of there."

"Have you got the key? How clever!"

"Nearly," she said, and squatted in front of the cell door.

"Charlotte? What on earth are you doing?"

"Picking the lock."

"Oh. But . . . how did you learn to do that?"

"A friend showed me."

"I'm not sure . . . I don't like to complain, Charlotte, considering the circumstances, but I don't think you have any business learning to pick locks. It doesn't seem . . . suitable, somehow."

"Yes, Father."

The lock groaned open with a rusty wheeze. The

door hinges screamed. Charlie pulled her father from the cell, picked up the lantern and began to run back towards the lift. "Come on, Father! Run! We have to get out of the Castle before O'Dair or Windlass find us."

"Alistair? What has he to do with any of this?"

*"Oh, Father!"*

# Thirty

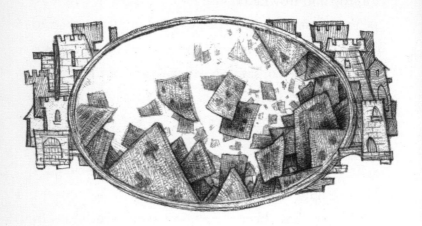

"I can't leave, Charlotte. I am the King." Her father trotted ahead of her, his slippers pattering on the marble floor of the state rooms. He was heading for his chamber. He ran with an easy grace, and she struggled to keep up.

She had pleaded with him, shouted at him, tried to haul him away physically, but when her father had insisted on returning to his chamber, she had abandoned the lantern and its telltale light and followed him.

"Windlass has spent the past hour writing your suicide note, Father!" Her whisper was harsh in the darkness. "Why can't you listen to me? He plans to kill you!" She caught him at last, clung to his arm. Her father slid to a stop and frowned down at her.

"You must have misunderstood. Alistair is a man of honour. I trust him implicitly. However, I have let him carry the burden of state alone for too long. I have been remiss. I have duties..." His voice trailed away, and he removed her hand from his arm, patted it. "I miss your mother." He sighed. "But that is no excuse." He began to run again. Charlie chased him across puddles of moonlight.

"O'Dair has been drugging you, Father. On Windlass's orders!"

He seemed not to hear her. "One thing I must do, Charlotte. After that, if it pleases you, we will discuss all your worries. I promise to listen to you. But first..." They had reached the antechamber door. The King opened it, strode through, flung open the door to his chamber. He stood in the acid-pale light streaming through the windows, gazing up at his castle of cards.

He sighed deeply. "I have failed. I have failed the Kingdom, and you, and myself. And if your mother is still alive, I have failed her. This castle is a symbol of that failure. I am going to destroy it, and then, I hope, I will be able to start afresh." He switched on the gas, took a packet of safety matches from his pocket and began lighting the wall lights. The moonlight retreated before the blue-white glow of the gas. When he had finished, he returned to stand in front of her. His face was calm but inexpressibly sad. "Do you forgive me, Charlotte?"

Her eyes welled with tears of love and frustration and fear. Her father reached out gentle fingers and wiped the moisture from her cheek. Then, for the first time in five years, he gathered her in his arms and held her tight. Her face was pressed against his shoulder, and she did not see the intruder. But she heard the creak of whalebone and the swish of bombazine across a dusty floor.

"Revolting!" Mrs. O'Dair stood behind them. Her skirts swirled to a stop, and Charlie heard the whisper of a thousand playing cards shivering. The housekeeper's face was the colour of stewed plums. "Ancel has escaped," she snarled. "But at least I have you, brat! You sent me on a fool's errand! Well, you won't have the opportunity to trick me again. Stand away from her, Your Majesty." Her right arm swept up. It held Watch's pistol.

"You're m-mad, woman!" the King stuttered with outrage. His arms tightened around Charlie. "You are dismissed from your post," he gasped. "You will leave the Castle at once! And stop pointing that weapon at my daughter!" He pushed Charlie behind him, walking them backwards, circling the castle of cards. "Get onto the scaffolding, Charlotte! Climb as high as you can. Keep the castle between the two of you. I shall disarm her."

"No! I—"

"Do as I say!" he roared. Charlie turned and ran.

*"Out of my way, you stupid man!"*

Something flew past Charlie's ear, and she heard the unmistakeable whine of a bullet, chased by the crack of a retort. She flung herself forward and scrambled up the nearest scaffolding ladder. She paused on the first platform, crouching down, her eyes searching for her father. And saw a huddle of blue dressing gown heaped against a wall, a tangle of auburn hair. Her heart stopped. The huddle stirred, and her father lifted his head. She heard herself cry out in relief. It was a mistake.

O'Dair was standing near the portcullis, pistol in hand, scanning the scaffolding. Now her head swivelled, and her eyes fastened onto Charlie like black leeches. The malevolence in them struck Charlie like a blow, and she clutched the scaffolding to keep from falling. O'Dair smiled—her lips parted in anticipation.

She lifted her arm, took careful aim.

"Put it down, Mrs. O'Dair!" Alistair Windlass stepped through the doorway. His face was flushed, and he was panting as though he had been running, but his voice was cold and precise. "I don't want to have to kill you," he said, "but if you fire again you may be sure I will." His right arm was fully extended, the pistol in his hand pointing at the housekeeper. His eyes were colder than his voice. Colder than Charlie had ever seen them. She could feel his fury from across the room. She shivered.

Charlie watched the triumph in O'Dair's face twist into a snarl of rage and fear. Watched her spin around in a whirl of black. The housekeeper's skirts flared out and whipped the dust, roused the air. She stood in the eye of a whirlwind. As Mrs. O'Dair took aim, a gust struck the card castle, and the portcullis trembled. It shifted, shuddered and fell with a dry clattering, like the rain of a thousand tiny bones. Charlie saw O'Dair flinch, and Watch's pistol spat a bullet into the plaster over Windlass's head. The housekeeper bellowed in fury and lifted her arm again. The Prime Minister did not move, but Charlie heard a second explosion. She felt a distant awe, a faint surge of surprise, as Mrs. O'Dair staggered, then collapsed onto the floor with groan of whalebone and a dusty sigh of bombazine.

In the silence that followed, Charlie stared at the body of the housekeeper. It lay with an unnatural stillness that made the breath catch in her throat. She looked up and met Windlass's eyes. In two seconds she was down the scaffolding and darting across the room. But he was there before her. She stumbled to a halt in front of him, watching with all the intensity of a trapped animal as he slid Watch's pistol into his pocket. She turned her head, seeking her father.

He was standing now, leaning against the wall, looking down at O'Dair. She lay on the remains of the portcullis, stretched on her back in a tumble of playing cards. Her face was peaceful, her eyes open. There was a small hole in the centre of her chest, and the surrounding bombazine was a darker black than usual. Blood puddled around her, seeping into the cards and staining them scarlet.

The King lifted his gaze. The Prime Minister looked at her father, and Charlie saw Windlass's mouth tighten as though he were in pain. "I'm sorry, Your Majesty," he said and raised his arm. The pistol pointed at the King's head. Charlie froze. Fear unlike any she had ever known flooded through her.

Her father's sea-green eyes widened and a look of deep sadness darkened them. "So Charlotte was right. Treason and regicide. Why, Alistair?"

The hand holding the pistol never wavered. A lock of Windlass's hair had fallen across his forehead, but otherwise he was as elegant as ever. His black frock coat was unbuttoned, showing a silver-figured waistcoat. His tiepin gleamed in the gaslight. His mouth tightened further, and he shook his head. But his eyes glinted cold as the winter moon. "It is necessary. Truly, I wish it were otherwise."

"I have failed," said the King, "so many people." He glanced at her, and she saw that his eyes held the distant look they had so often contained when he was busy designing a new tower. He was far away—somewhere she could not follow. He turned his head to gaze up at his card castle. "You'll not harm Charlotte?"

"I give you my word. As long as you do as I tell you. If you do not . . ."

The King nodded. "And?"

"Climb," said Windlass. "Take that with you." He

pointed to a coil of rope lying beside the door. The King walked to it, picked it up, and Charlie saw that one end had been knotted to form a noose.

"*No!*" she screamed and lunged at Windlass, hitting and kicking.

He gathered her to him with one arm, binding her arms to her chest so fiercely she could barely breathe.

"I'll kill you!" she panted. "If it takes the rest of my life!"

"Quite possibly." He was watching her father. The King strode to the nearest scaffolding tower and sprang up it. Tears burned in her eyes as she saw her father, graceful even in pyjamas, swing himself to the very top of his card castle, the rope strung about his chest like a royal sash.

"Don't, Father!" she screamed. "Fight him! Don't give in!"

The King did not look at her. Did not hesitate. He stretched up his arms and tied the end of the rope to the highest scaffold pole. Then, without the slightest pause, he loosened the noose and slipped it over his head.

Darkness swarmed over her eyes, and when she looked again she saw nothing but the glimmer of dust motes dancing in the gaslight. She was lying on the floor. She felt sick and weak. Her vision cleared, and she saw Tobias staring down at her in horror. Mr. Moleglass's face swam into sight beside him. His eyes were huge with shock. As she looked at him, his face sagged with relief, and he staggered. Tobias put out a hand, steadied him.

A movement caught her eye. Nell stood behind Mr. Moleglass. Charlie recognised other Resistance members behind her. They were crowded in the doorway but did not seem to be trying to push further into the room. Many of them carried muskets or rifles. Charlie struggled to her knees. She shook her head to clear the last of the giddiness from it and looked for her father.

Instead, she saw the Prime Minister. He stood near O'Dair's body, his face grim, his mouth pressed thin. His eyes glittered as he watched the intruders in the doorway. His arm was raised; the pistol in his hand pointing unwaveringly towards the top of the card castle. Charlie looked and saw her father. He had not moved. He was staring at Windlass as though the Prime Minister was a puzzle he was trying to solve. The noose was still around his neck.

"Stand back, Moleglass." Windlass's voice was as

cool and controlled as ever. "I mean it," he said. "Out of the chamber. Out of the antechamber and into the corridor. And keep the others out. All but Tobias. He stays. Do it, Moleglass, or I shoot the King!"

The crowd behind Nell began to shout. Angry voices crowded into the room.

"Nell!" Mr. Moleglass straightened. He turned from a small, frightened man into a butler. "Take these people out now! You put the King's life at risk with every second you stay here!"

"Please, Nell!" Charlie cried.

Nell's eyes met hers, softened. She nodded. "Very well, Mr. Moleglass. Until the King is safe. And Charlie. Then he's ours." She turned to look at Windlass, and Charlie saw a Nell she did not recognise—a Nell as ruthless as Peter, as the Prime Minister himself. There was a confusion of pushing and shouting, then Nell vanished into the antechamber, taking the Resistance and their bristling weapons with her.

Mr. Moleglass cast a last agonised look at Charlie, at the King, at the body of Mrs. O'Dair heaped upon the floor. Then he, too, backed out of the chamber.

Tobias threw his father a look of contempt, walked to

Charlie and took her hand. He squeezed it and tried to smile. His eyes were bright with anger, his jaw clenched. He pulled her to her feet. "You all right, Charlie?"

She nodded and turned to face Alistair Windlass. The Prime Minister was watching them, his mouth twisted in a faint smile.

"Well, Charlie," he said. "It appears you get your wish. Your father may live, but in exchange I must once more request the pleasure of your company. If you agree to become my hostage while I escape the country, I will not shoot him. If you refuse, I will. And my aim is deadly, Charlie. Trust me."

Her eyes climbed the castle of cards. Up and up they flew, twenty feet into the air, past rampart, crenellation and tower. Her father was looking at her now. He gazed into her eyes and smiled. "Charlotte," he said. "My little Charlie. I forbid you to do as Alistair requests. Do as I tell you, and leave this room."

Charlie shook her head. It felt like her heart was breaking. Her father was himself again, and she was about to cause him pain. "I can't do that, Father. You know I can't."

The King frowned. "Charlotte! Don't disobey me. I know you've had little enough cause to do so these past five years, but please trust me. I know what is best for you. You are my dearest treasure, and I cannot give you into the power of a man like Alistair Windlass. Leave this room!"

Tears blurred her eyes. "I can't."

"Moleglass!" roared the King. "Come back! Get Charlotte out of here! You, boy! Take my daughter out!"

"If you do, Tobias, I shoot the King." Windlass's voice was calmly precise. "Make no mistake. I will do it."

"You'll do it, all right!" Tobias shouted. His hand still gripped hers, and Charlie felt him trembling. "There's nothing you'll not sink to. Anything low and rotten as long as it's in the cause of Alistair Windlass. I wish Petch had been my father. At least he was an honest villain. If you need a hostage, take me, damn you! Leave Charlie with her dad. You owe her that much."

Windlass's mouth thinned. He smiled. "Sorry, Tobias. You're worth very little as a hostage, I'm afraid. Any soldier out to collect bounty would merrily shoot us both dead. It must be the Princess. Come here, Charlie."

"Charlotte!"

She let go of Tobias's hand and smiled up at her father to show him she wasn't afraid. Her eyes were as cold as Windlass's own as she walked towards him. But she looked away as she stepped past the mound that had been Mrs. O'Dair.

"Well done, Charlie," said Windlass when she stood in front of him. She stared into his eyes and saw him blink. This close, she could hear the quickness of his breathing, see the pulse beating fast in his temple. So the icy calm was mere pretence. She tasted bitter satisfaction, lifted her chin in defiance.

He looked back at her, and a gentle, self-mocking smile flickered across his face and disappeared. The momentary warmth faded from his eyes. "Turn around, Charlie." She turned and flinched as the cold mouth of the pistol pressed against the back of her neck. "Tobias," he said. "Go and get my carriage ready. You have ten minutes. Be prompt."

Tobias looked sick. He glared hatred at his father, turned and ran from the room.

"Charlie, start walking." The pistol dug into her neck, and she stepped forward.

"Windlass!" the King shouted. Something in his voice made her forget the Prime Minister and his gun. Made her whirl round and stare up at her father, hope and dread tumbling through her mind. He had taken the rope from around his neck and was holding the end in his hands. He stood straight and proud in his pyjamas, his long auburn hair flung back, his dressing gown draped around him like a ceremonial robe. He was gazing at the tallest and grandest of his towers, which speared upwards to scrape the ceiling twenty feet above them.

As she watched, the King bent his knees and leapt into space. The gaslight caught his shadow and cast it against the ceiling as he arced through the air. He reached the end of the rope and let go, spreading his arms, aiming himself like a human arrow. His feet punctured the tower. Cards exploded with the sound of a flock of birds taking flight. The tower crumpled and fell with reluctant grace. Tower after tower shuddered, buckled and collapsed in an avalanche of cardboard.

Six hundredweight of playing cards fell out of the sky, burying the man and girl standing in their path. Charlie didn't feel them hit her. She was already unconscious.

# Thirty-One

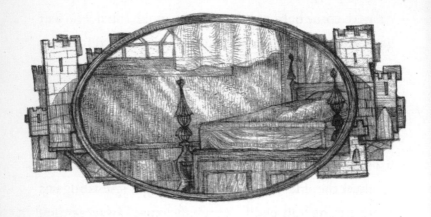

She opened her eyes and saw a ceiling she didn't recognise. Fat plaster rectangles marched stolidly around its perimeter in what she realised was an attempt at decoration. She turned her head, only a little, because it hurt, and saw a window she didn't know. Beyond the wavy glass, the sky floated, an uncertain blue. Soft, wispy clouds drifted across it, like legless sheep.

She heard a noise of someone moving, a door opening and closing. Whoever it was had left. She closed her eyes and slept.

When she woke, Mr. Moleglass was sitting in a chair beside her bed. He looked up from the book he was reading and smiled at her. "So, Charlie," he said. "You've come back to us." He put his hand in his pocket and pulled out the white queen. He reached down and tucked it into her hand. Her fingers curled round its cool, comforting weight. "I found this in your room," he said. "You forgot to take it with you."

"Sorry."

"I thought you might like to have it now." He smiled down at her. His seal's eyes answered her question, and the hurt she had been straining to hold away swelled into a monstrous weight and fell.

Moleglass's voice seeped through the layers of pain. "I don't suppose it will be of any comfort, Charlie, but I would only hope, that in the same circumstances, I would have had his courage. He acted as a father, out of love."

"It was pointless!" she cried. Tears burned her throat, but her fury kept them caged. She squeezed the white queen so fiercely it dug into her palm. "Windlass wouldn't have killed me. I would have got away from him eventually. Why couldn't he let me go?"

Moleglass looked towards the window. Sighed. "Parents are often bad at letting go of their children, Charlie. You may be right. It might all have worked out as you say. Or not. Neither you nor your mother would have been safe with Windlass free. Your father didn't feel he could take that chance. And he had a duty beyond you, my dear. He chose not to let a dangerous criminal escape: a man who had done great damage to the Kingdom and might do more. Your father lived the part of victim for many years, Charlie. He preferred to die as a king and father. Would you deny him that right?"

She couldn't hold on any more. Moleglass lifted her up and held her safe as the world tore into a million pieces and fluttered away in the wind like so many playing cards.

She sat in a chair by the window. A book lay on her lap. She wasn't reading it. There was a knock at the door.

"Come in," she said. Tobias stepped into the room, paused. She hadn't seen him for weeks. He looked taller than she remembered. The cut on his face had healed to a thin line. His eyes were a pale, pale blue. She shivered. "Will you see me?" he asked.

"Why shouldn't I?"

"You might not want to know me. Things being what they are . . ." He flushed and looked down.

"Don't be an idiot." She sighed. She was tired. "But you might have told me!" The sense of betrayal had seeped deep these past weeks. "You knew everything about me, and you didn't trust me with that. The most important thing of all."

"It's not!" He clenched his fists. "He's nothing to do with me! Only . . ."

"Only he's your father."

"He may be my blood, but he's *not* my father!" He took a deep, shuddering breath.

She had upset him. She hadn't wanted that. The tiredness grew.

"May I sit down?" It was stilted, formal. It didn't sound like him at all.

She nodded.

He sat in the other chair. Stared at his feet. "I'm sorry, Charlie. Maybe I should have told you. But it's over and done. And I got something else I need to say." He looked up and smiled at her, the ghost of his old, lopsided grin. "You won't want to hear it. You can call me a cloth-head afterwards if you like. But I can't rest till it's said." The grin faded. "He's my blood, and he's done you a terrible injury. I can't change what happened. I can only say I'm sorry for what he's done. He'll pay for it, if it's any comfort."

"He's alive, then?" She looked out the window.

"Aye. Topplesham's locked him in the dungeons till the trial. None of the prisons is safe. He'd be hauled out and lynched. Not that it matters. He'll hang. He knows it. I . . . been to see him."

"I don't want to know." Her voice was chilly.

"No. I'll go now then."

She heard the chair scrape. In a moment he would be gone, and it would be too late. She had lost so much already.

Charlie reached out, caught both his hands in hers and squeezed with all her strength. He winced but didn't pull away. She looked up, straight into his pale blue eyes, and found that she had been frightened for nothing. There was no trace of Alistair Windlass in them. There was only Tobias. Just like always. She smiled up at her friend. "Bless you, Toby Petch," she said. "You cloth-head."

She refused to move back into the Castle. "Not while that man is kept there."

"Your Majesty," said Lord Topplesham, mopping his

red face with an enormous handkerchief. "I'm pleased as Punch to have you for a guest in my house. You know that, lass. I'd love you to stay on. But you're right as a tick now, and the people need to see you. There's rumours you're dead as well. It won't do, Charlie. You're Queen now."

"I know I'm Queen! You don't need to remind me!"

"Forgive me, ma'am, but there's things needing doing. There's rumours that Esceania is preparing an armada. You must recall Parliament, and quickly! I've taken control of that dog's dinner Windlass cooked up, but it's a makeshift affair. We need the full Parliament reinstated and elections in due course. Then there's your coronation. The military needs looking to. I've managed to persuade the generals to support me, but only because there's no one else, and they're scared stiff of a revolution!" He puffed in dismay. "The Radicals and Republicans are brewing trouble, marching and pamphleting. No one's much interested at present. Your father's popularity, ironically, has never been greater. But that could change. The people need to be reassured that your father's daughter sits on the throne of Quale. You represent their desire to return to the prosperity of the past and their hopes for a brighter future.

"You can't do any of that from here, ma'am." He glowed red as a tomato beneath his white wig. "I'm sorry to have to say this, Your Majesty, but you owe it to your father!" He looked as though he might faint from anxiety at any moment.

Charlie turned and walked to the window. The garden of Topplesham's house lay below her. Its neat paths and rectangular beds wavered in the distorting glass. Beyond the garden wall, the tiled roofs of her city stretched downhill, tumbling into the distance further than she could see. For a moment it felt as though all the air in the room had been sucked away. She touched a finger to the glass, took a slow breath. "Order the Royal carriage, Topplesham," she said. "The landau, so that they can see me. I'm going back to the Castle."

It was midday. The sun had climbed to its highest point in the southern sky. Each day it rose a fraction higher. The earth was tilting on its axis towards spring. The carriage clopped past the Castle gates and down the cobbled drive. The snowdrops were in full bloom, the narcissus and jonquils just beginning to poke green heads out of the earth. She saw Foss in the distance, stabbing the ground with a spade. He would have to find a new boy. She was sending Tobias to school, although he didn't know it yet. Doubtless, he would be stubborn about it.

Her smile faded as the carriage rounded the last bend. The Castle didn't change. It was ageless, its turrets sprouting from the ground as though they had taken root in a time when trees were made of stone. For a second, Charlie saw the image of the Prime Minister standing beside the entrance, waiting for her. She shuddered. Her fingers crept into her coat pocket and found the white queen.

The carriage pulled up beside the shallow stone steps, and a footman ran to open the door and hand her down. It was not, she was pleased to see, Alfred. She jumped down and walked up the steps to the door. It swept open, and Mr. Moleglass, elegant in black and grey, the folds of his handkerchief sharp enough to cut an unwary finger, bowed his deepest bow and ushered her into her castle. As he helped her off with her coat, he murmured in her ear with consummate circumspection: "There is someone to see you in your office, Your Majesty."

It was a relief to have something to do. Moleglass followed her at a discreet distance, yet somehow manoeuvred himself to open the door before she reached it. She would have to have a word with him about all this butlering. It was already getting on her nerves. He would just have to save it for grand occasions. It was on her lips to tell him so when she saw the people waiting for her.

One was Bettina. She turned towards Charlie with a smile. "I told you, Charlie, did I not? I told you that you would find your mother."

The other person was a woman she had never seen before. The woman rose to her feet, took two steps forward. She was tall and too thin. Her face was careworn. She was dressed in a shabby coat and straw bonnet. Beneath her hat, mouse-brown tendrils escaped ribbon and hairpins and curled about her neck and ears. She smiled at Charlie with the smile she saved especially for her.

In a moment, Charlie was wrapped in her arms. The white queen slipped from her fingers and fell to the floor. It shattered with a sound like angels singing.

"Welcome home, Charlie," said Mr. Moleglass.

# Acknowledgments

This book exists because of the support and assistance of many people. I would especially like to thank:

Helen Corner, for choosing this story as winner of the Cornerstones Wow Factor competition.

My wonderful agent, Rosemary Canter; and Jane Willis and Jodie Marsh, her colleagues at United Agents. My editors, Sarah Lilly and Kirsty Skidmore; and the entire team at Orchard Books.

Lee Weatherly, for her generosity and guidance. William and Kit, for their patience and encouragement. My mother, for always being there.